T0374456

The Last Word

Richard Loofbourrow

iUniverse LLC
Bloomington

THE LAST WORD

iUniverse books may be ordered through booksellers or by contacting:

iUniverse
1663 Liberty Drive
Bloomington, IN 47403
www.iuniverse.com
1-800-Authors (1-800-288-4677)

ISBN: 978-1-4917-2550-4 (sc)
ISBN: 978-1-4917-2549-8 (e)

Library of Congress Control Number: 2014902757

Printed in the United States of America.

iUniverse rev. date: 3/13/2014

PART ONE:
Might Makes Right

Chapter One

It was the first day of summer, school was out, and the days were long. The twins looked like something right out of *Tom Sawyer* as they rafted the Missouri River. Both boys had on coonskin caps, jeans, and white cotton T-shirts. Charles chose to wear a navy blue bandana around his neck. David, his brother, opted for red. Tattered backpacks clung to their wiry frames as they boarded their handcrafted bamboo raft. It had been carefully lashed together with discarded cordage found behind the local hardware store. The bamboo was readily available, near and around their family farm. Last fall, the Soviets launched Sputnik, an event that kick started the twins' fascination with science. But today they were about to embark on another adventure.

They bobbed, drifted, and nearly capsized before beaching on a sandbar. The towheaded boys strained and cursed as they slowly dragged their raft out of the water and across the short expanse of sand. After crossing the narrow sandbar, the twins pushed the raft back into shallow water near the river bank and slowly floated through a short stretch of calmer waters. Fifty yards upstream, they spotted the mouth of a cave. Inspired by Huckleberry Finn and Tom Sawyer, the freckled-face brothers gathered their courage, grabbed their backpacks, abandoned the raft, and scrambled over boulders, jagged rocks, and loose soil before reaching a sandy ledge. Here they stood transfixed, staring into the darkness of the cave.

"The mouth of the cave could accommodate two adult bears," David yelled.

"Or a pack of coyotes," Charles answered.

David cried out, "You first."

They both laughed.

When their eyes adjusted to the blackness, David cautiously entered and found the interior to be more than double the size of their bedroom. Charles nervously followed. The ambient light was poor, but they did see the blackened, rocky walls of the cave. Smoke from earlier campfires was their best guess. Near the mouth of the cave were two flat boulders perched high above the mighty Missouri—perfect, they thought, for lounging and watching the river.

"Let's make a fire." David adjusted his coonskin cap.

"Did you bring matches?" Charles asked.

"No, but I have a lighter. Let's gather kindling and branches." David spoke with a slight drawl, his voice squeaking, vocal chords straining with excitement. He'd be a sophomore next year. He couldn't wait. He hated sounding like a girl. He felt mature. After all, he was twelve minutes older than his twin.

In less than twenty minutes, they had the kindling, branches, and two small pieces of driftwood in place. Their Boy Scouts training had paid off. Within ten minutes, the cave sprang to life, sparked by the light of a roaring fire.

Charles took off his backpack, opened a side pocket, and took out his prized Swiss Army knife. "Are you ready?" Charles said, trying desperately to keep his cool. His hand shook as he tightly gripped the pocketknife. Excited but fearful, he was not turning back. "It's time."

"Yes! We've dreamed of this for months," David shrieked. "Damn it all, we've been planning this since last summer." He was more nervous than when he had to dance with Margaret at last month's Boy Scout square dance.

Charles grimaced. With eyes nearly shut, he lightly drew the blade across his index finger. A few droplets appeared. He sliced it again. Now a stream of blood ran down his finger. "Hurry! Take the knife."

David followed his younger brother, but with a bit more flair. He first sliced a small x at the tip of his index finger followed swiftly by a deeper thrust. As the blood flowed down his finger, he reached out for his twin. They extended their arms, touched hands, and then awkwardly embraced. The brothers trembled with excitement as blood streamed down their fingers, turning their slender wrists red. With spaghetti legs, they wobbled to the flat boulders at the entrance of the cave. David loosened and then yanked the blue bandana from his neck. He quickly fashioned a compression bandage. Charles followed suit, quickly imitating his older brother. Beaming with pride, they raised their bandaged hands in a power pump. They both collapsed on the flat boulders at the cave's entrance, nearly passing out. Their mutual excitement had less to do with the loss of blood than their vivid imagination transporting them to a magical place where they would one day rule the world. In this magical world, courage, tenacity, and sheer delusion won out. After a brief moment of silence and reflection, they turned and grinned at each other. As if prompted, they both spontaneously yelled, "Semper fi." Their high-pitched adolescent voices echoed shrilly. In body and soul, they were of one mind.

Chapter Two

William St. George cringed. His bloodshot eyes strained from hours of staring at his desktop monitor. The newly released gun regulation polls irked him. He removed his glasses, rubbed his eyes, and squinted at the screen. A blurry summary of the latest stats lay lifeless before him. CNN reported that 80 percent favored stricter gun regulation. A recent *New York Times* editorial called for an assault weapons ban. The *Washington Post, Rolling Stone, Los Angeles Times, and Mother Jones* featured editorials calling for a ban on large ammunition magazines. "Pinko rags," he mumbled.

It was slowly sinking in. Nearly 90 percent of Americans wanted the gun show loophole eliminated. Now that a Sunday Fox News survey admitted that 78 percent of NRA members agreed with beefing up background checks, he lost it.

Wayne slammed his fist against the desk, swiftly switched to his Google account, and fired off an e-mail:

> *We are at war with the enemy. All members*
> *of the board of directors are summoned to*

*national headquarters Saturday, April 15.
That's right, that's less than a week!*

After hitting the send button, William turned off the lights in his home office and stomped down a long hallway to his favorite haunt, his man cave, a refuge from the political wars of Washington politics, a room dedicated to booze, sex, and guns. Only exclusive NRA insiders ever laid eyes on the *cave*, one dedicated to the eternal verities of masculine life. As he unlocked and opened the double doors, which were always locked for security reasons, light from the hallway revealed a spacious room. At the center of the room was a stately pool table, classical green felt playing surface, ornate hand-carved legs made of dark oak, and an overhead tiffany lamp. He switched on the bar lights and the tiffany lamp. The room instantly glowed with rich shades of red, amber, and green.

At the bar, he retrieved a lime from the fridge and sliced it into sections before opening a bottle of Silver Patron. He sat on one of the barstools, poured two fingers, *good for starters*, bit into a lime with a dash of salt, and downed it. The warmth spread throughout his upper body, starting at his mouth, and soon to his throat and cheeks. Within seconds, he felt his genitals warm. Fueled by the Silver Patron, his courage and euphoria escalated. *The goddamn bleeding hearts will not win the day. The hearts and minds of the American people are mine. No Pinko anti-gun movement will stand while I'm alive*, he thought.

With a smile and a sigh, he slid from the barstool and crossed the room for the gun cabinet that dominated the wall adjacent to the long bar. He plucked a brass key from the pocket of his hoodie, unlocked the massive cabinet's central glass door, and removed a Bushmaster AR-15. He looked like the infamous Unabomber, slinking about his man cave. He moaned like a bitch in heat as he stroked the hard steel of the barrel. "Oh sweet Jesus, I'm on fire," he blurted.

His public image was one of a bespectacled professorial type, slicked back dark hair with hints of gray, a stoical spokesman providing a kindly face for the NRA. But hidden from the eyes of prodding journalists, gun enthusiasts, and the supporters of gun control was a darker side—a side seen only by the inner circle. Here he was known as The Saint.

* * *

Matt Tyson had a date with the devil. *Well, maybe that's a bit premature*, he thought. He had a feeling there was more to William St. George than his media image. The public saw him as the public face for the NRA, a tough-talking, no-nonsense lobbyist for gun rights. Political insiders, lobbyists, and wealthy power brokers, however, saw him as a savvy and greedy businessman. Matt sensed there was more. He wanted to peel back the slick veneer and reveal the naked truth. After months of phone calls, e-mails, and brief conversations with lower-echelon NRA executives, he got his chance. It was 9:45. In fifteen minutes, he would sit down with *The Man*. He had been granted forty-five minutes to pick William St. George's brain. His managing editor at *The Socratic Rag* was delighted. *I finally got my shot*, Matt thought. He was pumped.

The receptionist at William St. George's Fairfax, Virginia, office blushed. She knew of Matt from his articles in *The Socratic Rag*. She preferred reading about music. But she occasionally skimmed a political piece or two. "Please have a seat. Mr. St. George will see you shortly."

Matt smiled. He enjoyed seeing the receptionist blush. He knew it wasn't his looks that caused all the redness; he had a robust readership.

The wait was short. Before he had opened his briefcase to check on his recorder, the secretary announced, "Mr. St. George will see you now."

The corner office was expansive. It offered only a pedestrian view of the surrounding community, providing only a bird's eye view of tree tops of a nearby parkway. But the ambient light showed off the photos of famous gun enthusiasts adorning the adjacent walls. A poster-sized photo of a clean-cut militia type, clutching an assault weapon to his breast, caught his eye. At the bottom of the photo, in bold print, was a quote from the man he was about to interview. "The only thing that stops a bad guy with a gun is a good guy with a gun."

"Mr. St. George, it's a pleasure to finally meet you." Matt smiled and shook the hand of the guy at the top of the food chain of the gun industry. Before Matt took his seat, he asked, "May I record our conversation?"

St. George took a seat at his desk, peered up at Matt through his wired-rim glasses, and bluntly said, "My legal office frowns on recording private interviews. Public interviews, that's okay."

Not wanting to get off to a bad start, Matt acquiesced. But timidity was not his strong suit, so after sitting down, he remarked, "The photo with the guy with the assault weapon got my attention. I especially like the caption at the bottom of the picture. It's got a lot of media play."

"There's a cold logic to it. We hire armed guards at airports and shopping malls. It works." William St. George removed his glasses and cleaned them, all the while seeming to study Matt.

"So, if somebody attempts a mass shooting in a movie theater, somebody else in the theater will be armed and shoot the shooter. Is that the rationale of the NRA?"

"I couldn't have said it better myself. There's nothing worse than a crazed nut with a gun, bent on mass murder in a room full of unarmed people."

Matt didn't want to get caught up in a Second Amendment argument. He wanted access to the real story, the NRA's connection to the gun industry. He wanted dirt. Follow the money. But he needed a subtle transition, a not so obvious way into William's private dealings. Stalling for time, looking for that moment to crack open the door to his private affairs, he said, "Since 1968 when Bobby Kennedy was assassinated, 1.4 million people have been killed by guns, one million since the murder of John Lennon. It doesn't look like gun owners should be trusted." Matt grinned boyishly and took a pen out of his coat pocket. Before Mr. St. George could respond, the office door burst open.

"Sir, there's an emergency. There's a bomb threat!" St. George's secretary face had turned pale. Her voice was high-pitched and strained.

A uniformed Virginia State trooper suddenly appeared beside the secretary and urgently pleaded, "Please, you need to evacuate now. The threat appears credible."

What happened next was a whirlwind of excitement. It was only that evening, while savoring his favorite cabernet at his Washington D.C. condo, that Matt realized the enormity of what took place earlier that day. It was the lead story on *CNN, Fox News,* and all the major networks. He surfed the Internet on his laptop and watched the evening news on his nineteen-inch Sony. He didn't have the time or taste for the latest in home-entertainment centers. He never rested. He was either digging deep for a story or writing one. His down time was consumed by playing chess. It sharpened his sense of strategy, logic, and structure.

The airwaves were overrun by stirring reports of a bomb threat, followed by talking heads speculating about the perpetrator. Little was known other than an anonymous call of the threat and the discovery of a live bomb in a women's restroom stall on the fifth floor. It had been disarmed.

Matt thought the evacuation of the office building went smoothly enough. A few shrieks and shouts could be heard while descending six flights of stairs at NRA headquarters. Two female employees thanked him for assisting them down the crowded stairway. *But no outright panic*, he thought. *No one trampled. I'm just bummed I didn't get a full crack at William St. George.*

Chapter Three

Tom Parker, director of the FBI's Washington D.C. Field Office, slid five folders across the conference room table, stood, and addressed the assembled agents. They were here because of the recent NRA bomb threat. "We have no leads. Just a pressure-cooker bomb, now unarmed, an anonymous phone call to a secretary at the NRA headquarters in Fairfax, Virginia, and a lot of heat from William St. George. In the folder, I've set up a preliminary list of priorities. Topping the list are several possible big-time players who hate the NRA. Most of them are legitimate political opponents. Three possible areas I want hit hard: extremist groups associated with Al Qaeda, the Islamic Brotherhood, and an emerging radical leftist group, Democracy Now."

"Democracy Now? What or who is that?" Senior Special Agent Alex Martini said. "Don't know *that* one."

"It's the latest thing. What's one more nut group? We're being hit upon by both extremes, left and right," said Director Parker. "You'll find in each folder a list of concerns and priorities. Get on it. Big Daddy downtown is breathing down my neck."

After the director left the conference room, the agents shared their frustrations at the lack of information. Big Daddy was the director of the FBI. He wasn't J. Edgar Hoover, but he was pretty damn close. They looked forward to the forensic team's report. Agent Martini was the last to leave the field office. He'd be at NRA headquarters bright and early in the morning.

* * *

Before heading out to NRA headquarters, Agent Alex Martini downloaded the FBI forensic report finished less than an hour ago. It was short but riveting. Fingerprints were too numerous to be completely checked. The pressure-cooker bomb was ordinary. The ingredients could be easily found at Home Depot. There was no fresh blood found, no suspicious fibers, nothing unusual except a message scrolled in lipstick on a fifth-floor restroom mirror. Written in bold capital letters, it read:

WILLIAM ST. GEORGE, STEP DOWN
NOW. YOU ARE NOT THE PROTECTOR
OF THE SACRED COW.

"Gibberish," Agent Martini blurted before taking his first sip of coffee. *I'm no poet, but this looks like nonsense. Why the message?* he thought. *If the bomb had detonated, there would be no lipstick message to be found. Maybe it wasn't meant to go off.*

He studied the report, looking for something to hang his hat on. Nothing stood out. He decided to start with the secretary, the only one who talked to the anonymous caller.

The eighteen-mile trip from his condo in Alexandria to Fairfax was uneventful. Just one traffic snarl after another. It was a way of life. It was 8:30 when he parked in front of the multi-winged glass complex, just behind several TV news trucks, a handful of Virginia State cruisers, and two FBI forensic vehicles. The NRA headquarters looked like a house of mirrors. The reflected morning sun was a visual nightmare. It was no high rise, but it reached skyward about five floors. At the top of the central tower were the letters NRA spelled out in red. It stood out clearly against the blue-tinted glass windows.

He took the elevator to the fifth floor and immediately looked for Kevin Armstrong's office. He was William St. George's special assistant. And it was his secretary that received the bomb threat. He entered the outer office where he hoped to find Mary Sandoval. Bingo—the nameplate on the receptionist's desk confirmed he was at the right place.

"Mary Sandoval?" he asked pleasantly.

"Yes."

"I'm Senior Special Agent Alex Martini. I'm here to ask a few questions."

"Yes, I've been advised. But I have to confer with my supervisor."

Alex glanced at his notes. The coffee had not done a good job this morning. He had a bad case of brain fog. "Yes, that would be Kevin Armstrong?"

"Yes. Please excuse me for a moment." She glanced back over her shoulder.

Alex watched the leggy secretary retreat behind the inner office doors. He liked what he saw. What the heck. He was divorced, no kids, and had an active libido. A couple of minutes passed before Mary and her boss, Kevin Armstrong, emerged from the inner office.

"Special Agent Martini?" Kevin Armstrong asked.

"That's close. Actually, it's Senior Special Agent Alex Martini." He didn't like to brag, but he was certainly not wet between the ears.

The special assistant to St. George cleared his voice and said, "I think it's appropriate that we conduct our interview in our fifth-floor conference room."

"Suits me. Let's go." The agent had to crane his neck. Kevin looked like he had once played basketball. *Has to be at least six-foot-six*, Alex thought.

The trio walked by several offices before entering double doors. The conference table was huge compared to FBI standards. It extended nearly twenty feet and accommodated nearly two dozen soft-backed swivel chairs. They settled in at the nearest end, Kevin Armstrong opting for the head of the table, while Mary and Agent Alex Martini sat across from each other.

Alex smiled, opened his notes, briefly cleared his voice, and asked, "Mary—may I call you Mary?"

"Yes, please do."

"At what time did you receive the call in question?"

"It was a bit after 10 a.m."

"Could you be more specific?" Alex smiled.

"Yes. I had just faxed a report to a US congressman. That was at 10:15. I have records of the fax."

"Good. And the time of the mystery phone call?"

"That would be five minutes later. It was about 10:20." Mary looked over at her boss, who was poker faced.

Agent Martini looked down at his notes and nodded

agreeably. "Yes, our phone records have pinpointed the call. Exactly 10:21. Tell me about the call."

"What do you mean?" Mary looked confused.

"Describe the voice, the message, the length of the call."

"It was a low, raspy voice, masculine in tone. Not quite like Darth Vader, but similar. Not as loud, but breathy."

"Perhaps disguised?"

"That would be my guess. But I'm no expert, you know." Mary again glanced at her boss.

"Yes, and what did the person say?" Agent Martini scribbled something in his notes. He looked up at Mary and was suddenly transfixed by her pale blue eyes. *I'd have a hard time dealing with those blue beauties*, he thought. He sensed that she could read his mind.

"The man said, wait, ah … I'm not sure. Man, woman … Oh, well, I know that the voice was low and throaty. Anyway, the person said that William St. George had gone too far. He literally said, 'I'm here to tell you that his time on earth is numbered. A bomb has been set to go off in thirty minutes. Better alert the big wig. Jack be nimble, Jack be quick. Jack jump over the candlestick. St. George's life and work is nothing but a dirty trick.' That's exactly the message."

"That's *exactly* what the caller said?" Agent Martini fiddled with his pen, clicking it rhythmically against the tabletop.

"Very close. I've been told I have a good memory. High school friends bragged that it was photographic."

"That's good. I'd love to have one of those. You know, with all the detail and minutiae I have to deal with every day." The senior agent smiled and then said, "So you're confident that's what he said?"

Kevin Armstrong answered for Mary. "Yes, that's what was said. She indeed has a prodigious memory. I can attest to that." Kevin smiled at Mary Sandoval. She beamed, bathing in the glow of his compliment.

"Was there anything else that stood out?" Agent Martini made a few more notes, scribbling at a rapid pace. He had his own method of shorthand, unintelligible to almost anyone else.

"That was it. Oh, wait. The call ended with a farewell. 'See you in the funny papers.' Weird." Mary's eyes widened, eyebrows raised.

"What?" Agent Martini leaned closer to Mary, looking her directly in the eyes.

"Yes, 'See you in the funny papers.' Strange, don't you think?" Mary looked over at her boss.

"Strange indeed," said Agent Martini. "Yes, strange indeed. My grandmother often said that."

Kevin Armstrong scooted back his chair and stood. "I take it that we're finished."

Agent Martini thumbed through his notes. "For now, but could you do me a favor?"

"Of course. What's your pleasure?" Kevin Armstrong looked down at the agent. Alex read his facial expression; it said it all. His lips were curled and eyebrows narrowed. He resented the inconvenience. He wanted the bomb scare solved, but not at his expense. He was a busy man.

"Show me the way to William St. George's office." Agent Martini stood, smiled at Mary, and graciously thanked her for her cooperation.

* * *

As Alex waited in William St. George's outer office, he looked over his notes. The mystery caller disguised his voice, liked nursery rhymes, and seemed to play the part of a joker. He'd check with some of his buddies on this. Agent Jeff Walker had an ear for rap, poetry, and word games.

The inner office door opened, and two executive types hurried out. Both were frowning. Seconds later, a bespectacled man of average height appeared, wearing an expensive, dark blue business suit and starched white shirt, set off with a blood-red tie. He approached the waiting agent. "Agent Alex Martini?" he said, his hand extended.

"Yes." Alex stood and shook his hand.

"Please come in. We've much to discuss."

Once in the office, William St. George took a seat behind his massive desk and motioned for the agent to sit. "Is the Bureau making any headway?"

Taking a seat, he said, "We're just getting started. I've talked to Kevin Armstrong and his secretary, Mary Sandoval."

"Were they helpful?"

"Yes, very. Maybe you can help me, too." Agent Martini retrieved his notes from his coat pocket and thumbed through the pages. "Here it is. The mystery caller said, 'Jack be nimble, Jack be quick. Jack jump over the candlestick. St. George's life and work is nothing but a dirty trick.' Can you help me here?"

William St. George leaned back in his chair, removed his glasses, retrieved a small, gray cloth from his desk drawer, and slowly cleaned them. "Sounds like a nursery rhyme. Childish, don't you think?"

"Perhaps, but there appears to be a hidden meaning.

Is the caller pushing any of your buttons?" Agent Martini looked up from his notes and stared down William St. George. The NRA's head man looked agitated. His cheeks were flush, his eyes glassy, and he made a fist with his right hand.

Agent Martini broke the silence with more questions. "Have you received any threatening letters, e-mails, or phone calls? Any nasty confrontations?"

"No, nothing significant." St. George slumped in his chair, put both his elbows on his desk, and made a steeple with his hands. He appeared to be praying. His voice lowered and he spoke slowly, clearly weighing his words. "Some left-wing political rants. I have my adversaries. But they're just haters of the Second Amendment."

There came a brief knock at the office door before it swung open. Kevin Armstrong took two quick steps in, stopped, and said, "I just received this letter." He held it up and waved it in the air. "You have to read it."

William St. George motioned for Kevin to come in and then took the letter and scanned it, taking only seconds before throwing it on the desk. His face was red with rage.

"Agent Martini, here's another threat." He shoved the letter across the desk.

Alex picked it up and read it aloud. "*When the cat's away, the mice will play. Now it's your turn to pay. Better go home before it's too late.*"

"More nursery rhyme nonsense," St. George snapped.

"May I see the envelope?" Alex reached across the desk and snatched the envelope. He looked it over, front and back. "It's addressed to the NRA in care of William St. George. There's no postmark. Who first received the letter?"

"My secretary. She just got it." Kevin narrowed his eyes.

"Where'd she get it?" Alex looked first at Kevin Armstrong and then over at St. George.

"It was delivered from the mailroom." Kevin looked over at St. George and shrugged his shoulders.

"Mr. St. George, is there anyone at your home—a maid, butler, chauffeur, anyone?" Agent Martini spoke with a sense of urgency.

"No, it's the staff's day off. Why?"

"Looks like a threat. 'Better go home before it's too late.' That's a big red flag. Please excuse me while I make an emergency call." Agent Alex Martini hastily made his way to the outer office and a few steps down the hallway, where he dialed an FBI emergency hotline. He requested help. Then he dialed 911 and alerted Virginia State troopers. It appeared he was too late. A text message alert flashed on his smartphone. A bomb blast and fire were reported at the residence of William St. George.

Alex dashed back to St. George's office. Both he and Kevin Armstrong were gone. He looked for St. George's secretary. She wasn't at her desk.

Chapter Four

M att Tyson grinned, stretched out his arms, and shouted, "Feeling good!" He then playfully kicked closed the study door behind him. Shouting for joy felt good. He had wrapped up his latest article for *The Socratic Rag*, and to beat all, it was cocktail hour. He opted for a cabernet, knowing from experience that a bit of heavenly nectar would take the edge off. Writing for six hours without a break was bloody hard work, but he was at his best when totally held captive by an important assignment.

More personally, he'd been held captive by the hopeful dream of someday owning a California winery. Maybe it had something to do with a 2009 road trip he made with friends through the rich wine country of Napa, Sonoma, and Mendocino Counties.

He uncorked a 2009 Betts and Scholl, a fine California cabernet, and with glass and bottle in hand, he headed for the sofa where he switched on old faithful, his aging TV. He punched in CNN on the remote and was shocked by what he saw. Anderson Cooper was reporting on a bombing in

Fairfax, Virginia. Behind the well-known anchor was live TV feed of a house that had nearly burned to the ground. It wasn't the home of some anonymous victim. It was the residence of William St. George.

A CNN reporter on the scene got access to Fire Chief Bill Nelson. He said, "We have few details at this time, but we've been in contact with Mr. William St. George, and he confirmed the residence was uninhabited at the time of the explosion. Several neighbors reported hearing a loud explosion a little before noon. No other structures were damaged due to the timely work of City of Fairfax Local 2702. At 11:50, rescue Engine 433 and Battalion 443 were dispatch to control the burn. The type of explosive device used is unknown at this time."

A well-known pair of talking heads joined Anderson Cooper to shed some light on the tragedy. Their comments were speculative and superficial. But Matt had a hunch. He sensed something nefarious lay beneath the surface of the life and times of William St. George. *I'm going to eat and sleep anything and everything to do with this guy*, he thought. He finished the first glass of cabernet and grabbed the half-empty bottle. *I'll finish this tonight. Tomorrow, I'll become a bloodhound.*

* * *

William St. George was in a bad mood. His main residence, prized gun collection, and man cave had been wiped from the face of the earth. His vacation home in Vail was too far away, so his temporary residence was the Capital Hilton, two blocks from the White House. Proximity to the president was of little help, but the hotel was well positioned for convening the inner circle, key players in Fire Power. There were no official records of this group. It was known only to a handful of people at the center of the gun industry. It was deep pockets for the NRA, the driving financial engine of one of the most powerful political lobbies in the world.

In his top-floor suite, he fired off an e-mail cancelling the emergency meeting of the NRA board of directors. During the next hour, he placed a series of calls to contacts that had indirect access to Fire Power. An elaborate maze of routine-looking business and social calls ended with five invitations to a birthday party. This was no ordinary birthday celebration. It was an emergency call for a sit down with Fire Power.

* * *

After studying the forensic report from the bomb scare at NRA headquarters, Alex Martini turned his attention to the Fairfax Fire Department report. Preliminary results indicated that a bomb similar to the one disarmed at NRA headquarters was the likely culprit in the destruction of the St. George residence. He checked the FBI database on explosive devices and cross-referenced that with terrorist groups. Last night, while blowing off steam at The Red Fox, a favorite watering hole, fellow agent Jim Simmons planted a seed. He asked, "What do George Clooney, Chaka Khan, the AMA, and Bon Jovi have in common? Answer: they're among five hundred names on the NRA's new enemies list."

Curiosity getting the better of him, he checked the

official NRA web page. Sure enough, on a back page was the NRA's official anti-gun "enemies list." He studied the list and cross-referenced it with the FBI data. He put together a list of top contenders with violent propensities. Alex settled on a dozen. The enemies came from the world of music, movies, comedy, and television. But it didn't stop there. The NRA had its crosshairs on just about the entire country. Women: National Organization for Women. Law enforcement: the National Association of Police Organizations. A Sports team: the St. Louis Rams. Teaching organizations: the American Federation of Teachers. Religious organizations: American Jewish Committee.

It was a longshot, but he would leave no stone unturned. The political spectrum was fair game, both the far right and the far left.

*   *   *

Thank God this day has come, William thought. *It's party time.* William St. George had a trusted insider make discrete arrangements to rent a guesthouse at Pine Shore Estates on Buggs Island Lake, less than four hours' driving time south of Washington D.C. The birthday party had to be far from the eyes and ears of the general public, especially the press, adversaries, and his bellicose enemies. *God do I ever have enemies*, he thought. *First it was the fucking bomb threat at NRA headquarters. But that wasn't enough for the bastards. They bombed and razed my home. Jeez, the loss of my gun collection hurts the worst. Shit, some of the guns were irreplaceable antiques. And without a doubt, I'm getting a new man cave.*

William had a trusted contact inform the rental agency that it was a birthday party for a former classmate from college. No real names were used. Even at the party, only Greek letters identified the revelers.

St. George pulled up into the circular driveway in his rented Lincoln Town Car, admiring the two-story log cabin. The massive stone chimney, roughhewn logs, dormer windows, and lush landscape dotted with Virginia pines reminded him of his getaway in Vail. He was early. He'd have an hour or so before the guests arrived.

Inside, he checked out the interior. The six bedrooms were well appointed, king- and queen-sized beds, private bathrooms, and three large decks overlooking the lake. Knotty pine walls and large, oak-planked floors provided a frontier atmosphere. There was even a bear-skin rug in the master bedroom. *I'll take that one*, he thought. *It's masculine through and through.*

The living area had a huge stone fireplace, a large sectional sofa, and a sixty-inch flat-screen TV. But it was the den where they would blow off steam. It featured a massive saloon-style bar running the entire length of one wall, pool table, jukebox, and rugged, stone fireplace a bit smaller than the one in the living room. He went outside and retrieved the refreshments from his rented Lincoln Town Car. The roomy trunk and backseat were stuffed with goodies. It took several trips to stock the bar. Another couple of trips and he had packed the freezer with prime rib and salmon. He loved to barbecue.

The partygoers all showed up within a few minutes of one another. They were disguised. No one knew of the others' real identities. Only William St. George knew. At least that's what the others thought. William ultimately answered to two mystery brothers, whose identity, profession, nationality, location, and politics were unknown. All he knew was that they were incredibly wealthy, and they always had the last word. He addressed them as Gemini.

The first to arrive were two burly dudes dressed as bearded bikers, riding late-model Harleys. They looked intimidating in their faded jeans, leather vests, and tattoos. They introduced themselves as Zeta and Theta. The remaining guests exited from their respective rented vehicles wearing dark charcoal gray business suits. They identified themselves as Alpha, Beta, and Delta. They wore dark sun glasses, brimmed hats, and carried brief cases. It was like a scene out of the *Blues Brothers*, Wall Street style. At this point, the only thing they agreed on was the nature of their disguises. Bikers and Wall Street types ruled the day.

William greeted each guest with a high five and a hug. They enthusiastically addressed him as The Saint. He was dressed as a circus ringmaster. And of course, they knew who he was. He was their front man for the world of guns. They were the profiteers.

The two bikers, Zeta and Theta, were playing pool while the trio of Wall Street types were at the bar nursing their drinks. All the partygoers were packing heat. They were proud NRA members. But above all, they were rich because of the lucrative gun industry. Fire Power called the shots. So they thought. William St. George was responsible for ensuring their leadership was at one with the biddings of Gemini, the almighty mystery twins.

After several hours of drinking and gorging themselves on William's tasty barbequed salmon, they sat down to do business. The ringmaster had the revelers gather in the living room where he had prepared a roaring fire. He stood before the alcohol-fueled members of Fire Power and made his call for action. "The NRA is under siege," he announced. "Headquarters has endured a bomb threat, and my home and treasured gun collection were burned to the ground. It's payback time."

"Hear, hear!" cried out Fire Power in unison.

"It's time we institute Armageddon." The ringmaster pumped his fist heavenward.

"Hold on. That's only as a last resort," countered Zeta.

"It's time. The heart and soul of our enterprise is at stake." William reached behind him and retrieved a whip from the wall next to the fireplace. It was staged, but The Saint had a flair for theatrics. He turned to his left side, away from his guests, and snapped the leather whip with the authority and power of a lion tamer.

A Wall Street type stood, wobbling a bit from the booze, and exclaimed, "Alpha is in!"

The two remaining businessmen, Beta and Delta, looked at each other, hesitated, and then stood. "We're in."

Zeta and Theta shot off a couple of skeptical questions, but the ringmaster had a compelling reply. It came down to money and power. Feeling satisfied with The Saint's appeal to their bank accounts, they agreed. They knew damn well that their enormous wealth was wedded to the NRA. And their connections were not merely local. Fire power was like a giant octopus, its tentacles wrapped around the face of the globe. Wherever there was friction, one guy at another guy's throat, be it a gang or a terrorist group, guns were there. Guns made the world go around.

William St. George was ecstatic. Gemini had already authorized the implementation of Armageddon. *Thank God*, William St. George thought. *Their will be done.*

* * *

Evidently, William St. George felt the urge to fight back. Matt Tyson was holed up in his study, immersed in anything related to the NRA, when he received a surprise phone call from St. George's secretary. She offered him a Friday interview at ten. Tomorrow, he realized. He jumped at the chance.

He closed his smartphone, rocked back in his swivel chair, and stared up at the ceiling, lost in thought. *Another crack at the face of the NRA,* he mused. *Something juicy— that's what I want.* Everything in the gun world was black and white. St. George's supporters saw him as a loyal Second Amendment purist; critics, however, cast him as a conspiracy nut who believed the president of the United States was out to confiscate their guns. *There's more to the story*, Matt thought. *Much more.*

The next morning, he went to the interview ready to pepper St. George with well-rehearsed questions. Once again, he took a seat across from the NRA's front man. He flipped open his notebook, ready to fire the first question, when St. George made a surprising move. He played the sympathy card. It was definitely not his style, but it was indeed effective.

"My world has been turned upside down. Since the bomb scare, the entire staff at NRA headquarters is a nervous wreck. My house is gone, my gun collection ruined, damaged beyond repair, and my doctor has me tranquilized. I feel like I'm slipping down the rabbit hole."

The hard-ass spokesman who once warned that government agents were nothing but "jackbooted thugs" was on the verge of tears. He removed his glasses, took out a handkerchief from his coat pocket, and dabbed at his eyes.

Matt Tyson felt conflicted. He came for blood and got nothing but tears. *It's nothing but a sham*, a *burst of showmanship, a red herring. It smells—bait and switch. I'm not buying it*, Matt thought.

Attempting to curb his emotional gushing, he asked about the status of the investigation. "Have you heard any news on the identity of the culprit? Anything come in from the FBI, Fairfax police, or the ATF?"

"Nothing. A big, fat zero. The authorities are on it, but nothing concrete." He put on his glasses, shook his head sadly, and slumped down in his chair.

"May I ask a direct question?" Matt wasn't going to be bamboozled.

"Sure. Fire away." St. George's eyebrows arched. *He's going to make a move*, Matt thought.

"Well, with due respect, I'm baffled," Matt said with a Cheshire grin. "There's been a great deal of talking about the 'enemies list.' I know it's now been removed from the NRA web page. But I saw the original. Hallmark Cards, the PTA, teachers, and social workers have all made the list. Why use the shotgun approach? Won't it backfire?"

"We've experienced severe negativity from the most innocuous places." St. George shook his head. "We're on high alert."

"Is it really that sinister?" Before St. George could

answer, Matt went on. "Some of the people on the list are deceased. And I'm shocked to see you target retired game-show host Bob Barker as 'anti-gun.' I've read that Mr. Barker sleeps with a loaded gun next to his bed."

St. George straightened up and said, "The NRA is suffering. First, there's a bomb threat. Now, someone's burned my house to the ground, and I have a jittery staff afraid to come to work. *We have enemies.*"

Matt could see that St. George was upset, so he tried to steer the interview to lobbying senators and representatives in congress. St. George calmed down and dished out his patented free-speech defense. He praised the First and Second Amendments as bulwarks of freedom and security. The interview became political. *No new revelations. No real dirt*, Matt thought.

Chapter Five

David and Charles had not visited the cave since childhood. They hoped the trip down memory lane wouldn't disappoint. After renting a small outboard motor boat, one good for fishing, they headed south on the Missouri River toward Blackbird Bend. The twins, sandwiched between the two great Midwestern states of Iowa and Nebraska, were giddy. They weren't going fishing. They were going caving.

"You think the cave is still there?" David shifted on the hard bench seat at the stern, looking for a comfortable spot. He moved the tiller slightly to the port side. He got what he wanted—a starboard tack. "Gosh, it's been fifty-five years."

"Yeah, time flies when you're having fun." Charles laughed and added, "Recent floods might have changed things a bit. The cave could be buried in sand."

After a half hour of slowly moving through choppy waters, they spotted the sandbar they had been beached on as kids. David yanked the tiller. The small boat lurched, and the twins made a beeline for the diminutive island of sand. David backed off on the throttle and slowly eased the bow of the boat onto the soft sand. Charles jumped off and tied the boat to a large chunk of driftwood. The twins enthusiastically threw on their backpacks. They both wore fishing boots, so splashing through shallow water and short stretches of sand wasn't a problem.

Charles scanned the embankment, looking for something familiar. "See the cave?"

David shook his head. "No. Let's hoof it downstream. I think we're too far north." David led the way. After about a hundred yards, he spotted a grouping of boulders and jagged rocks.

"Over there." David scrambled up the embankment, stumbled, regained his footing, and pushed through some heavy brush. "I see an opening," he said. His legs felt heavy. *Old legs*, he thought. Charles pulled up the rear. The twins were close.

They had about thirty minutes of daylight before dusk. The shadows and dying light of the setting sun played tricks on their eyes. The brothers hopped over the last two boulders. "Fucking great, it's here," David yelped.

The twins approached the mouth of the cave, paused, and retrieved small flashlights from the front pockets of their jeans. Time stood still; they were instantly transported back to their childhood. But this time, they had halogen flashlights. Back in the summer of '58, halogen lights were just being developed. They certainly weren't available to the general public. David and Charles, still out of breath, aimed their compact flashlights at the interior of the cave and entered.

"Look at the walls." Charles moved the beam of light around, revealing the blackened rock.

"Do you remember our campfire?" David moved his light about, stopping on some graffiti. At the rear of the cave, painted in red script, was the old standby, *Kilroy was here*.

Toward the front, a more recent message resonated with the brothers. In bold white spray paint was the call for gun freedom: *Guns don't kill people, people do.*

The twins yelled out in unison, "Here, here!"

"Let's break out the beer." Charles looked around.

"Not yet," David chided. "First, let's make a fire."

"Right on," Charles agreed. "That floats my boat. A blazing fire and a cold one would hit the spot. You can't beat that. And, let's leave corporate talk for business. Schools out, so let's party."

The twins busied themselves gathering the essentials. In little time, they found suitable kindling, branches, and driftwood. Charles retrieved a small can of lighter fluid from his backpack, squirted the wood, and stood back. His brother cautiously bent down and lit some kindling. Within minutes, they had a roaring fire.

"Do you remember our blood oath?" Charles grinned at his twin.

"How could I forget," David said. "Semper fi. Tomorrow we rule the world." He opened his backpack and removed a bottle of Hennessy XO (Extra Old), one of their favorite cognacs. They opted for drinking directly from the bottle. They would chase it down with Samuel Adams. The beer was cool, but not ice cold. The Samuel Adams had been iced when they rented the fishing boat. "And today we've got beer."

"But have we succeeded?" Charles sat down on one of the flat boulders at the cave's entrance, took a snort of cognac, then reached for a beer, and downed a third of the bottle in one gulp.

"Be serious my man. Why the self-doubt? We *are* the world of guns. Anything that goes *bang* goes through us," David said. "Guns have made us fucking rich."

Charles shook his head. "Maybe, but we have bigger fish to fry."

Chapter Six

Allen Carter pulled onto PCH, punched the accelerator of his late-model corvette convertible, and headed north toward Malibu. It was late spring, the weather was mild, and California poppies were in bloom on the hillsides near his Malibu estate. The moist ocean breeze blowing off the Pacific ruffled his hair. *Thank God it's Friday,* he thought. Forty hours of legal drudgery, endless documents, chaotic courtrooms, and pushy clients made him question why the hell he became an attorney. His thriving legal practice in Santa Monica was now temporarily on hold. *Office closed. Party time,* he thought. Booze and sex were okay, but they had lately lost their luster. He longed for three-day weekends. They allowed him to indulge himself.

He made a hard right on Las Flores Canyon Road and climbed the steep hillside. He loved the deep-throated sound coming from the Blue Devil ZR-1Vette engine. As he pulled into his gated drive, he glanced down at the Pacific Ocean, its deep blue water crowned by shades of red. It was sunset, his favorite time of day.

Twenty-five years of defending and advising wealthy

Hollywood types, actors, producers, and investors, made him very wealthy. His four-thousand-square-foot home, perched on an outcropping of granite rock, provided him an unobstructed view of Malibu, Santa Monica, and on a clear day, the Palos Verde Peninsula.

He pulled the Vette into his four-car garage, alongside his pride and joy, a 1935 Duesenberg, model SJ La Grand, dual-cowl Phaeton. The sleek red and burgundy convertible was the quintessential essence of functional art. *Hell, Picasso lovers, eat your hearts out,* he thought. *I'd pit the aesthetic elegance of my Duesey against the art treasures of the world. Clark Gable drove a Duesenberg. So did the Great Gatsby.*

He hurried upstairs to the master bedroom, showered, shaved, and prepared to dress. He had special company tonight. He laid out his clothes—purple blazer, green vest, blue collared shirt, funky orange tie, and gray and purple striped slacks. In the bathroom, before donning his costume, he tinted his dark hair green. Before applying makeup, he paused and admired his reflection. Several girlfriends had mentioned that he looked like Mel Gibson. *A stretch,* he thought. But he liked what he saw. He had no trouble attracting the opposite sex.

"Let the transformation begin," he said. He added red lipstick around his mouth and cheeks, molding wax for the scar, and dark black liner around the eyes. The makeup class he took five years before had sure paid off.

In the master suite, he got dressed. When everything was in place, he turned and gazed at himself in the full-length mirror. *Fuck, I love role playing. And Motley Wag, he's the cat's pajamas,* Allen thought. But tonight, Allen Carter was away. When the cat's away, the mice will play. *God bless Comic book characters.* The Joker and Spiderman were fun, but Motley Wag was his main man. Heath Ledger was his favorite Joker. Jack was not far behind. But they could not match the villainous Motley Wag. Movies, however, took a backseat to his colossal comic book collection. It had been appraised at well over a million bucks. He was enormously proud of those comic books from the Golden Age: the late 1930s to the late '40s. He recently purchased a Batman no. 1 for 275,000 dollars. He just had to have it. His latest acquisition was a first edition of *Motley Wag.* Bedlam's Best, an up and coming comic book publisher, was challenging D.C. Comics for current popularity. *Motley Wag* had recently received The Creep of the Year award from *Comics in Review.*

Downstairs in the den, he grabbed an open bottle of Johnnie Walker from the bar, retrieved some ice cubes from the fridge, and poured two fingers' worth. He hesitated and then poured a smidge more. He glanced up at two photos of himself standing near a Cessna 172 Sky Hawk. He missed flying, but his workload had cut into his free time. He hadn't been up in nearly three months.

With drink in hand, he walked outside to the wraparound deck. He stood silently and gazed at the distant lights of Santa Monica. *How in the hell did I get here ...* At UCLA, he was a philosophy major, a budding socialist with the dream of becoming a famous philosophy professor. Now, he was a multi-millionaire, lover of vintage cars, word games, nursery rhymes, and comic books. Violence was the blood and guts of comic books and video games. But it was just pure fantasy.

He sipped his drink, lost in reverie. He often lectured

his friends about the evils of gun violence. He'd say, "Guns are Satan's gift to mankind. If there's a God, she should ban them. It would surely take a feminine God to ban guns in America." Motley Wag shook himself. He was prone to daydreaming. At times, he lectured the bathroom mirror. He glanced at his watch. *Fuck, it's seven. They'll be here in a half hour.*

For the next thirty minutes, Motley Wag breezed through his estate. From pantry to fridge, he assembled the hors d'oeuvres, party favors, and chilled the champagne. The catering service had prepared everything. *God bless Millie for making the arrangements. Too bad she can't be here tonight.* He knew damn well that tonight's doings would blow her mind. Millie, his loyal secretary, had the looks and sensibilities of a fresh-scrubbed farm girl from Indiana. She was a dear.

By ten o'clock, the hilltop estate was jumping. The revelers, ten in all, were in full swing. They had all come as their favorite comic book character. The fairer sex was well represented. The Black Widow, Electra, Wonder Woman, and Bat Girl were kicking up their heels on the dance floor with their male partners. The expansive den featured hardwood floors—perfect for dance lovers. Moody Muse, Motley Wag's long-term girlfriend and accomplice in crime, was at his side, nursing her drink. In looks, she was at the top of her game. Her cunning smarts were not far behind. Tonight, she chose her slinkiest attire. Her red tights were indeed skin tight, showing off her full breasts and bubble butt. Her court jester hat bobbed as she moved her head.

Balancing out the female side were the male characters: Spiderman, Superman, Batman, Lex Luther, and the ringleader, Motley Wag. Allen Carter lowered the volume on the sound system, cutting in on Tommy Dorsey's "String of Pearls." The forties swing music, he thought, complemented the Golden Age of comic books. He cleared his voice and made a toast. "Here's to Dionysus. Tonight we party. Tomorrow we get down to work."

The guests shouted in unison, "Down with guns, up with hedonism, and long live Motley Wag!"

* * *

Alex Martini picked up the phone. His answer was flat. He threw a neglected file across his cluttered desk. He was frustrated, tired, and getting nowhere on the NRA fiasco.

"Max Heller. I've got some news."

"Hey, top of the morning to you." Again, his voice was flat and lifeless. Alex and Max went way back. Some twenty years ago, he and Max endured a twenty-week-long training camp at Quantico. They'd put down a few cold ones and exchanged horror stories in their time, both professional and personal. Max now worked at the FBI Laboratory at Quantico.

"You sound hung over. Bad night?" Max liked pushing his buttons.

"There's a fat chance of that. I'm buried in minutiae. I'm getting nowhere on the NRA thing."

"Well, Max to the rescue. I've got the latest on both bombs. The deactivated bomb discovered in the restroom at NRA headquarters and the bomb that leveled St. George's home are linked. Both have the same signature—same material ingredients."

"Tell me more." Alex needed some good news.

"Sophisticated bombs? Maybe. They're very clever bombs, no doubt." Max paused, clearly waiting for a response.

"You got my attention." Alex suddenly sounded more chipper.

"We both know that black powder isn't sophisticated, ah, compared to C-4 or other modern plastic explosives." Max paused again.

"Okay. Go on." Alex was antsy.

"Black powder was used. It's readily available. As you know, C-4 is difficult to get and traceable. Black powder and a pressure cooker purchased at Wal-Mart, a piece of cake. Why reinvent the wheel? Use a readily available casing, pack it with nails and ball bearings, and you have a two-directional bomb. Add electronics—in this case, a control unit from a remote-control car. It's available at any hobby store: common wiring, timing and firing mechanisms. Just like that, and bang, you're in business."

"Well, that makes my day," Alex said sarcastically. "Black powder is as easy to buy as ammunition. Check the Internet. Suppliers will have it delivered to your front porch. BTAF allows up to fifty pounds of black powder in single-family residences. And hell, you can get a pressure cooker anywhere."

"Good luck, pal. I'll fax you the complete report. Maybe something will jump out at you."

"Thanks. I might make a visit to your lab soon." Alex drummed his fingers on his desk.

"Great. I'll buy you a cold one."

"You're on."

Alex said good-bye and headed for the fax machine by

his desk. He examined Heller's fax, looking for something to bite into, some juicy morsel that would kick start his search. After a first look, he felt empty. The report revealed a very common bomb with a long history. A pressure-cooker bomb was easy to build, and any Joe Blow could buy the components at just about any place. And they wouldn't look suspicious.

Alex was up against a wall. A pressure cooker was simply a container. Any fool could put a lid on it and create an airtight seal. *Oh, good golly, Miss Molly!* Alex thought. *A common pot can be turned into a bomb in a matter of minutes.*

Chapter Seven

Allen Carter's master plan had reached part two. His loyal subjects were in place. They knew their roles. Allen entered his spacious living room, stepped behind the bar, threw a switch, and the drapes retracted, revealing a panoramic view of the Malibu shoreline. The Pacific Ocean glimmered in the late-morning sun.

Memorial Day weekend had just begun. But there was much work to be done. They had just finished a sumptuous brunch, Thanks to California Catering, a four-star service in Malibu. The superhero costumes were gone. What was left was a wide-eyed group of anti-gun fanatics. Fanatics might be too kind a description—terrorists fit better.

"It's time to go to work. The next step in our master plan is at hand," Allen Carter announced. He stood before his court, grinning. He was pumped. His law career was a drag. It was a moneymaker, no doubt, but that was merely a means to an end. Operation Gotham City, however, was his life's blood. It was now in its second phase.

"The NRA is paranoid, frozen with fear. It's time to strike. You know your missions. We've practiced it for the past year. Today we spread out across this glorious land; tomorrow we strike. By Sunday night, the NRA will be hamstrung. The gun-toting front for the gun industry will be neutered. Their fake masculinity revealed. Their greedy capitalism exposed. Decent folks don't make their living on the backs of corpses."

Allen Carter's longtime girlfriend, Alexis Williams, stood and made a last-minute plea for discipline, alertness, and courage. She had shed her intriguing Moody Muse costume, revealing a woman blessed with natural beauty. Her dark hair, almond-shaped brown eyes, and voluptuous figure were Playboy quality. But it was her mind that made her unique. She was not only smart but sinister. Her intellect was easily matched by her unconscious demons.

"When we meet again," Alexis said, "the gun world will be ripped asunder."

*   *   *

Matt Tyson had checked into the Beverly Hills Hotel, hoping for a breakthrough on the William St. George assignment. Larry Fielding, an old college buddy now working for Paramount Pictures, had enticed Matt west to Beverly Hills with a hot tip. That's what he called it anyway. It was only a hunch, but he wanted to know more. The NRA had enemies everywhere, especially in Hollywood. Besides, he thought, it gave him an excuse to rub elbows with history. The Pink Palace, the bar where W.C. Fields, Humphrey Bogart, and the Rat Pack frequented, was a must see. Matt pictured Joan Crawford pulling up for lunch, of course, chauffeured in her Rolls Royce, and he recalled stories about

John, Paul, George, and Ringo slipping through the back door for a dip in the pool.

It was Saturday, the first day of the three-day Memorial Day weekend. Larry Fielding had heard through the grapevine that Matt was working on a story about William St. George and the NRA. He had a hot tip. But he had only a couple of hours of free time. He was leaving town at noon, so he agreed to meet Matt at the Polo Lounge at 8 a.m. It was undoubtedly a bit early for Matt's taste. But this was a business trip, and *The Socratic Rag* wanted a story. Even if Larry's lead was a dud, he had some Hollywood types on his short list.

After a warm greeting, they decided on breakfast outside on the patio. The old college roommates were thrown back in time, swapping wild stories of youthful indiscretions.

"So, Larry, tell me more about your lawyer acquaintance." Matt grinned, pushing back his plate. He motioned to the waiter for more coffee.

"Well, I have this buddy I play racquetball with. We meet every Tuesday after work. One day we were talking about flying small aircraft and target shooting when the NRA came up. We agreed that the NRA propaganda is bullshit." Larry paused, sipped his coffee, nodding to a starlet walking past. "You know that lady?"

Matt glanced up, checking out the girl slinking by their table. "Hell, with dark shades, floppy hat, and jeans, she could be the girl next door. Haven't a clue." Matt looked over at his old buddy.

"Shannen Doherty. She was on *Beverly Hills, 90210*. Canned for feuding with cast members. She's a real Hollywood bad girl." Larry shrugged his shoulders, shaking his head.

"I'd rather hear about your lawyer guy." Matt wasn't much into TV shows.

"In the last six months, my friend and I have played three racquetball tournaments in Santa Monica. In the course of competition, I befriended this lawyer from Santa Monica. He's one hell of a competitor. But anyway, we got friendly and went out for beers after the last two tournaments." Larry paused, checking out a tall brunette walking by. "If her skirt was any shorter or her blouse any skimpier, she'd be in a bikini," Larry whispered.

"You were saying." Matt wasn't interested. He was hungry for a lead.

"Well, while blowing off steam at an Irish pub in Santa Monica, he goes on this rant about the NRA. He called it a propaganda machine, a front for the gun industry, and the biggest public health menace of the past hundred years."

"He's not the only one with those sentiments." Matt rolled his eyes. "I need something far juicier."

"After about three beers, he says he knows how to slow down the NRA and send William St. George packing for the hills. You've got to fight fire with fire." Larry paused, sipping his coffee.

"Go on."

"He said there's this guy that's well connected, has lots of cash, and has a following of willing comrades eager to wipe out St. George." Larry leaned in closer, lowering his voice. "And do you know what I asked?"

"Yeah, who's the guy and where are his comrades?" Matt Grinned, eyebrows raised.

"Bingo." Larry leaned back in his chair, grinning.

"You asked him directly?"

"I did. He looked me in the eye and said, 'You're looking at him.' That sent shivers running through me." Larry gently shook his shoulders.

"That's all?" Matt was skeptical.

"That's all? Isn't that threatening? The way he said it sounded downright evil." Larry shrugged. "It sounded creepy to me. But there's more. *His eyes,* they give me the creeps. For a moment, he looked like Manson."

"Okay, what's the lawyer's name?" Matt pulled out a notebook from his coat pocket.

"Allen Carter. His law office is in Santa Monica. I looked him up on the Internet. His clients are well-to-do Hollywood types. Big names."

Matt and Larry reminisced for another hour and then bid farewell with a warm handshake and hug.

"Good hunting," Larry said as he left the Polo Lounge.

"I hope that's a pun," Matt said.

They both laughed.

* * *

William St. George breathed deeply, savoring the alpine air. *It's been too long*, he thought. He had finally found the time to visit his beloved vacation home in Vail. He eased the full-sized rental car into his three-car garage, next to the bright yellow Hummer. He glanced at two snowmobiles, one blue, the other red, before dashing through the garage entrance of his three-thousand-square-foot log home. He headed directly for the bar, popped open a new bottle of Silver Patron, grabbed a lime and some ice from the fridge, and poured a stiff drink. He sliced the lime, took a bite, and washed it down with his favorite drink. He was home. *Well, home away from home*, he thought. He may have lost his primary residence to the bomb, but he still had his favorite getaway. He had retained two bodyguards, at the request of the NRA board of directors. They'd be here any minute.

He walked out on the rear deck. The sun was setting behind the Sawatch Range. He finished his drink and went out to his front deck, just in time to see a white late-model Ford sedan pull into the driveway. He felt safer. His armed guards were on the premises.

He was informed by his secretary that the board of directors had arranged for female entertainment. Wayne was ready to let his hair down. The last couple of weeks had been rough indeed.

Before greeting his security force, he got a text message on his smartphone. Gemini had put Armageddon on hold. The caller ID had been concealed. *I hate delayed gratification*, he thought.

Chapter Eight

Allen Carter and Alexis Williams bid farewell to their comrades-in-arms. Both the costume party and the Saturday morning business meeting were over. It was early in the afternoon. Gotham City was on. The cocaine-hyped couple sped along Malibu Canyon Road in Allen's Corvette convertible, hooked up with US 101, and headed north. If all went well, they'd check into their budget motel in San Francisco well before midnight, under an assumed name.

The Corvette's top was down. Wind whipped, and the dynamic duo was all smiles. Allen had cranked up the sound system. "Brown Sugar" echoed off the canyon walls while they were cruising through Gaviota Pass. The crazed couple joined in, imitating Mick Jagger. The only thing they lacked was a microphone and Mick's big mouth.

Drugs and rock and roll propelled them north, getting them to San Francisco well before midnight. After parking the Vette at airport parking, they removed two gray gym bags and two backpacks from the trunk, hopped on a tram, and picked up the rental car at the main San Francisco

Airport terminal. All arrangements were made using bogus identification. Tired, but still stoked, they checked into the budget motel. The co-conspirators showered together, horsing around and enjoying the sensual play. After toweling off, they once again went over the details of tomorrow's attack. Exhausted, they collapsed onto the well-worn bed. Despite the cheap and lumpy mattress, they were both asleep in less than five minutes. Their dreamless sleep was deep and satisfying.

Gotham City was in play. There would be no sex tonight; they'd get off tomorrow afternoon. The gun show at Candlestick Park was their target. No baseball game was scheduled. The San Francisco Giants were on the road.

*   *   *

No one, not even their closest friends, would recognize Allen and Alexis. He had shopped at a Santa Monica Goodwill store, spotted some oversized clothing, and picked out some extra-sized duds. The baggy overalls and work shirt were filled out with a pillow and carefully sculpted foam rubber. He wore makeup that darkened his skin, a straw hat festooned with NRA pins, and sunglasses.

Alexis wore an oversized sweat suit. Underneath, she had on four layers of loose-fitting cotton shirts and pants. The ensemble was excruciatingly confining and uncomfortable. But the bulky disguise did the trick; it flattened out her voluptuous body. The curvaceous body that Allen adored simply disappeared. She now looked middle aged and fat. Her face, like Allen's, was darkened. She wore a pink, floppy, cloth hat adorned with embroidered daisies. Oversized, dark sunglasses hid her beautiful eyes.

They waddled through the gun show, each carrying an oversized gray bag. In bold red capital letters were the initials NRA. The duo was quite impressed by the displays. Firearms stretched as far as the eye could see. It was opened to the public, crowded with eager buyers looking for a deal. Near the center of the gun show, they split up, planning to rendezvous near the entrance in five minutes.

They individually moved around the displays, closely examining the merchandise. Each was hypnotically drawn to the assault weapons, particularly AR-15s. At the set time, to the second, with coldblooded calmness, both Allen and Alexis departed their respective exhibits, leaving the gray bags. Within ninety seconds, they regrouped at a booth featuring hunting knives. They were a mere twenty yards from the main entrance. Looking like a couple of absentminded hay seeds, they calmly exited Candlestick Park.

* * *

Regular Sunday afternoon television programming came to a screeching halt. "All hell has broken out," reported weekend CNN anchor Don Lemon. The major networks erupted with terrifying news. The airways were inundated with images of mayhem. Videos of the grisly aftermath were horrific. Paramedics, SFFD trucks, emergency medical vehicles, and local police cruisers dotted the area. The first responders were overwhelmed by the human carnage. Smoke and debris covered the grounds of the gun show. Brief images of scattered human body parts had to be blurred out from TV news. A stadium that had hosted cheering baseball and football fans was turned into a killing field. Innocent victims lay lifeless on the ground. Helicopters filled the San Francisco sky, hovering above the critically wounded and dead like vultures. Within an hour, the casualty toll had reached ten dead with seventy-five wounded. Attendees of the Crossroads Gun Show at Candlestick Park were in shock.

Before the afternoon was over, the San Francisco tragedy was dwarfed by identical stories and images flooding the airways from gun shows across the country. Don Lemon paused, shaking his head in disbelief. "I've just been informed that a gun show in Carson City, Nevada, has been bombed. The casualty toll is not known at this time."

Within an hour, numbing reports came in from Albuquerque, New Mexico, Rockford, Illinois, Evansville, Indiana, and Detroit, Michigan. They all suffered bombings within a time span of six hours. The country had come to its knees. Pundits immediately questioned whether the brutal attacks were the work of foreign or domestic terrorists. The Department of Homeland Security announced an emergency lockdown of all airports and international border crossings. A large swath of the United States looked like a war zone.

At the close of day, the nation had been paralyzed with fear. "Memorial Day is tomorrow. But today will live on in infamy," said CNN's Anderson Cooper. His stoic face showed pain; he was nearly brought to tears.

* * *

Homeland Security, the FBI, and local police agency were immediately placed on high alert. The director of the FBI, Horace Rich, quickly established a national task force. Director of the Washington D.C. Field office, Tom Parker, joined forces with John Bartolla, assistant director of the Detroit Michigan Field Office. Under their leadership, all the sites hit would be thoroughly investigated. Homeland Security, FBI, ATF, and local authorities would not rest until the culprits were apprehended.

Alex Martini had just finished dinner when Tom Parker called. "Pack your bags. I want you at Candlestick Park by Monday morning. You'll be working with the San Francisco Field Office. Good luck. I want results."

*   *   *

William St. George's mind raced, conjuring up revenge fantasies in rapid succession. He was livid. He needed to vent. His mind became a kaleidoscopic nightmare. Blurred images of bloody body parts strewn about the grounds of gun shows across the nation were driving him crazy. *Revenge, revenge, oh sweet revenge, I want to shoot someone*, he thought. *Fuck the bastards.*

William's smartphone buzzed. He frantically grabbed it, hands shaking. He stood on the rear deck, leaning on the railing. The sun was setting, casting dark shadows across the rugged alpine landscape. It was a text message, and it was urgent. It was terse and startling.

> *Stay put. Fire Power has been alerted. Armageddon has been put on fast track, but with a couple of new twists. Details soon.*

It was from Gemini. And it was cryptic. *Stay put*, William thought. *No way*. But defiance was useless; he knew he wasn't in charge. He had to talk to someone. But no one at the NRA, board of directors included, knew about Fire Power. And he was the only person in the world who knew of Gemini—though he had no idea who they were.

Chapter Nine

It was early Monday morning. All entrances to Candlestick Park had been shut down. News trucks, police cruisers, and black sedans with government plates were everywhere in sight. FBI and ATF agents were huddled in small groups. Forensic technicians covered the bomb site like Monarch butterflies swarming their favorite tree. Yellow tape cordoned off the area, keeping the curious at bay. Blue wooden barriers marked the investigation site.

Alex greeted Special Agent Mario Gonzalez from the FBI San Francisco Field Office. They skipped the small talk and got right down to work.

Alex said, "Do you mind showing me around? You were here yesterday, right?"

"Sure," Mario said. "But it's grisly. Follow me."

The two agents walked about the playing field, once green, but now stained with blood, blackened by fire, and littered with burned wood, twisted metal, and broken glass. Metal that was once a gun barrel poked up through the debris. Ammunition clips riddled the ground. Bullet casings were strewn about like pebbles on a rocky beach.

Mario pointed to an area a few feet away. "Over there, the forensic team found a damaged metal pressure cooker, mangled and dented by the blast. Close by, they discovered scraps of nylon. The explosives might have been carried in a nylon backpack or bag."

Alex looked about, surveying the killing field. "Did the forensic team find nails and ball bearings?"

"They did, and in abundance. We both know that those things increase the carnage. Some victims had multiple fragments of pellets and nail-like shrapnel embedded in their bodies. The perpetrators were out to not only kill, but maim." Mario shook his head.

After several hours of scouring the area and talking with other agents, Alex got a phone call from Tom Parker. He wanted Alex to check out a Hertz rental agent at the San Francisco Airport. The manager working the front counter, a Donald Driver, reported seeing something suspicious. Alex told his boss he would be right on it.

* * *

After a quick stop at Subway for a half sandwich and coffee, he headed over to Hertz Car Rentals at the San Francisco Airport. Because of the recent lockdown, the rental agency was like a graveyard at midnight. The only one around was the manager, a Donald Driver. He chuckled to himself. *With a sir name like Driver, how in the hell did he end up at Hertz?* He was balding with a thick, dark brown moustache. He looked like Groucho Marx on a bad day.

He approached the manager. "I'm Senior Special Agent Alex Martini. Could I have a word with you?"

The Hertz manager looked around. "I'm swamped, as you can see." He shrugged, laughed, and then gestured with his hands. "Weird. It's a ghost town—y'know, with the bombing and all. I called the FBI only hours ago. You guys don't waste any time."

Alex smiled. "So, you were on duty Saturday?" Alex pulled out his notebook and flipped it open.

"Yeah, one of our agents called in sick on Saturday. I was here until midnight. Another agent worked graveyard." He tilted his head and grinned. "I avoid the graveyard shift at all cost."

"Gotcha. My supervisor said you saw something suspicious Saturday night?"

"Indeed. It was about 10:30. A flashy couple came to the counter. The guy looked like Mel Gibson. Dark hair, about six feet tall, and dark eyes." Donald Driver paused and rolled his eyes upward, searching for his next words. "His companion was a looker. A voluptuous vamp, you might say."

"I've seen all kinds at airports. Is that all you got?" Alex's patience with this guy was wearing thin.

"Well, what caught my eye were the bags they were carrying. Bulky, dark gray gym bags with NRA plastered on the sides." He nodded his head. "Yep, the bags had NRA in big ol' red letters. The National Rifle Association. I think I've seen the bags for sale at gun shows."

"You frequent gun shows?" Alex didn't figure Donald Driver as a gun enthusiast.

"Maybe two a year." Donald arched his neck, thrusting out his skinny chest, proud.

"You own guns?" Alex asked.

"Why?"

"I was just curious."

"Do you really want to know?" Donald seemed pleased that the FBI agent was interested in his guns.

"Give me what you got." Alex sensed that Donald would make a good witness.

"Okay. I own a Glock 27 handgun and an AR-15 Bushmaster. Are you surprised?" Donald clearly liked their repartee.

"No, not at all. They fit you." Alex grinned. "Tell me more about the couple you saw." Alex scribbled down a few things in his notebook.

"That's it. Big bags with NRA plastered on each side. Looked like jumbo-sized gym bags. They handled them carefully."

"What?" Alex narrowed his eyes.

"Well, let's say they were very protective of the bags. They threw their backpacks around. But they were very careful in handling the NRA bags."

"Do you have their paperwork?" Alex finally cut to the chase.

"Sure. Want a copy?"

"Absolutely." Alex small talked with the manager for a few more minutes. Before he left, he gave Donald his card. "Call me if something comes up—anything. Something new or something you've overlooked."

* * *

Alex checked out the paperwork he picked up at Hertz. The flamboyant couple lived in Bozeman, Montana. They signed in as Ben and Ava Tomlinson. He tried a couple of phone numbers, but no luck. The service had been disconnected. He checked the address. The house was for sale. He contacted the real estate agent. The couple had been killed in an auto accident six months ago. *Bingo*, he thought. *They used fake IDs.*

Chapter Ten

Allen Carter breezed through his Tuesday calendar. He sailed through a two-hour courtroom appearance in the morning, followed by afternoon consultations. He had finished his paperwork by four. *Cocktail time in one hour,* he thought. His mind was racing. He punched on his desktop computer, looking for the latest on the gun show bombings. The *New York Times, Wall Street Journal,* and *Huffington Post* featured bloody pictures of the carnage. The *San Francisco Chronicle* detailed the Candlestick bombing with chilling firsthand accounts. Pictures of mutilated bodies, grown men weeping, and bloodied children made up the bulk of the day's news. The Candlestick scene was repeated in city after city, extending as far east as Detroit.

Allen was wrenched from his daydream when he thought he heard a knock at his office door. He frowned. He didn't want to be disturbed. He heard it again. The door opened, and his secretary peeked in. "Mr. Carter. There's a gentleman from *The Socratic Rag* outside. His name is Matt Tyson. He would like a couple of minutes."

"Tell him to make an appointment. I'm busy." Allen waved his secretary off. He was in no mood for an interview.

"He's insistent. He wants to talk about William St. George." Millie, Allen Carter's secretary, was in her early sixties. She wore her gray hair in a bun and spoke softly with a British accent.

Allen leaned back in his chair. "Okay, send him in."

Matt appeared at the door, smiling. "Please, just a few moments of your time."

"Please, come in." Allen was calm and collected.

"Thanks." He took a seat across the desk from Allen. "We've a mutual friend."

"Oh, how's that?" Allen leaned forward and turned off his computer monitor. He'd seen enough. After all, he'd seen it firsthand.

"Larry Fielding and I are longtime friends. We went to college together."

"What college?" Allen knew where Larry went to school. He was just checking the veracity of his surprise guest.

"Bard College, the great academy on the Hudson," Matt said proudly.

"Your parents were no doubt well off. The place is known for its tuition."

"Not at all. I was on scholarship." Matt looked about the office and gestured to the bookshelf that displayed two trophies. "I bet you won those playing racquetball."

"I love a friendly game. So, what's the interest in William St. George? And why talk to me?" *It's time to cut to the chase*, Allen thought.

"I'm on assignment with *The Socratic Rag*. They want an inside story on the gun industry. St. George's the front man.

61

No better place to peel back the veneer than investigating the NRA's top dog."

"I've read several of your pieces. Riveting piece on Wall Street, especially the great line about Goldman Sachs."

"Thanks. The bit about the great vampire squid raised some hell. My editor nearly canned it." Matt leaned forward. "Larry Fielding says you have a thing about the NRA."

"You got that right. The right of the people to keep and bear arms is a myth fabricated by the NRA. Follow the money. The NRA is all about protecting the profits of gun manufacturers. In 2011 alone, industry-wide gun sales were a whopping 4.3 billion."

"Well, the Second Amendment *does* have the 'right of the people to keep and bear arms' clause," Matt said.

"Sure, following the clause about 'a well-regulated militia being necessary to the security of a free state.' Back in 1991, former Supreme Court Justice Warren Burger referred to the NRA Second Amendment myth as one of the greatest pieces of fraud pushed by a special interest group on the American people. He said, 'I repeat the word fraud.' He was emphatic." Allen stared at Matt, eyes wide and glazed over with controlled rage.

"Politicians don't seem to have the will to take on the NRA," Matt said. "As the deaths pile up, the gun industry reaps the economic rewards. What can be done?"

"I say, fight fire with fire." Allen clinched his fist.

"Money or violence?"

"Whatever works. Look, in all foreign wars during our history, about 650,000 soldiers died. But get this; in the forty-five years since Robert Kennedy and Martin Luther

King were assassinated in 1968, there have been 1.3 million deaths in our country caused by firearms. It all goes back to that weasel William St. George. He's worse than the Grand Inquisitor." Allen could feel his heart pounding. He needed to back off.

"Impressive stats, but all this is like water off a duck's back. The political powers are either not listening or have been bought off." Matt leaned back.

"Congress houses sycophants and whores. They'll either kiss ass or sell their souls to the devil. Say, I'm thirsty. Want to join me for a cold one? I know a cozy Irish pub where we can blow off steam." Allen stood, smiled, and said, "Come on. It's close by."

"Sure, why not." Matt smiled.

*　　*　　*

Allen offered to drive. It was not much more than a mile, but the ride over to the pub in his flashy Corvette Convertible was a blast. The combination of the balmy weather and moist salty air blowing off the Pacific made Matt thirsty. But he was thirsty for more than a drink. He needed a story.

The ambience of Mulligans reminded Matt of an old Boston haunt. Pictures of famous literary, political and sports celebrities covered the dark wooden walls. A four-leaf clover flanked by two dancing leprechauns graced the wall behind the bar. Strains of "Danny Boy" caught his ear. A bit over the top, but Matt wasn't about to complain. He was thirsty. The bar was crowded, so Allen picked a corner booth and ordered Guinness. Matt approved.

"So, what do you know about William St. George?" Matt tugged on his beer, liking the pub and the brew.

"I've studied him from afar." Allen took a sip of beer.

"And what did you find?" Matt didn't want to be pushy. Not yet.

"Attorney-client privilege keeps me from citing names and places. Let's say, hypothetically, I have a couple of clients who have access to the NRA's cash cow. They personally know two big-time players in the organization's deep pockets. It's awkward for my clients. They hate the NRA. But these guys are big-time players in the NRA's gravy train. But here's the hitch. They're also the source of my clients' funds. They walk a razor's edge. Career and principles collide like protons in a CERN accelerator. Boom, goes the collision. They're playing with fire." Allen's rambling soliloquy was perplexing. It was also pregnant with possibilities.

"You're teasing me. You've led me to the trough, but I can't drink," Matt said.

"Sorry, old chap. But I'm a high-profile lawyer, and I represent high-profile clients. I'd love to help. But I play by the rules. Attorney-client privilege trumps all for me." Allen finished his beer. "How about a second round?"

"I've never said no to a Guinness."

The two new drinking buddies had another round before saying good-bye. Matt's curiosity was piqued, but he left the pub unsatisfied. Who were Allen Carter's high-profile clients? What were their politics? Who did they do business with? Who owned them? Were they just Hollywood whores?

* * *

Allen arrived at his Malibu estate a little after sunset to find Alexis glued to the small television in the kitchen. She was seated at the counter, hunched in front of the thirteen-inch Sony, mesmerized by CNN's endless coverage of the Memorial Day Massacre. Six gun show bombings from San Francisco to Detroit rocked the nation. Pundits had decried the event as the most far-reaching assault on American soil. The bombing of Pearl Harbor and the destruction of the World Trade Center were localized. Memorial Day Massacre spanned the heartland of America.

"What's up?" The Guinness had taken the edge off. He felt on top of the world.

"What have we done?" Alexis gazed up at Alex. Her eyes were bloodshot. She'd been crying.

Alex leaned down and gently kissed her cheek. "Want to talk?"

"I need more than talk." Alexis's full lips quivered. "I need you."

"You've got me." Allen smiled, gently raised her from the barstool, and hugged her.

Alexis whispered in Allen's ear. He kissed her again, this time more passionately. The lovers headed upstairs to the master bedroom. An hour later, Alexis checked herself out in the bathroom mirror. Her full lips were red and swollen. Her back was scratched, bleeding slightly, from shoulders to hips. Her silky smooth thighs were bruised. She was satisfied. Allen had made the pain go away.

When Alexis emerged from the bathroom, she found Allen propped up on a pillow, naked, gazing at the ceiling. He exhaled a white plume of smoke, sighed, and said, "*Mary Jane*. She's only second to you, babe."

Alexis rolled her eyes. "Thanks for the compliment. I'm hungry. Want a snack?"

"Later. I'll be down later. But I got an idea. Want to fly up to Santa Barbara Saturday? I'm getting rusty. I haven't flown the Cessna for months."

"Maybe. The Biltmore Four Seasons sounds good."

Downstairs, Alexis grabbed a Dannon raspberry yogurt and some fresh strawberries from the fridge. The strawberries were juicy and plump. She had picked them up today at Whole Foods in Malibu. As she snacked, the events of the Memorial Day Massacre took hold of her once again. Transitioning from Operation Gotham City to teaching Ethics at Pepperdine University was stretching her psyche to the limit. She had gone to college thinking of becoming a psychologist. When she took abnormal psychology as a sophomore, she had seen glimmers of herself in a case study about a female sociopath. The revelation was so traumatic that she had switched her major to philosophy. The analytic bent suited her better. Ideas were friendlier than emotions. She lived in her head.

Chapter Eleven

Professor Alexis Williams was only on campus Monday, Wednesday, and Friday. The schedule allowed her to write at home and to carry on her true mission. Beneath her professorial appearance was Moody Muse, loyal follower and lover of Motley Wag. But at the university, she dressed down, hiding her femininity by wearing finely tailored suits. She never wore skirts or tight blouses on campus or at university functions. Makeup was avoided at all cost. And tortoise-shell designer glasses obscured her eyes. Allen once walked right by her at Whole Foods in Malibu. He didn't see her until he heard a shrill whistle and whirled around. Alexis took off her glasses and howled. "Gotcha! I just fooled the expert," she said.

Her last class of the day was over. *Thank God*, she thought. The students were nervous, unfocused, and not in a mood to talk about Immanuel Kant's moral philosophy. They wanted to vent about the Memorial Day Massacre. The ethical discourse advanced by the German philosopher rang hollow; his analytical arguments seemed sterile and lifeless. Discussion of the second formulation of the categorical imperative, the part about treating others as persons, beings with free will and rationality, seemed untimely.

The nation was under attack; people were being slaughtered, bloodied, and maimed. The students wanted to talk about what makes a human being a monster, a wholesale killer of innocent human beings. She let them vent. Alexis was uncomfortable dealing with emotions. She could only be an impartial observer. She was at best a referee, controlling the free play of dialogue, distancing herself from the raw edges of emotion.

She taught undergraduates at a private university, kids from upper-middle-class and wealthy families. They had been raised by helicopter moms, pampered, spoiled, and handed social and educational opportunities on a silver platter. They hadn't experienced the underbelly of society. They hadn't walked on the dark side. Little did her students know that the monster they wanted to understand was standing right before them. Evil was right in front of their innocent eyes.

*   *   *

Alexis needed to talk. Her girlfriends knew little of her professional life, and they knew nothing of her secret life. Her colleagues saw her as an intellectual. The handful of close female friends saw her as an avid gym rat that never skipped an aerobic dance class. It was unanimous—her close female friends were envious. She had a body to die for. Her students and colleagues saw none of this. They saw only a bespectacled professor who had great taste in suits, hats, blazers, and slacks. No one at the university had even caught a glimpse of her long, shapely legs, let alone her full breasts. She needed to vent. Other than her other comrades, Allen was her only outlet.

That evening after dinner, Alexis and Allen sat outside on the deck of his Malibu estate and watched the sun disappear into the Pacific Ocean. Allen lit a joint and offered it to Alexis. She inhaled deeply, holding it in for several seconds, only letting go of the trapped smoke when her lungs began to burn. He took the joint and inhaled.

Alexis took a sip of cabernet and then said, "We need to talk."

Allen smiled. "I'm listening."

"The Memorial Day Massacre haunts me. I turn on the news, and there we are. Every news outlet, every hour, has our deeds meticulously covered for everyone to see. When we planned all of this, it was thrilling. I was pumped, eager to push the envelope of existence. *Fucking fantastic!* That was then. Now I feel lonely and depressed. The excitement is over." Alexis leaned forward, grabbed the joint from Allen, and took a drag. She held it as long as possible and then leaned back in the deck chair, sending smoke heavenwards. "If there's a God," she said, "she's outraged. If Lucifer rules the universe, then all is well. I need an answer."

Allen laughed. "You're a philosopher. Good at asking questions. I'm a lawyer. We're shysters. We're good at looking for loopholes. And how do you know the gender of God? "

"I don't fucking know. Shit, do you think we can get away with this?" Alexis shrugged. She felt lightheaded. The cannabis was taking hold. She felt like drifting off into the black of night.

"Why not? We hold all the cards. The members of our

team are rock solid." Allen reached for the bottle of Colgin Cellers, one of his favorite cabernets, and poured another glass.

"I need to touch base with our team. I haven't talk to anyone. I need to check in—compare notes and test their will. One break in the chain, and we're toast." Alexis felt a mounting paranoia. She felt like she was being watched.

"Perhaps a meeting is in order. Better yet, how about another costume party. It could be the drug of choice." Allen laughed. "I love being Motley Wag."

"I need a fix." Alexis stood, took a couple of steps toward Allen, and slowly turned around, showing off her generous curves. Her sensual movements, accentuated by the soft light of the rising full moon, sent shivers through Motley Wag.

"Your request is my command. I'll see you upstairs in five. That's minutes, not hours. Oh, by the way, I've made reservations for a flight tomorrow."

"The Cessna again?" Alexis said.

"No way! It's a surprise." Allen smiled. "You'll love it."

An hour later, sounds of yelping coyotes echoed off nearby canyon walls, and whimpers of sexual ecstasy rocked Motley Wag's world. Moody Muse got her fix.

*   *   *

Allen had Alexis stay behind in the Santa Monica Airport waiting room. He was preparing her surprise. After the flight preparations were made, Allen went back to the waiting room and escorted her to the tarmac. He had her cover her eyes, and when they pulled up alongside the plane, he said, "Open your eyes."

Alexis gasped. "This is our ride?"

Allen pulled out a bandana, tied it around his neck, and said, "The Red Baron at your service."

"Wow! She's a beauty." She gazed at the by-plane, taking in her classic lines.

"It's a Grumman G-164 Ag-Cat." Allen bowed and said, "My lady, shall we?"

The vintage by-plane stood out among the other more conventional private planes. Her wings and struts were a bold red, and the fuselage was midnight black with yellow lettering and numbers. It shared the same classical elegance as his beloved Duesenberg.

Within fifteen minutes, they had the aging by-plane in the air heading west over the Pacific Ocean. They wore goggles, leather jackets, and gallantly donned colorful bandanas of red and blue that flapped in the wind.

"Want to see the Hollywood sign up close?" Allen didn't wait for a response but banked the by-plane to the right and headed east toward Hollywood. After buzzing the famous landmark, he circled Hugh Heffner's Playboy mansion and then headed north toward Malibu.

"Look over to your right," Allen said in the intercom.

Alexis looked down at the sprawling seaside campus of Pepperdine University. "I can see my faculty building!" she said. "It looks so different from this perspective."

Allen gave Alexis a thrill ride, putting the vintage plane through its paces. He loved looking down at things.

*   *   *

Senior FBI Agent Alex Martini shook his head in disbelief. He was only halfway through his first Miller Lite when another tragedy hit the nation. "Ricin attack turns deadly. Five US Senators targeted. Now one dead," reported CNN's Anderson Cooper. All eyes in the bar stared at the two TVs behind the bar.

It was Friday, his fifth day on the Memorial Day Massacre case. Alex was planning a day off. He was stressed. *Perhaps a little sightseeing. Maybe a bike ride across the Golden Gate Bridge*, he mused. Only moments ago, Bender's Bar and Grill had been buzzing with excitement. But now a chilling quiet gripped the patrons. T.G.I.F. took a sudden nose dive. Five democratic senators received mail at their senate offices containing a poison thought to be ricin. Unfortunately, a letter addressed to California Senator Elizabeth Huntington slipped through surveillance. She was found alone in her Washington D.C. apartment, sprawled across the bathroom floor. She was pronounced dead at the scene.

Agent Martini had just polished off his first beer and was considering another Miller Lite when his phone rang. "What's up?" he said.

"It's Tom Parker. You're needed in D.C. We've made arrangements for a 9 p.m. flight. The ricin-laced letters are right up your alley. We need you here. Drop the gun show and report to my office bright and early. I'll brief you then."

"I was planning a bike ride across the Golden Gate," Agent Martini said, trying to play the sympathy card. It was dead on arrival.

"Funny guy, I'll see you in D.C., and as I said, bright and early."

He tipped the bartender and returned to the downtown Marriot and packed. He felt important. He got an emergency FBI escort to the airport and through security. He'd be in

Washington D.C. for a very early breakfast. After boarding the Boeing 747, he popped an Ambien.

* * *

The FBI's Washington Field Office was on high alert. The rash of gun show bombings had everyone pulling overtime. Now the ricin attack forced the Bureau to enlist the help of Homeland Security and local police. The conference room was packed with agents. Director Parker rapped his knuckles on the conference room table.

"Time's of the essence," he barked. He was tense. His voice was hoarse. "I have the preliminary lab report. Ricin powder was discovered in an envelope within an envelope. A smaller manila envelope inside the larger one contained a silk scarf. Thank God four of the envelopes were intercepted and sent to the lab. Lab technicians discovered that each scarf was covered with a fine white powder. It was ricin."

"What happened in Elizabeth Huntington's case?" Agent Martini was quick to speak. He had three cups of coffee and was agitated and jittery.

"Elizabeth Huntington's envelope had no postmark. That's the mystery. We don't know how the envelopes got to her office, if they did. She was found dead in her apartment's bathroom. In the bedroom, two opened envelopes were found along with a scarf covered with ricin. On the nightstand was a half-empty bottle of sleeping pills and a near-empty bottle of cabernet."

"What about the other US Senators?" Agent Gary Carlson had worked with Agent Martini on other poison cases. "How were they intercepted?"

"Office personnel were alerted by the lack of postmarks. Somehow, the deadly envelope slipped by Senator Huntington's staff. There's a chance that either she brought it home or it was delivered to her apartment. That's what we know. I want Agents Carlson and Martini to investigate Senator Huntington's death. The rest of you will follow up on the other senators. Let's get going. I've got gun show bombings to worry about."

Agents Martini and Carlson headed straight to Senator Huntington's office. They needed answers. The office was somber. The staff had just lost their senator. The two agents waited ten minutes before they could talk to two key staff members. After a closed-door interrogation that lasted nearly an hour, they came out with more questions than answers. The staffers saw nothing unusual. No unidentified guests, no unusual mail or packages. It was just business as usual. Three lobbyists swung by, but all were well-known. A columnist for the *New York Times* interviewed Senator Huntington for forty-five minutes before lunch. She left for home around 6 p.m. with her briefcase and purse.

Leaving the senate offices with little to go on, they checked out her residence. At The Horizon, the agents cornered Horace Williams, the doorman at the senator's apartment complex. He worked the day shift yesterday. He was eager to help and very cooperative. Horace provided Agents Martini and Carlson with a detailed account of his shift. He started at 2 p.m. and worked until 10 p.m. He named almost all the people who entered and left the building. The only people he couldn't name were two guys from Shamrock Cleaners and a cable repairman. This got the agents' attention.

"Did the cable guy have on a uniform?" Agent Martini asked.

"He had on faded blue jeans and a dark blue work shirt." The doorman took off his brimmed cap and wiped his dark-skinned brow. It was an unseasonably warm June day.

"Did you see any logos, business identification, or nametag?" Agent Carlson said.

"There was a name on the back of the guy's shirt. It didn't ring a bell. I can't recall. I do remember a nametag. Henry. I remember because it's my twin brother's name." Horace put back on his cap and said, "I hope I've been helpful. Senator Huntington was such a nice person. She was always respectful and polite. Every year she gave me a Christmas present."

Upstairs in the senator's apartment, Agents Martini and Carlson joined a team of FBI and Homeland Security agents. It was claustrophobic. After hanging around for an hour, the frustrated FBI agents left with no real leads. They interviewed the doorman for a second time, trying to elicit the name of the cable company.

"How about we split up. You check on the cable company that services the apartment complex, and I'll interview Senator's Huntington's maid," Agent Martini said.

"Okay, Alex. I'll get right on it."

Chapter Twelve

The Saint was back at NRA Headquarters. He gazed out his office window, enjoying the warm spring morning. His mood was good. Operation Armageddon had commenced with a bang.

St. George walked down the hall to the main conference room where he had a 9 a.m. meeting with the board of directors. He swung open the door and greeted the assembled board members. "Top of the morning to you," he said. He was beaming like a teenager on the last day of school before summer vacation. "The Second Amendment is much safer today."

He took his place at the head of the conference table and grinned. "It's sad that a United States Senator had to die," Wayne St. George said, "but Elizabeth Huntington had pushed the envelope far too long. She meddled with the US Constitution, tried to confiscate the guns of law-abiding citizens, and tried to establish a national gun registry. She lost her way. If she had prosecuted criminals and fixed our mental health system, she'd be alive today."

St. George bowed his head and asked for a minute of

silence. He loved dramatic endings. He also loved sarcasm and irony. After a mock moment of silence, he got down to business. And as always, it was the business of promoting guns.

* * *

Matt Tyson phoned his old college buddy, Larry Fielding, and got a short list of names that Allen Carter played racquetball with. He interviewed three on the phone. The third guy, Mel Adams, said that Allen Carter, in addition to his anti-gun rants, had a passion for comic books. He suggested talking to the owner at Dream World Comics. "Don't be misled by the cheesy exterior of the shop," he said. "Inside you'll find treasures from the Golden Years and an enthusiastic owner. In the back of the shop, there's a bat cave. The geeks love it."

That was enough to pique Matt's curiosity, so he made an afternoon visit. The shop's interior did not disappoint. It was jammed full of collectibles. A wall-to-wall treasure trove of action figures, graphic novels, trade paperbacks, and comics. Collectibles from the Bronze, Silver, and Golden Age were housed behind a large glass case. Behind the counter was an older guy, with disheveled gray hair, wearing bright red suspenders and a faded blue shirt. The place had only two customers, who were methodically sorting through old comics in bins at the back of the store.

"Good afternoon," Matt said. "I've been told you have some comic books from the Golden Age."

"Yes, sir, that and more. We have the biggest and best collection west of the Mississippi. How may I help you?" The owner closed a catalogue and shelved it.

"I'm doing an article for *The Socratic Rag*. Matt Tyson's the name. Are you the owner?"

"Yep, but what's *The Socratic Rag's* interest in my shop?"

"We've an interest in one of your customers." Matt glanced about the store, impressed by the inventory of comic books and graphic novels.

"Is he in trouble?" The owner cocked his head. His eyes narrowed with instant suspicion.

"Oh, I hope not. No, I'm on assignment, and Allen Carter is key to my story."

"What's he done?" The owner squinted.

"It's not what he has done. It's what he has. I'm interested in his comic book collection." Matt smiled, trying his best to stay on the good side of the owner.

"It's a winner. He found a couple of rare beauties here. They rounded out his collection. You thinkin' about buying his collection?" The owner turned and picked up a catalogue from the counter behind him. He plopped it on the desk and opened it. "See this *Batman* comic?"

Matt turned the catalogue slightly to get a better look. "It's an oldie. *Batman #1* (1940)."

"It's the centerpiece in Allen Carter's collection." The owner smiled and added, "I sold it to him about a year ago."

"I bet it went for a pretty penny." Matt knew very little about comics. As a kid, he preferred *Mad Magazine*. He loved the political and cultural satire.

"You might say. I can't tell you what he actually paid. That's between him and me. I do know that it's been appraised for $49,000. Allen's collection, as I recall, is on the far side of a million." The owner closed the catalogue. "So, how can I help you?"

"Well," Matt looked about the shop and continued, "is he in it for the investment? Or is he a real lover of comics?"

"I'd say both. There's a reason he popped for big bucks on the 1940 first edition. It featured the first appearance of The Joker and The Cat, better known as Cat Woman. He also owns the first edition of Motley Wag. " The owner turned to help a customer.

Matt walked around the shop. He peered into the Bat Cave and just shook his head. It was a real cave-like space full of Bat Collectibles.

Back at the counter, he asked the owner his name.

"I'm Charles Cohen. And you?"

"Matt Tyson. It's a pleasure Mr. Cohen," Matt said.

"Call me Charles," he said.

"Can you tell me more about his interest in The Joker and The Cat?" Matt pulled out his notebook.

"Nah." Mr. Cohen chuckled and added, "Well maybe. His interest in The Joker and The Cat is both business and pleasure. But his real passion is for Motley Wag. He mentioned a couple of times that he loved costume parties because he could dress up like Motley Wag, purple blazer, funky orange tie, and eerie facial make-up. He had even taken several classes to learn the finer points of make-up artistry. His eyes lit up and he broke out into laughter describing a recent affair. He was a talker, that one."

"Were these private parties?" Matt scribbled something in his notes.

"Hell, I don't know. None of my business, but he did go on about his estate in Malibu. He often bragged about how his place had a great view of the Pacific. Lucky guy."

"When's the last time he was in the shop?"

"Couple weeks back, he bought some action figures." Charles again turned to assist a customer.

After he finished with the customer, Charles retrieved another catalogue from the counter, opened it, and flipped through some pages, muttering to himself.

"One last question. Why did he buy the action figures?" Matt asked.

"Party favors. That's all I know. Nice talking to you." Charles Cohen headed for the back of his shop. He had to sign for a new shipment of comics being delivered by UPS.

"Thanks. You've been helpful." Matt left with a hunch.

* * *

After leaving Dream World Comics, Matt Tyson stopped at Starbucks for some caffeine and then made a couple of calls to *The Socratic Rag*. During the second call, he got what he wanted—the address of Allen Carter.

He wished he had rented a convertible. Driving north on PCH toward Malibu was a trip through paradise. But his budget demanded prudence. His rented Honda Accord had navigation, so finding Los Flores Canyon Road was no problem. The Honda strained as it climbed the steep hillside overlooking Malibu. Near the top of Los Flores, he spotted his destination, a sprawling estate cloistered behind high walls and a massive iron gate. The white exterior and red tile roof stood out sharply against the scrappy and thick chaparral.

Matt pulled passed the gate and rounded a sharp curve

in the canyon road. There he looked down on the Carter estate. *There's got to be a way for me to get in there,* he thought.

On his way back to Santa Monica, he brainstormed. He knew what he wanted. That was the easy part. *Now,* he thought, *how do I get it?*

Chapter Thirteen

FBI Director Tom Parker had studied the map of the United States for the past week. He had immersed himself, relived, and suffered through the gory details of the gun show bombings. The human devastation was mind numbing—at least 149 confirmed dead, and 307 injured.

The material used to construct the bombs and the logistics were well documented. The combined efforts of forensic teams from the FBI, Homeland Security, and local law enforcement had paid off. The specifics of the tragedy were detailed, dissected, and understood. All the bombs were pressure-cooker bombs containing ball bearings and nails fueled by black powder. They were detonated by components from a remote control car, common electrical wiring, and a cell phone. What the experts didn't know was *who* did it and *why*.

Director Parker stood before a large map of the United States pinned to a bulletin board in his office. The cities of San Francisco, Carson City, Albuquerque, Rockford, Evansville, and Detroit were circled in red. He took a couple of steps back, grabbed a red marker and paper from his desk, and printed the first letter of each city in capital letters. SCARED. The acronym, boldly scrolled in red marker, stunned him. Was it pure chance or a hidden message? He needed confirmation. He called for an emergency meeting of agents heading up the Memorial Day bombings. Within in an hour, he got his confirmation. This was no accident.

*   *   *

David and Charles were on retreat. It was time to celebrate. And there was only one place for that— Shangri-La. That was the pet name for their log cabin tucked away in the Bitterroot National Forest in South West Montana. Log cabin was an understatement. It was their private retreat, playground, and master control center of their financial empire. The twins sat on the deck of their two-story getaway, enjoying the sun dipping beneath the jagged saw-tooth ridge of the Bitterroot Mountain Range. Phase one of Armageddon was in the books. It was time for phase two.

"Shall we notify The Saint?" David tugged at his second beer, pleased that there was more to come.

"Let's have him meet us here." Charles leaned back in his chair and followed a red-tailed hawk diving toward the lily pad pond at the rear of their property.

"*Here?* That's crazy. He doesn't even know who we are. All he knows is that Gemini calls the shots." David was mystified.

Charles looked his brother in the eye. "Maybe it's time to change the rules of the game."

"What if he cracks, breaks down, or loses the faith?" David finished his second beer and pulled open the cooler at his feet. He popped open a third.

"His career and power are tied directly to us. Without us, the NRA would sink, overpowered by the rising tide of anti-gun sentiment. Plus, we own his soul." Charles followed his brother's lead and retrieved another beer.

"True. He entered a Mephistophelian bargain years ago. He knows he's done if he betrays us," David said.

"What's the benefit of inviting him here?" Charles asked.

"He's been a loyal soldier. It's time to reward him." David laughed.

"You have something in mind …" Charles smiled, suddenly interested in David's proposal.

"I think we should introduce him to the *War Room*. I've been dying to share our brain center with someone for years. Are we on the same page?"

"Have we ever been on a different page?" Charles laughed. "How about we have him over the day after tomorrow?"

David finished his beer. "Let's do it."

* * *

Professor Alexis Williams was running late for her therapy session in Santa Monica. The morning traffic along PCH was a nightmare, congested because of road work. She parked her late-model Lexus in the parking garage off Seventh Street, sprinted up four flights of stairs, and breezed into Dr. Emily Hollingsworth's waiting room one minute early. She abhorred tardiness.

Her weekly sessions were a treasured secret. Even Allen Carter was clueless. The inner door opened slowly, about halfway, allowing Dr. Hollingsworth enough room to peek into the waiting room.

"Good morning. Shall we get started?" Dr. Hollingsworth opened the door wider for Alexis to enter.

The therapist had a corner office, windows along two sides, and adjustable horizontal blinds. She could adjust the lighting electronically based on the time of day or the mood of the client. This morning they were opened, allowing the early-morning sun to brighten the room. Books lined one windowless wall, and along the adjoining wall was a sofa and two wingback chairs. At the center of the bookcase was a large fisheye aquarium. Colorful tropical fish lazily swam about.

Alexis plopped down on the sofa, near a wingback chair where Dr. Hollingsworth sat. She sighed and then said, "I'm in crisis."

"I thought things were going well. You were gearing up for one of your costume parties." Dr. Hollingsworth crossed her legs and smoothed out her skirt. She was always fashionably dressed. Christian Dior on Rodeo Drive made sure she looked elegant. They had never failed her. Her clients called her Doc. She was slim and attractive and cherished her appearance. Her dark brunette hair, styled and dyed by a Beverly Hills salon, artfully disguised her age. She had turned sixty just last month.

"Last week, I was on top of the world. We had a great party with good friends. We had a blast," Alexis said. "But since then, I'm a basket case. The only thing that eases the pain is my bloody sessions with Allen."

"You're using sex as an escape. You blow off steam, feel good for a while, and then crash. It's a vicious circle." Dr. Hollingsworth paused and then added, "Your university work, aerobic dance, and costume parties are healthy activities."

"I know you're right, but when my world turns dark, when I feel lonely and hollow, the only fix is Allen. He knows how to extinguish the darkness. He drives the devil right out of me." Alexis looked Doc in the eye. "I know cognitively what's going on. But my emotions have a mind of their own."

"It's time," Dr. Hollingsworth said. "Are you up for it?"

Alexis stood and positioned one of the wingback chairs directly in front of the fisheye aquarium. She collapsed into the chair, took a deep breath, and gazed at the tropical beauties. *Perhaps we can grab the devil by the tail*, she thought.

Blue neon guppies, blood-fin tetra, electric yellow cichlid, and dwarf gourami glided lazily about the aquarium. Their repetitious circling was indeed hypnotic. The colorful meanderings of the tropical fish were not lost on Alexis. She was soon in an altered state, relaxed and receptive, ready for her therapist's suggestions.

In less than five minutes, Dr. Hollingsworth had skillfully transported Alexis to her sophomore year in college. It was a familiar touchstone, that fateful day she read the case study of Anna in her Abnormal Psychology class. Anna was a sociopath, a term modern psychologists loathed. The DSM-IV, the bible of the psychiatric profession, preferred the label "antisocial personality disorder." After reading about Anna, she fell into a funk and changed her major from psychology to philosophy. Reading about Anna was like reading her biography. When Alexis looked in a mirror, she saw a beautiful woman. When she glimpsed her unconscious mind, she saw the devil himself.

"Tell me about Anna." Dr. Hollingsworth sat on the sofa behind Alexis. "Tell me how you felt when you first read about her."

"At first, I was fascinated. Anna could float through life, flitting about like a brightly colored butterfly, unfazed by challenges and pitfalls. It felt good to read her story. I wanted to be her. She was in control, master of her destiny." Alexis's voice suddenly lowered, becoming throaty and sinister. "But Anna's elegance and beauty were shattered when her motives were revealed. Friends and acquaintances were merely stepping stones. They provided a path, a convenient way to get what she wanted. The butterfly image was a mirage. She was a snake, slithering, cunning, and deadly. Beneath the surface charm was the heart of a demon, a violent viper creeping through the shadows of life."

"How did this make you feel?" Dr. Hollingsworth asked.

"I was terrified. I became an emotional wreck. Psychology became a threat. I feared going to class. I had nightmares, missed classes, and ended up talking to a school counselor. So, I changed my major." Alexis tracked the tropical beauties making lazy loops in the aquarium. Her trance had deepened numbing her thoughts. She had finally let go and had sunk deeper into her being, losing contact with the eternal roof brain chatter that ruled her life.

After a lapse of several minutes, Dr. Hollingsworth asked, "How do you feel now?"

"Afraid."

"Why are you afraid?"

"I'm terrified of the unknown. I'm terrified of what's behind my thoughts. I'm afraid to look inside the black box." Alexis's voice cracked, and her hands trembled.

"What black box?" Dr. Hollingsworth asked.

"In the attic."

"What attic?"

"At my grandmother's house, in the attic."

"What was in the black box?" The psychiatrist leaned forward.

Alexis screamed. "I can't look. No!"

Dr. Hollingsworth calmly asked, "Tell me, please. What's in the black box?"

"A head, the head of a clown," Alexis blurted. She sobbed, gasping for air. "It's got a wide mouth, painted red, distorted by scars into a permanent smile. No, no, no. I can't go on."

"Please tell me. Who's the clown?"

"I don't know. The eyes! Oh, God help me." Alexis wailed, hands trembling. "The sunken eyes bore right through me. They stripped me naked. They saw the real me." Alexis slumped down in the wingback chair, nearly disappearing into a ball of quivering flesh.

Dr. Hollingsworth reached forward and handed her a tissue. "Today, we've made progress."

Chapter Fourteen

The Saint boarded an early-morning flight to Bozeman, Montana. He was nervous. Not about the flight. That was old hat. Today was judgment day. He was about to meet Gemini for the first time. All he knew was that the twins were incredibly wealthy, powerful, and ruthless. They were the blood, guts, and brains of the gun industry. Without the twins, the NRA would be nothing but a safety-minded gun club. In a matter of hours, he'd meet them face to face.

Driving by car toward the Bitterroot Mountains was a thing of beauty. But the stunning Montana landscape offered little solace. St. George was trembling.

He pulled off the main highway and traveled a couple of miles down a dirt road better suited for an off-road vehicle than a Lincoln Town Car. He wanted a Hummer. He had slim pickings at the rental agency in Bozeman. He had settled for luxury.

The Saint pulled the black Lincoln down a secondary dirt road and stopped at a massive wooden gate. It had the look of a medieval fortress. The gate was composed of thick logs, connected and fortified by steel crossbars. Steep log walls disappeared into the pines on both sides of the driveway. On the right side, atop a supporting log column was a surveillance camera. On the left side, a buzzer and speaker were mounted on a much shorter stone and concrete structure. He buzzed, identified himself, and was let in.

After traveling a quarter mile through a dense forest of pines, an oval patch of land dramatically appeared. There he was overwhelmed by the biggest log structure he'd ever laid eyes on. It was resort-sized. The architecture reminded him of a hotel he had once stayed at in Glacier National Park.

Across from the entrance of Gemini's retreat was a white helicopter with blue trim. He was sure he'd seen one like that before. It was a Bell 222, a sleek, fast helicopter good for private service. Two weeks ago at NRA Headquarters, he'd greeted some lobbyists out of Washington D.C. using the same model. Next to the chopper, atop a gigantic flag pole, was Old Glory. Beneath her stars and broad stripes was the Montana State flag, and lower still was a smaller NRA banner. The place had the aura of a military outpost.

The view to the west was spectacular. While approaching the getaway, he had noticed a lily pad pond. Beyond the pond was the Bitterroot Range, a rugged saw-tooth mountain range, a smaller version of the Rockies.

He parked the Lincoln and slowly approached the entrance. Fear gripped him. He slowly climbed a series of steps before reaching the front door. He looked for a door bell but saw none. He rapped at the door. No response. He rapped again, somewhat more forcefully, and the heavy redwood door slid open a foot or two. He called out, "Anyone home?"

An ethereal voice came from deep within the fortress. "Please take the spiral stairway to the second level. You'll find us outside on the rear deck."

At the top of the stairs, The Saint stepped into a large living area with high ceilings and an impressive stone fireplace. At the far end of the room, he found the double doors open and two men seated with their backs to him. They were drinking beer.

William called out, "I'm here. The Saint's at your service."

"Come on out," one of the men said. "And pull up a chair."

St. George stepped out onto the deck and moved in front of Gemini. He smiled and slowly approached the twins. They stood, each greeting the NRA bigwig with a hardy handshake.

"Please, get comfortable. Join us for a beer. We have a lot of catching up to do." David opened the cooler and took out an ice-cold Miller Lite and handed it to The Saint.

"Thanks," St. George said. He was flabbergasted. He immediately recognized the twins. They were the one and only Berrigan brothers, billionaires, petroleum moguls extraordinaire, and producers of the best American whiskey. The twins ruled Berrigan Industries, the second largest privately owned company in the United States, with an iron fist. He had never seen pictures of them lounging around in baseball caps, faded blue jeans, and T-shirts. The brothers looked like retired buddies, throwing down cold ones after a long day of fishing. They were gray haired, freckled, and showed age spots on their hands and forearms. Both had put on a little extra weight around the middle.

"Welcome to Shangri-La." Charles smiled and gestured toward the mountains. "Great country, don't you think?"

"Yes indeed." The Saint took a tug on his beer. His nervousness was replaced by elation. He had always admired the Berrigan brothers. "The vista is spectacular. But what's more awe inspiring is your libertarian philosophy. I feel an immediate connection."

"We know of your fondness for libertarianism. That's why you're the *chosen one*." David looked at his brother. "Isn't that right?"

Charles smiled. "Free enterprise and personal freedom, that's what it's all about."

The trio spent the next hour drinking and sharing their thoughts on libertarianism. A common thread ran through their philosophical ramblings—distrust of the US government.

"We should put an end to the government meddling in our lives. Scrap social security, minimum wage laws, and gun control," Charles said.

"Here, here," echoed David. "And fuck the scientists. Climate warming is a myth perpetrated by pointed-headed nerds. They'd be out of work if it weren't for government grants. Shit, they suckle at the tit of government handouts. They're nothing but pinko left-wingers, the lot of them. "

Charles stood to emphasize his point. "Slash personal and corporate taxes. And for God's sake, let us alone. We must legalize prostitution, recreational drug use, and suicide. I'm the decider. I own my body. I am my freedom." Charles looked The Saint in the eye and then sat down. "That's my two bits for today."

David took his turn at the libertarian rant. "A

night-watchman state is all we need. The purpose of a just state is like that of the duties of a night watchman. Just keep the bad guys away and protect our private property and individual rights."

"Enough of the philosophical bullshit," Charles said. "Let's visit the War Room."

"May I ask a question?" The Saint stood.

"Go ahead," David said.

"When do we launch phase two of Armageddon?" The Saint was eager for payback. The gun show bombings made his hair stand on end. He wanted blood.

"In due time. In due time, my friend." David motioned for The Saint to follow. "We've something to show you."

The slightly inebriated trio descended two flights of stairs, passed by the game room, and entered the study. Charles stepped into a closet, and seconds later, a section of the study's bookshelf slid open. The trio entered a concealed door and walked down a long, narrow passage to a second door. Charles punched some numbers on a wall-mounted keypad. There was an electronic hum, and then the door slid open. The Saint's eyes widened in amazement. The room looked like an electronic cave. It was dark except for a group of built-in lights that illuminated desks and counters crammed with the latest in electronics. A bank of flashing lights glowed eerily in the semi-dark room. The top half of the wall was covered with flat-screen monitors. The bottom half accommodated desks and counters filled with computers, desktops, laptops, fax machines, copiers, and surveillance controls.

David stepped up to the central control panel, punched in a code on the keyboard, and the monitors sprang to life.

The darkness of the cave vanished, replaced by a blur of bright light. The monitors filled the room with an array of diverse images, ranging from surveillance video of the front gate and the Bell 222 helicopter out front, to the major networks, cable news, and a private feed from their hotline. The hotline connected the Berrigan brothers to key operatives on five continents. From the War Room, they could monitor the world, especially their world of wealth.

Charles broke the silence. "What do you think?"

The Saint's eyes said it all. He knew the Berrigan brothers were big-time players. It was common knowledge that they operated oil refineries in Alaska, Texas, and Minnesota, and controlled some four thousand miles of pipelines in the US. They had their hands on everything from paper towels to Lycra. *Hell, they own the gun world*, he thought. This was the central nervous system of their capitalistic playground.

"So this is where it happens ..." The Saint fell silent. He was speechless.

Chapter Fifteen

Alex Martini rang the doorbell of apartment 22 at Gardner Drive in Alexandria, Virginia. He had phoned ahead and confirmed that Alice Washington was home. She was the maid on duty the day Senator Elizabeth Huntington was murdered.

Just as he rang a second time, the door opened halfway, and a light-skinned African American woman with brilliant white teeth and a broad smile said, "You must be Special Agent Martini."

"Yes. Senior Special Agent Alex Martini at your service."

"May I be so bold to ask for ID?" She smiled. Her tone of voice was soft. There was definitely no hint of hostility.

After he showed his badge, she stepped aside. "Please come in and have a seat."

She sat on one end of a long sofa while he settled in an overstuffed chair across from her. It was exactly the kind of chair that could put him to sleep in minutes. When married, his wife quipped that he preferred the comforts of his favorite chair to her. He had made the mistake of saying that at least the chair didn't talk back. The exchange escalated, eventually ending their ten-year marriage. Of course, sixty-hour workweeks at the Bureau didn't help much either.

"So, Alice Washington," he paused and pulled out his notebook, "may I call you Alice?"

"Yes. Please do." She leaned back and casually stroked the doily on the arm of the sofa.

"You were on duty the day Senator Elizabeth Huffington was found dead. Is that right?" He looked up at Alice and smiled.

"That's correct." Alice continued stroking the doily. She fidgeted, obviously still shaken by the loss of her employer.

"Did you notice anything out of the ordinary? Unexpected visitors, phone calls, or service personnel carrying out their duties?" Agent Martini glanced at some photos on a nearby table. She was in the pictures along with a Caucasian gentleman with a large, dark moustache. They were flanked by a couple of good-looking youngsters. "Is that your family?" Alex pointed toward the photographs.

"Yes. My husband is dead, killed in an auto accident. The kids are grown. I live here by myself." The way she smiled signaled that she was doing just fine. "But to answer your question, it was a typical day."

"You didn't notice anything out of the ordinary?"

"Well, one little thing sticks out." She stopped talking and took a deep breath.

"Go on," Agent Martini encouraged her.

"I was about to leave for the day. It was 4:30. I was doing a last-minute check of the premises when I noticed a large manila envelope tacked to the kitchen bulletin board. I paused, checked out who it was addressed to, and shrugged.

I've seen many large manila envelopes in the apartment. I just didn't remember one tacked to the bulletin board. Don't recall seeing it when I cleaned the kitchen earlier. But I was tired and hungry. My blood sugar was low—brain fog, y'know. Anyway, I shook it off thinking I was being silly. I locked up and left for home."

"And who was the envelope addressed to?" Agent Martini scribbled furiously in his tattered notebook.

"Senator Elizabeth Huffington." She looked down. Her right hand worked the doily, wadding it up in a ball.

"Was there a postmark on the envelope?"

"I'm not sure. I saw her name and address, that's for sure. It was printed in bold capital letters. Postmark? Can't say. As I said, I was tired and ready for my commute home."

"Think back. Close your eyes and try to visualize what you saw on the kitchen bulletin board." He smiled and spoke softly.

"I saw a manila envelope addressed to Senator Elizabeth Huffington. That's all." A small tear ran down her right cheek.

"Are you willing to testify in court? Will you admit to seeing a manila envelope in the senator's kitchen?"

"Yes." Alice Washington looked down. She seemed ashamed of not noticing more.

"So, no one entered the apartment when you were on duty. Is that right?"

"No. I saw no one." Alice spoke softly. "I'm sure of that."

"You've been extraordinarily helpful. Here's my card. If you recall anything more, please don't hesitate to call me. Any time of the day or night is just fine." Agent Martini stood and looked back at the photos of her family. "You sure do have a beautiful family."

"Thanks. The kids are fine. But I do miss Mark. He was a great husband and father."

Senior Special Agent Martini said good-bye. He needed more. How did the envelopes get into the apartment? Did Senator Huffington bring it home? Was the envelope tacked to the kitchen bulletin board the cause of the senator's death? Did someone have access to the apartment?

* * *

Matt Tyson checked his e-mail before heading out for an interview with a left-wing Hollywood producer. The guy was tight with the likes of Susan Sarandon, Tim Robbins, and Richard Gere. The e-mail read:

> *Saturday, June 5, Allen Carter and Alexis Williams are hosting a costume party. Please come as your favorite comic book hero.*

Manna from heaven, Matt thought. *If I were religious, I'd fall to my knees with thanks.* He'd racked his mind for a way to check out Allen Carter's villa. Twice this week he'd awaken from a deep sleep, obsessed with finding a way in.

Matt didn't hesitate. He fired off an e-mail accepting the invitation. His next challenge was selecting the appropriate hero. As a kid, he was a big fan of Spiderman. But he needed an ephemeral personality, a character of many faces, and a character for any man. He chose Hypnos, God of sleep, and the Lord of Dreams. He went by many names, but none were really his: Sandman, Dream King, and Dream Cat. They all projected a different image.

Hypnos was the personification of stories and dreams. *Perfect*, Matt thought.

The next two days were a whirlwind of interviews with Hollywood agents looking for clues about NRA backing and visits to costume stores. He was prepared. The party was tonight. He had two hours to apply his makeup and dress. The original plan was to dye his hair. He scuttled that and opted for a black wig with spiked hair. That had a dramatic effect. It literally doubled the size of his head. After applying face paint and dark paint around his eyes, the transformation was complete. The reflection in the mirror of a tall man with bone-white skin and black spiked hair, wearing a billowing black cape, stared back at him.

Matt was fashionably late. The party was in full swing when he made his entrance. Motley Wag greeted Matt enthusiastically, temporarily stopping the music to introduce the mystery guest.

"Please give a hearty welcome to Matt Tyson, *The Socratic Rag's* best, agent provocateur, and the fourth estates' noblest warrior." As Motley Wag bowed, the partiers applauded wildly.

Hypnos bowed. "I haven't donned a costume since my college days." Matt felt empowered. Sharing the evening with a room full of superheroes was definitely a first. His last costume party was a Greek orgy in the honor of Dionysus. His sophomoric antics got out of hand. He ended up falling into a vat of cheap wine. It was the first and last time he ever passed out from an overdose of booze. "I'm looking forward to meeting all of you."

Motley Wag turned back on the music, and the place erupted with cheers. Moody Muse pulled a hesitant Hypnos out on the dance floor to the pulse-pounding strains of the Bee Gees, "Stayin' Alive." After a cautious start, Hypnos found his groove and gave the beautiful Moody Muse a spirited dance. It was hard to keep his eyes off the fluid moves of such a stunningly beautiful woman. The next song was a romantic ballad. Motley Wag broke in, reclaiming his love.

Hypnos made the rounds, sharing stories, dances, and booze with the other characters. But he felt conflicted. All the partygoers were protective of their true identities. He left the party knowing only that Allen Carter was a lawyer with a practice in Santa Monica, had a hard-on for gun enthusiasts, and a love of hedonism and costume parties. Motley Wag loved to play the mystery card. He'd throw you a morsel, whet your appetite, and then abruptly change the subject. He loved laughing and making sarcastic puns. His date, the beautiful Moody Muse, was as tantalizing and elusive as a mythological Siren.

Chapter Sixteen

Alexis Williams's eyes glazed over as they watched the tropical beauties making lazy circles in Dr. Hollingsworth's aquarium. The radiant colors and fluid movements of the exotic tropical fish were indeed hypnotic. It was only here with the guidance of her psychiatrist that she left behind the comfort of her highly structured rational mind. She was at ease at the helm of her rational mind. It was here that she conversed with the intellectual giants of philosophy, holding her own with Plato, Kant, David Hume, and Nietzsche. The elegance of a logically compelling philosophical argument resonated with her rational sensibilities. Within the boundaries of lucid conceptual distinctions and rigorous logical structures, she felt at peace. No ambiguities, no loose ends, no unaccounted-for variables. Everything neatly stacked, sorted, and classified. But beneath this logical superstructure, far below her conscious mind, was a seething mass of conflicting urges and desires. Beneath the veil of words and thoughts simmered a cauldron of molten passions and feelings.

"Alexis," Dr. Hollingsworth said softly, "breathe deeply

and follow the movements of our little beauties. Look, feel, and see. Notice the color and feel the fluidity of their graceful meanderings. Allow yourself to enter their world. Feel the water, glide along, and be at one with the wiggly world of nature, unrestrained, unfiltered, and unstructured. Just be."

Alexis drifted into a kaleidoscopic show of bright colors and sounds. It felt like she had entered an amusement park. Everywhere she turned, she heard a jumble of music, saw a blur of colors, and detected aromas from hot dogs and mustard to peanuts and cotton candy. The tropical fish beckoned her to the fun house where she saw reflections of herself, distorted, twisted, elongated, and compressed. She passed by many mirrors, reflecting her twisted and stretched image. Suddenly everything went dark. She tried to scream, but nothing happened. Out of the darkness, a clown suddenly appeared, laughing wildly, thrusting his index finger inches from her face. His lips were twisted into a sinister scowl, his yellowed teeth clenched tightly, and his white painted face wrinkled under his green tinted hair. He laughed and said, "The joke is on you."

With Alexis's piercing scream, Dr. Hollingsworth leaped from her chair, pulled Alexis to her feet, and hugged her warmly, saying repeatedly, "You are safe. You are with me. Everything is good."

After long moments of consoling her patient, she encouraged Alexis to sit down and recount what she experienced. After hearing her account, Dr. Hollingsworth said, "Did you recognize the clown?"

"No, but he's scary."

"Describe to me again what you just experienced."

"I saw a fun house of horrors, a freakish clown, one with green tinted hair and a hideous face, twisted lips, scowling. It was horrible."

"Who was the clown?" Dr. Hollingsworth calmly waited for an answer.

After a long period of silence Alexis mumbled, "Him."

"Who?" Dr. Hollingsworth paused, and then repeated softly, "Who was the clown?"

"Him."

"Please Alexis. Who was the clown?"

"Motley Wag."

"Do you know Motley Wag?"

"Yes. He's the one that likes to impersonate Motley Wag, throws costume parties as that creepy clown, Motley Wag. He's the one who makes the pain go away. He's the one I saw in my grandmother's attic. He's the master of my dark side. He's the one in the black box, the one with the distorted smile." Alexis slumped further into the chair, hands shaking, not immediately understanding what she had just blurted. It was an eruption from somewhere deep within her.

Alexis was stunned and confused. When she realized what she had just said she back peddled, frightened by her confession. All she could say was, "Allen is good. He makes the pain go away. We are one. We will overcome. Down with guns."

Dr. Hollingsworth talked Alexis down from the glimpse of her dark side. After ending the session, the psychiatrist made some notes.

* * *

William St. George strolled into NRA headquarters with a new sense of empowerment. The Berrigan brothers had his back. It was indeed a promotion. David and Charles were two of the wealthiest and most powerful men in the world, and he had been invited into their inner circle.

He had less than twenty-minutes to put the final touches on his grand proposal before leaving for Shangri-La. The twins were expecting him this evening for dinner.

After a helicopter ride to Dulles, he took a commercial flight to Salt Lake City, where he was whisked away by private jet to Bozeman and then helicoptered into the Bitterroot Mountains. Shangri-La was waiting.

He wasn't greeted by the twins, but met by a butler formally dressed in a dark gray coat, gray and black striped pants, red bowtie, and top hat. The Saint was promptly escorted upstairs to his room where he was instructed to prepare for dinner. Laid out on the king-size bed was a tux, white shirt, blue tie, and top hat. The butler informed The Saint that cocktails would be served in the study at five. He had forty-five minutes to shave, shower, and dress. The formal attire was a surprise. On his first visit here, the twins guzzled beer and wore jeans, T-shirts, and baseball caps. Tonight was the Saint's initiation into the twins' world.

George, the butler, greeted The Saint at the top of the stairs and showed him the way to the study. After opening light-stained knotty pined double doors, The Saint entered a room lined with books from floor to ceiling on two walls, and a bar stretching the length of the room adjacent to a floor-to-ceiling stone fireplace. The room featured high ceilings and rugged log beams. In the middle of the room was a grouping of leather chairs and two large sofas. The arrangement of furniture created an intimate area perfect for conversation.

Before The Saint took a seat, the twins appeared, wearing identical formal wear. It looked like a reunion of Arctic penguins.

"How was your trip west?" David said.

"Yes. I hope you enjoyed the efficient service. I never tire of approaching Shangri-La by chopper. There's nothing better than being greeted by Old Glory, the Montana State flag, and the NRA banner," broke in Charles.

"I didn't expect all the formality." The Saint hadn't gotten his bearings yet.

"There's more to come." David went behind the bar and asked, "What's your pleasure?"

"Do you by chance have Silver Patron?" The Saint hadn't truly savored a Silver Patron since his man cave had been bombed from the face of the earth.

"Lime and a touch of salt?" David beamed a friendly smile across the study.

"You read my mind."

The trio of conspirators got comfortable, the twins taking a seat across from each other on the facing sofas, while the Saint faced the bar with his back to the stone fireplace.

"Here's to the NRA." Charles raised his glass of cabernet for a toast.

"Hear, hear!" echoed David.

After a couple of rounds, Charles made a surprise announcement. "David and I have made our decision. With all due respect to your master plan, and we've both read your preliminary draft, we've decided on our version of Armageddon. We'll discuss the details of phase two tomorrow. But tonight we've arranged for some entertainment."

"Yes indeed. We have brought in three guests to add a feminine touch to our weekend retreat. They're waiting for us out on the deck." David stood and motioned to the far end of the room where the butler stood quietly. "George will show us the way," David said.

The sun was setting behind the Bitterroot Mountains, leaving a soft brushed sky of oranges and reds. Three very attractive women stood leaning against the railing, enjoying the last few rays of the setting sun. Their dress was less formal than the men, and far more provocative. Two were brunettes, and the other a blonde. Their short black skirts and plunging necklines wouldn't be stylish at a Beltway gala. But they were very popular with the twins.

"I like your taste in entertainment," The Saint said.

"The night is young. Carpe diem! Tomorrow we get down to business. Tonight we enjoy the spoils of victory. Long live the NRA," David said before approaching their special guests.

Chapter Seventeen

gent Martini flipped on CNN. His TV might be small and unimpressive, but the images it produced were truly stunning. Andersen Cooper was either stoical or in shock. His ashen face and thin lips had the look of a mortician. What he said was worse.

"Justice Helena Bartoletti was found dead in her chambers at the US Supreme Court. Clerks found her slumped over legal documents. A letter addressed to the justice along with photos of assault weapons were found at the scene. No more details are available at this time."

Agent Alex Martini's phone chirped. "Alex here."

"Supreme Court Justice Helena Bartoletti was murdered," Director Thomas Parker said. "The scene is a copycat of the murder of Senator Elizabeth Huntington."

"I know. I just got home and turned on CNN. Was there a handwritten envelope without a postmark?"

"Bingo. I want you on it now. Turn off the TV and report to headquarters. I'll be there with about two dozen other agents."

Director Parker signed off without a good-bye. Alex

took a quick shower and was out the door in less than five minutes.

At the meeting, details of the murder scene were dissected, analyzed, and discussed. As in the Senator Huffington case, two envelopes with no postmarks were found, but this time no ricin-laced scarf. The inner envelope contained a small album of photos featuring assault weapons. The cloth-bound album contained ricin and a hand-printed note. Its message was terse and blunt:

> *The Second Amendment is sacred to all lovers of American liberty. Any attempt to weaken the right to bear arms is an act of treason. Supreme Court Justice Helena Bartoletti has violated her sacred oath to honor and uphold the constitution. She will now answer to a higher court.*

Agent Alex Martini and his colleagues were confounded, not only by the message, but by how the perpetrator of this heinous crime got access to Justice Helena Bartoletti's chambers. The FBI, NSA, and CIA were put on high alert. Agent Alex Martini was assigned six additional agents to investigate anyone having access to Justice Bartoletti, her office, and her residence. Government offices, the Supreme Court, and congressional offices were under tight security. The president of the United States was scheduled to address the nation tomorrow evening. Washington D.C. was paralyzed with fear. The heart and soul of the nation had been violated.

* * *

Allen Carter, outraged and disgusted, tossed the *New York Times* into the trash. Everywhere he looked, he was met with the same nauseating imagery. The grizzly assassination of Justice Helena Bartoletti was an assault on the rule of law. The tenuous threads that had once held the savage irrational forces of men in check had been shredded. The United States of America had become a nation of men, not laws. It was no longer governed by the wisdom of our founding fathers. *We've been condemned to bedlam. Crazed inmates now run the asylum*, Allen thought.

He was about to leave his Santa Monica law office when his cell phone rang. He glanced at the caller's number and immediately picked up. "Well, Matt Tyson. Have you seen the latest on Justice Bartoletti?"

"Shocking! That's why I'm calling you. I thought you'd have a new angle on the murder," Matt said.

"I'm stunned. Where are you?" Allen needed to vent. He needed someone to blow off steam with.

"I'm at Mulligans, your favorite watering hole. Care to join me?"

"I was about to close shop. I'll be there in fifteen minutes." Allen signed off, washed his hands and face, slicked back his thick, dark hair, and headed for Mulligans. Within fifteen minutes, he was seated at his favorite Irish Pub with a Guinness in hand.

"You're certainly a man of your word. You made it here in fourteen minutes and change." Matt grinned and added, "So, what's your take on Justice Bartoletti?"

Allen took a tug on his Guinness, raised his brows, and briefly studied Matt's facial expression. *The Socratic Rag's* best looked like an aging grad student. His boyish grin, however, was deceptive. It cleverly concealed the grit and tenacity of a seasoned bloodhound. But somehow he felt at ease in his presence. "I'm stunned and pissed off. I feel like punching someone. But I don't know where to lash out. You got any ideas?" Allen frowned, once again visited by images of the grisly murder.

"I'm puzzled by what investigators found at the crime scene. A small cloth photo album containing pictures of assault weapons was found on her desk. The album was saturated with ricin. But what's up with the pictures of weapons?" Matt grinned, raised his mug, and drained it.

"That's not all. The *New York Times* reported that there was a handwritten note. The note said something about the Second Amendment being sacred. The *Times* also mentioned that the note called out Justice Bartoletti as a traitor." Allen paused and added, "There's evil written all over this cowardly attack. I sense that there are radical right-wing thugs behind this shit."

"Can you name names?" Matt flashed Allen a mischievous grin before taking another sip of Guinness.

"There are a few out there that are truly *out there*." Allen frowned.

"Who tops your list?"

"The Berrigan bothers." Allen didn't hesitate in his response.

"David and Charles?" Matt said.

"They're libertarian crooks. Their power and money is vast, limitless!" Allen's voice strained and deepened. His face flushed, and lips curled downward in a wicked scowl.

"What's your proof?"

"My Hollywood contacts keep me informed. I have

loyal clients with intimate knowledge of the workings of the inner circle." Allen grinned. He felt self-assured.

"The inner circle? Is this a private club?" Matt took another sip.

"There's a group of about a dozen of the world wealthiest that call the shots. These good-old-boys control the flow of money and power. They own Wall Street, the lobbyists on K Street in D.C., and Congress. The Berrigan brothers are key players in the inner circle."

"Who's your source?" Matt obviously wanted names—again.

"As I've told you before, I treasure my attorney-client privilege. It's sacred in my professional world." Allen leaned back. "Say, do you like to fly?"

"What?" Matt was clearly taken off guard.

"I occasionally fly up to Santa Barbara or over to Catalina. I mainly fly a small Cessna, but I've been checked out in a Lear jet."

"You're a pilot?"

"You look surprised," Allen quipped. He took a sip of beer and studied Matt's face.

"No, I just wonder where you get the time to fit in all your hobbies." Matt grinned.

There were several more rounds consumed before they called it a night.

*   *   *

After six hours of searching mainstream publications for something juicy on the Berrigan brothers, Matt Tyson called his contact at the *New York Times*. Charles Breeze, a regular contributor to the *Times* opinion section, owed him a big favor. He pleaded his case, and within two hours, Charles Breeze called back with the best news of the year. He had been granted a twenty-minute interview at the Beverly Hills Hotel tomorrow at noon. The Pink Lady, as she was known during Hollywood's golden era, was becoming a touchstone for his search for dirt on the NRA. It was over breakfast at the Pink Lady that his college buddy turned him on to Allen Carter. Now a cashed-in favor from Charles Breeze got him a date with Charles and David Berrigan. Two of the wealthiest and most powerful people in America were in town for a fundraiser for the NRA. But there were some ground rules. The three of them would meet in the brothers' bungalow, no recording of their conversation was permitted, and the dress was casual. The brothers were going swimming after their meeting.

Matt was early for his meeting with the Berrigan brothers, so he took a tour of the hotel grounds. He was nervous. Tight was a more apt description. He wanted a story, but discretion being the better part of valor, he would settle for anything that would open the door to their private lives. If Allen Carter wasn't blowing smoke, the Berrigan brothers were sitting on the story of the century.

It wasn't just a hotel room. It was a home, with a large living room, dining area, bar, and patio. Matt Tyson was greeted at the door by a valet who led him to the patio. David and Charles were wearing matching white bath robes, sandals, and baseball caps. They stood, shook his hand, and motioned him to take a seat at a circular wooden table with an opened umbrella.

"Charles Breeze is a friend." David smiled and added,

"Perhaps a friendly political foe. He's a bit liberal for our taste. But he's honest."

"My brother's dead on. Our libertarian views make him squirm," Charles said.

"Thanks for granting me a few minutes of your valuable time. I'm doing a piece on the NRA for *The Socratic Rag*."

"We've both seen your work. You like to nail Wall Street's best." David took a sip of coffee. "You care for some coffee?"

"No thanks."

"That bit about Goldman Sachs was a howler. You wrote something about a vampire squid wrapped around the face of humanity. You've got a way with words. William St. George warned us about you."

"I hope he was kind." Matt smiled, hoping to stay in the brothers' good graces.

"He liked you. So, what brings you to us?" David leaned back in his chair and crossed his legs.

"I'm just hoping for some inside info on your dealings with the NRA."

"We believe in the Second Amendment. We have business investments we would like to protect," Charles bluntly said.

"We don't like big government," added David.

"But there's a price to be paid." Matt Tyson cleared his voice and said, "People are being murdered at an alarming rate. According to the FBI Uniform Crime Report, between the years 2006 and 2010, 47,856 people were murdered in the US by firearms. There are 88 guns per 100 residents."

"Are you here to lecture us on firearm stats? This isn't our problem. We need a better mental health system. Crazy people kill people. Guns don't kill." David's face turned red.

"Sorry. I'd just like to know more about the wealth and power that fuels the gun industry." Matt shot the brothers a grin and added, "I would like a story." Matt felt like he blew it. For the first time in his life, he was lost for words. Allen Carter had planted a conspiracy seed in his mind. *Perhaps I'm being presumptuous and impertinent,* he thought.

"That's public record. The ins and outs of the gun industry have been well documented. Besides, our backing of the NRA has everything to do with the Second Amendment. The First and Second Amendments are safeguards of American liberty." Charles helped circle the wagons with his brother.

"But it seems that there's a unifying force at work here. The gun industry is a worldwide phenomenon. It's a monster with tentacles wrapped around nations throughout the world." Matt had dug a hole so deep he couldn't see the light of day.

"Are you accusing us of being part of an international cabal?" David's question and look of disgust sent shivers through Matt.

"No, sir. I'm just looking for something provocative for my story on the NRA." Matt grinned, trying desperately to diffuse the tension that had the interview in a death spiral. "By the way, I'm trying to get an interview with Martin Angelo. Do you know him?"

"Never heard of him," Charles snapped.

"How about Larry Petersen. Have you heard of him?" Matt made up the name, seeing if he was getting a straight answer.

"It doesn't ring a bell." David frowned.

"I know you have dealings with Jerry Rizzo." This was

Matt's last chance. Jerry's name came up when he researched Allen Carter's big-time clients. He knew he had financial dealings with the Berrigan brothers.

"What?" David and Charles both said. They looked alarmed.

"I talked with him earlier this week," Matt lied. He was fishing, and it paid off.

"What about?" Charles flashed Matt a concerned look, brows narrowed and lips twisted into a look of absolute disgust.

"We discussed your financial connections with the NRA and your close ties with William St. George." Matt was on a roll. It was pure fabrication, but it was working.

"You're treading in dangerous waters. Our financial transactions with William and the NRA are a private matter."

"Well, I think my readers would like to have a look." Matt sensed he had hit a sore spot.

"Well you'll just have to take your questions elsewhere. We're businessmen and patriots. God bless free enterprise and the Second Amendment. I think this discussion is over." Charles stood, and his brother followed his lead. The valet was called, and Matt was shown the door in short order.

He paused at the front door of the bungalow, savoring his breakthrough. He wasn't in the habit of lying, but his investigative bravado sure worked. He lingered by the pool before taking another tour of the grounds. In the lobby of the Pink Lady, he called his office and got Jerry Rizzo's work number at Universal Studios. He called and left a message with his secretary, requesting an interview.

Chapter Eighteen

Allen Carter was about to leave his law office in Santa Monica when his cell phone chirped. It was Matt Tyson. He immediately picked up. "What's up, Matt?"

"I had an interview with the Berrigan brothers." Matt was in a cheerful mood.

"What? You met with the big boys?" Allen's tone was one of genuine surprise.

"I think I rang their bell." Matt laughed.

"What happened?"

"I threw out a couple of phony names. They didn't bite. But when I brought up Jerry Rizzo's name, things got tense."

"Jerry Rizzo! How did you get his name?" Allen nearly shouted his question.

"I did my homework. There are a lot of financial dealings going down with Rizzo and the Berrigan brothers. I might add that you're in the mix."

"What?" Allen's voice was strained.

"Allen Rizzo is one of your juicy clients."

"What do you mean?" Allen felt his heart skip a beat.

Rizzo was off limits. He was a member of the inner circle. Allen wasn't, but he had a peek into its diabolical dealings. After a night of drinking, Rizzo had loose lips. Allen had made a solemn promise to keep quiet. If he didn't, he would be history. That was a given.

"I have a history of court cases, names, and financial dealings. He's your biggest client and benefactor."

"*Benefactor?* What are you getting at?"

"He's the life blood of your law practice," Matt shot back.

"He's a good client." Allen had talked enough. He didn't want Matt turning his inquisitive eye on him anymore.

"Well, I called to see if you could help with landing me an interview with Jerry Rizzo."

There was silence before Allen said, "As I said before, I honor my attorney/client relationships. I can't and I won't play John Alden here."

"Okay, have it your way. I just called to gloat about landing an interview with the Berrigan brothers. I'll catch you later."

Allen Carter needed to talk with Alexis. He knew that talk wasn't all he would get. She always needed a fix.

* * *

The Berrigan brothers had made a rare move. Tonight, Shangri-La played host to the first sit down of the inner circle. It was Saturday night, and the dress was casual. Jerry Rizzo was the first to arrive. He met the Berrigan brothers at the bar and opted for an Amstel Light. He was on a diet, strayed from the hard stuff, but on occasion put down a six pack. He was apprehensive about a face-to-face meeting with other members of the inner circle. The international cabal, six in number, had never assembled under one roof. Jerry represented the entertainment side, CEO of Universal Studios Hollywood. He had deep pockets and golden connections. He kept a low profile politically. Only members of the inner circle knew of his hatred of big government and his love of guns.

Carlos Grande joined the Berrigan brothers and Jerry Rizzo at the bar. His mood was good. He was ready to party. He had just returned from a profitable meeting with Saudi investors in Jubail, Saudi Arabia. Carlos Grande's wealth and power were legendary; he had been ranked by Forbes as the richest person in the world from 2010 to 2013. Only six people in the world knew of his membership in the inner circle. And they were all here tonight.

The last to join the sit down were George and William Stinger, by far the youngest and most mathematically gifted of the inner circle. The brothers used their high-power mathematical skills to propel their hedge fund company into a game changer. Over the last three years, they delivered 32 percent returns per year. Not bad for a company with the name of Pirate Capital. If the name hadn't turned people's heads, their earnings sure had. Their boyish looks disarmed their competitors. They were young, barely thirty, but their ruthlessness, hatred of big government, and fascination with guns were known only to the members of inner circle. Their bravado amused the elder statesmen of the group. Their mental acuity and financial brilliance, however, were taken seriously.

After drinks at the bar, the inner circle was ushered into the War Room. Other than the Berrigan brothers, only William St. George had laid eyes on the marvels of their electronic nerve center. Charles approached the main console, flipped a series of switches, and the room erupted into a dazzling display of flashing lights. The monitors, both satellite and closed circuit, filled the massive wall. At any moment CNN, MSNBC, Fox, and the major networks were on. A special feed linking Wall Street trading was always on. The only thing they lacked was a direct line to the Oval Office. They did, however, have a special hook up to the Supreme Court. This was unknown to the NSA, CIA, and FBI. The assassination of Elizabeth Huntington Fine relied heavily on this secretive connection.

George Stinger gasped, "You even have video surveillance of the chopper that brought us here."

"My brother and I leave nothing to chance. We can't rely on others. We especially don't rely on the government," David said. He joined his brother at the center console and switched to a channel showing a line of trucks entering a compound, a barbed-wire fence enclosure with guard towers at the entrance. "This is a weapons depot we run in Mexico. We sell everything from AR-15s to rocket launchers to the highest bidder. We distribute weapons to South America, the Middle East, Russia, Syria, and Mexican warlords. We deal in everything from light arms to heavy artillery. Most of our producers are small. The vast majority of our providers are located in Third World countries. There's little regulation at the international level. Our buyers represent the underbelly of society, organized crime, terrorists, rebel forces, and renegades of all stripes. Lately we've been quite successful supplying upstart countries mired in civil war. Of course, this is done in all of our names. My brother and I wanted to show off a bit. We wanted the inner circle to see how their prudent investment was paying off. We are fastidious about details. And it's all about trust and honest communication. We believe in straight talk. And to be honest, we need to pool our resources more effectively."

Carlos Grande cleared his voice and said, "The Fast and Furious operation was a great red herring. The failed and bungled ATF sting focused the media and government's attention on a small-potatoes attempt to track firearms illegally crossing the US/Mexico border. We have a pipeline that efficiently supplies the warlords with their insatiable thirst for arms. Hell, we know that 68 percent of all weapons recovered at Mexican crime scenes over the last five years were from US manufacturers or dealers."

"We've got a fucking pipeline of guns flowing across the border. The politicians fell for the Fast and Furious bit," William Stinger said with great pride. He added, "The inner circle came up with the idea. We owe the ATF for their brilliant naiveté. They took the spotlight off of us."

The night was young. The inner circled retired to the bar where they all celebrated.

"Tomorrow we'll institute the next phase of Armageddon," Charles Berrigan announced. "Here's to a new world order."

* * *

Allen Carter parked his Vette next to his canvas-covered Duesenberg, avoiding scratches at all cost, entered the house through the garage, and called out, "Alexis, where are you?"

"I'm in the kitchen."

Allen entered the kitchen to find Alexis cradling a half-empty glass of white wine. Her eyes were glued to the small TV, seemingly lost in a sappy *Oprah* rerun. "You've lost your sense of taste. How can you swallow her swill?" Allen shook his head in distain.

"What?" Alexis didn't budge, her eyes fixated on the screen.

"We need to talk."

"Later. This is important," Alexis said. "Grab a glass and help me with the Chardonnay."

Rather than demanding her attention by flipping off the TV, Allen headed for the bar, grabbed a glass, and opted for Cabernet. White wine was thin. It lacked the full-bodied taste he had a hankering for. He went upstairs and changed into jeans and a T-shirt, then washed his face and combed his hair before joining Alexis in the kitchen. *Thank God Oprah is over,* he thought. Her sentimentality unnerved him. She was only good at slopping around in the insipid pop culture that dominated the airways. The country's taste and intellectual respectability had died long ago. *It's a fucking cultural wasteland*, he thought.

"Join me," Alexis said with a half-smile.

Allen had seen that cheap imitation of a smile before. To him it was a smirk. *She's depressed and about to whine*, he thought. "So did Oprah ring your bell?" Allen smiled, but his sarcasm was apparent.

"She had on a psychologist. She made a lot of sense." Alexis took a sip of wine.

"I thought you dumped psychology years ago. You're a philosopher. You live in your head."

"What?" Alexis glared back.

"Come on, you've told me how you read a case study about a psychopath that scared the crap out of you. You saw yourself walking in the nutcase's shoes."

"Allen, you're being impertinent." Her eyes narrowed.

"I deal only in the truth. Don't you like what you see?"

"You're looking for a fight. You're being a horse's ass." Alexis downed the rest of her wine and poured another.

"So what did the psychologist have to say?" His sarcasm was emphasized by his animated body language and tone of voice.

"We need to listen to our inner voice." Alexis started to say something more but stopped short.

"And what does your inner voice say?" Allen sneered, being deliberatively combative.

"You must stop and listen. You must remember the black box," Alexis blurted, clearly surprising herself.

"What black box?" Allen leaned back and downed the remainder of his wine. He knew he'd need to anesthetize himself in order to survive the night.

"In grandma's attic, there was a black box. It scared me."

"What was in the black box?" Allen poured a second glass of Cabernet.

"It had the folded body of a clown." Alexis attempted to say more but couldn't. Her lips quivered, and her hands trembled, forcing her to put down the glass of wine.

"Maybe it was *Howdy Doody*. I remember seeing reruns in the late sixties. It was a children's show." Allen actually liked *Howdy Doody* when he was about eight or nine years old.

"No way! The clown in the black box had an evil look. It was scary. I still have nightmares about the black box." Her neck and cheeks were flushed red.

"Maybe you need professional help. Have you thought about seeing a therapist?" Allen wasn't serious. He was trying to measure the depth of her anguish. She seemed genuinely agitated.

"I've thought about it," Alexis said.

"What?" Allen was speechless.

"It might help." Alexis took another sip of wine.

"Fuck! We can't afford some therapist rummaging around in your mind. We have secrets, a mission, and fidelity to our comrades at stake here. Alexis, for Christ sake, you're jeopardizing our very reason for being."

"I'm scared. I'm confused. What the fuck have I done?" Alexis began to cry. Tears trickled down her reddened cheeks.

Allen shifted gears. He dropped his confrontational manner and lowered his voice. "I'm here for you. I'm listening." He had to comfort her. If she cracked, his world would end. He had to control her. Whatever the cost, he had to control her. He already had blood on his hands. A little more wouldn't destroy him. But he did care for Alexis. Love might be too strong a word. Although there was no doubt that she satisfied his lustful side. Maybe she needed a fix. He knew damn well he needed one.

Chapter Nineteen

Agent Alex Martini reread the *New York Times* article for the third time. He and his team had hit a homerun. The headlines said it all:

Supreme Court Justice Helena Bartoletti
was Hacked, not Poisoned.

The front-page article revealed that Justice Bartoletti, as well as the other eight justices of the Supreme Court, had had their privacy hijacked. The *Times* article detailed how the FBI and the NSA had uncovered the fact that ricin didn't end up murdering the late Supreme Court justice, but malware had been found on her laptop computer and cell phone. It was a Trojan horse that compromised her insulin pump. The late Justice Helena Bartoletti was a type-one diabetic and employed a computer program to monitor and control her insulin dosage. A hacker had compromised the system and reprogrammed the software that ran the insulin pump, resulting in a massive overdose.

The *Times* disclosed that not only had Justice Bartoletti

been hacked, but the eight other justices had their phones, e-mails, and computers compromised.

Alex's phoned chirped. He picked up and was greeted by Max Heller, his FBI buddy at Quantico. "Hey, Alex, a big congratulation is in order. Great work on the Bartoletti case."

"Thanks, but we had a lot of help," Alex said. "And a special heads-up to you."

"Hey, not everyone makes the front page of the *New York Times*. How about an autograph?" Max laughed and then added, "If you're not careful, you'll get kicked upstairs."

"Not a chance. They know a grunt when they see one." Alex knew he was a bloodhound, best suited for the gritty life of the streets.

"Well, I just wanted to touch base." Max paused and added, "Besides, you owe me a beer."

"Hey, without your help and the great work of the FBI lab, especially I.T., I wouldn't have discovered the cyber-attack on the Supreme Court. You're the one that turned me on to the fact that hackers can break into programs that run medical devices. The bastards behind the assassination threw us a red herring. The ricin was diluted and incapable of killing Justice Bartoletti. The program that controlled her insulin pump was the real culprit. That was a first for me."

"Hey, old sport, this is the twenty-first century. There's more crime happening in cyberspace than on Main Street. So when's your next trip to Quantico? I'm thirsty for a cold one." Max laughed. They had quite a history of bending elbows after hours.

"Soon, but the fact that eight other Supreme Court

justices had their security compromised has the Bureau on edge. They got me working overtime. "

"Don't be a stranger." Max signed off.

Alex's phone chirped again. "Alex here."

"We need you and two members of your team at the Supreme Court," Director Parker barked. "Two clerks and three secretaries need questioning. I want you there now. Chop, chop."

Alex stared at his cell phone. Director Tom Parker signed off without even a good-bye. His boss was at his wit's end and running out of patience. Everyone associated with the Washington D.C. Bureau was working overtime. The only thing Director Parker said to Alex was "Great Job." *It's sure better than getting chewed out*, Alex thought.

* * *

The Berrigan brothers had a problem brewing. Matt Tyson had rubbed them the wrong way. *The Socratic Rag* writer had invaded their private space and was snooping around in sacred territory. The interview with the upstart writer at the Beverly Hills Hotel left a bad taste in their mouth.

Just yesterday in his blog, Matt Tyson referred to the Berrigan brothers as modern-day robber barons. He called out the brothers as fixers: fixing everything from international exchange rates to buying off rating agencies. He accused the brothers of being architects of the Wall Street crisis of 2007–2008. *It wasn't a natural disaster*, he wrote, *but a carefully orchestrated scheme to implement risky bets, complex financial products, and foster a climate of undisclosed conflict of interests. The infamous Berrigan brothers*, he wrote, *are opportunistic tycoons. They inhabit a shadowy world of cloak and dagger. They wheel and deal in smoke field rooms where they plot to undermine the vast majority of Americans on issues ranging from social security to the environment and voting rights. They are shot callers. They call their shots from Wall Street, not prison. But prison is where they belong. The billionaire bullies represent the upper 1 percent at its worst.*

Charles and David had just finished breakfast and were about to be whisked away by helicopter to the Bozeman Airport. But they had agreed to make a decision about Matt Tyson before leaving Shangri-La. Matt's latest blog sealed the deal.

"What's your call?" asked Charles.

David grinned and said, "We go after him. He's nothing but trouble. The bastard has a big mouth."

"Do we take him out or just scare the fuck out of him?" Charles finished the last of his coffee and said, "It's your call. I'm fine with either alternative."

"Let's start with a good old-fashioned scare. If we have to escalate until he disappears from the face of the earth, that works too," David said.

"I'll make the arrangements." Charles looked into his brother's eyes and added, "He'll regret ever meeting us. The might of the written word is overrated. We have the power and wealth to make anything happen."

As the brothers prepared to leave Shangri-La, Charles shouted over the deafening sound of the chopper, "I love to see a liberal do-gooder squirm, and squirm he will."

"I'm with you," David shouted back.

The brothers took flight, briefly hovering over the entrance to their Montana compound. As they headed for the Bozeman airport, they caught a brief look at the flags flapping in the wind at the head of the heliport. The sight of Old Glory and the Montana State flag took a backseat to their favorite banner. The sight of an eagle clutching crossed rifles in a field of red followed by the letters NRA in bold white sent a chill down their spines. *God bless the Second Amendment*, Charles thought. David glanced at his brother and instantly knew what he was thinking.

* * *

William St. George had his orders. Alert two members of Fire Power. It was time to wage war with *The Socratic Rag's* best. Matt Tyson was out of hand and needed to be put in his place. The Saint was itching for action.

He loved being the ringmaster, directing the strong arm of the NRA. He hadn't met with Fire Power since their successful birthday party at Pines Shadow Estates on Buggs Island. The five members had convened at the orders of Gemini. At that time, William St. George only knew that they called the shots. He didn't know who or what Gemini was. But now he knew, and the Berrigan brothers wanted Matt Tyson silenced.

William assigned Zeta and Theta the task of instilling the fear of God into *The Socratic Rag's* agent provocateur. They had carte blanche on tactics. They should traumatize or maim, but not kill. The Saint didn't know the identity of Zeta and Theta. He knew only that they were ruthless. At the birthday party at Shadow Pines Estates, they dressed as bikers. They looked and acted the part; they could talk the talk and walk the walk.

Chapter Twenty

Allen Carter was worried about Alexis's state of mind. Her anxiety and self-doubt had escalated, causing her to miss two days of classes over the last couple of weeks. This was a first. Alexis's public identity was wedded to her profession. She loved being a philosophy professor at Pepperdine University. Missing a day at the university was unheard of. So he had her tracked. He bugged her phone and, with the help of Loc-Aid, was able to pinpoint her exact location. Tuesday afternoon, a little past three, his surveillance paid off. After typing in her cell phone number, her precise location popped up on his Droid. *Shit, she's here in Santa Monica, not more than a mile from my office*, Allen thought.

He Googled the address and found a Dr. Emily Hollingsworth. Her website touted her as a clinical psychologist who specialized in anxiety disorders and depression. She had received awards from the American Psychological Association and the Association for Research in Personality. She had published three academic books and many articles in leading journals.

Alarm bells went off in his head. His heart rate jumped up, and his chest tightened. *If a shrink gets in her head, all hell will break loose*, he thought. He needed a plan of attack. This nonsense had to stop. He couldn't directly confront her. That would panic her. If she lost a grip on herself, she could spill the beans. Christ, Gotham City would come down like a house of cards.

Allen called Bill Paxton. He had employed Bill for a dozen years. He was a first-rate private eye and surveillance expert. Allen explained he was on a big case for a Hollywood bigwig and needed some inside dope. That was a ruse, but he didn't want to implicate Alexis. He needed to find out the nature of the sessions, so he had the shrink's office bugged. It was a rush order, but Bill Paxton came through. The surveillance was completed the very next day, well before the sun set over the Pacific.

Within a week, Allen had heard enough. The surveillance equipment had picked up a Tuesday afternoon session that sent Allen over the top. During a hypnosis session, Alexis had revealed to Dr. Hollingsworth that there was more to the costume parties than was apparent. They were a front, a charade, a primal party for celebrating their mission. She didn't reveal to Dr. Hollingsworth what the mission was, but hinting that there was a secretive mission sent Allen into high gear. *This psychology shit has to stop*, he thought.

That Tuesday night, after dinner and a two glasses of wine, Allen called Alexis out on the deck to watch the sun disappear over the Pacific. It was an exceptionally clear summer night in the Santa Monica Mountains, the moon had just crested a nearby ridge, and a few stars dotted the darkening sky.

"We need to talk," Allen said. "Pull up a chair."

"Why so gruff? Did you have a bad day?" Alexis awkwardly sat down, juggling a half glass of Chardonnay. It was her third glass. Her drinking had surpassed his over the last few weeks. She was obviously self-medicating.

"Why didn't you tell me you were seeing a shrink?" Allen's tone was grave and his diction sharp and edgy.

"What?" Alexis's eyes widened.

"You heard me. I know you're seeing Dr. Emily Hollingsworth." Allen stared her down. "Don't give me the runaround."

"You followed me?" Alexis's voice squeaked. She took a gulp of wine. Her hands shook.

"I had you tailed. So what gives? Why the shrink?" Allen leaned back in his chair, enjoying her drunken nervousness. She looked pitiful. The strong woman he once adored was slipping away, melting into a slimy pool of nothingness.

"I need someone to confide in." Alexis's voice was soft, nearly inaudible.

"And I'm not a good listener?" Allen shook his head and added, "What's so bad that you have to talk to a shrink?"

"I'm upset. I can't sleep. I've missed work. I can't think straight." Alexis's words slurred together. She dropped her head and stared at her empty glass of wine.

"God damn you. You look like a cheap drunk. Maybe you should cut back on the booze." Allen's anger mounted. He balled up his right hand into a fist and slammed it into the table.

Alexis jumped up, pushed her chair away from the table, and moved toward the kitchen door. She tried to open it, but Allen intercepted her. He grabbed both her wrists, yanked her across the deck, and shoved her back down into the chair. She yelled, "Leave me alone, you *bastard.*"

"Not until we get to the bottom of this. So what's biting you?" Allen needed to hear her admit to her indiscretion. He wanted to hear it from her lips.

"I need a sympathetic ear, not a thug like you." She glanced up at him, her lips curled into a wicked snarl.

"You betrayed me, you bitch. You told the shrink that our costume parties are, and this is quoting you, 'a front, a charade, a primal party for celebrating our mission.'"

"Where did you get that shit?" She glanced at him. Her face twisted with horror.

Allen reached into his shirt pocket and pulled out his Droid. He flipped it on, found the appropriate app, and said, "Listen to this."

The voices of Dr. Hollingsworth and Alexis filled the evening air. She was stunned into silence. She heard the very words that Allen just uttered. She began to cry.

Allen was suddenly confounded. He had to silence her, but how? Alexis's sessions with Dr. Hollingsworth had to be terminated. But that left Allen Carter with a woman drowning in a sea of despair and confusion. But Alexis was not just any woman. She was his woman, a woman with blood on her hands, a woman at the center of Gotham City. *If that shrink gets wind of Alexis's true past, she'll be bound by law to notify the authorities. This can't and will not happen.*

Allen stood and slowly walked to the edge of the deck, gazing up at the ascending moon. In the distance, a coyote howled as if celebrating the magnificence of the moon. Behind him, he could hear the whimpers of Alexis wallowing in her drunken despair. He thought back on a previous conversation about a session with Dr. Hollingsworth, a session where the black box in the attic came up. In the black box was the head of a clown. Allen knew it wasn't Howdy Doody; it was him. It was Motley Wag.

Why me? he thought. Why was the head of Motley Wag stuffed into a black box? This psychobabble had to be extinguished. The insanity must be kept at bay. There existed a cause bigger than the both of them. They had to reconnect with the truth. Guns and gun violence had to be stopped. *The NRA will pay*, he thought. *And Gotham City will be saved.*

Allen turned away from the growing light of the rising moon, pulled Alexis to her feet, picked her up, gently cradled her in his arms, and took her to bed. By the time her head hit the pillow, she was out.

He was alone with his thoughts, terrifying as they were. He flashed on the first time his father threatened his mother with a doubled barreled shotgun. His father had just returned from a hunting trip, had removed his jacket, and was cleaning his shotgun when he heard muffled cries and whimpers coming from the bedroom. Alarmed, Allen's father checked out the cries coming from the bedroom. There, sprawled across the bed was Allen's mother, tears running down her cheeks, clutching several love letters penned years earlier, before Allen's birth. Allen, who was eight, scrambled to the bedroom where he found his father standing over his mother waving the shotgun. Tears flowed down her cheeks, lightly splashing the love letters. She defensively coiled into a fetal position, hugging the tear stained letters to her breasts, bawling uncontrollably.

His father yelled at her. His voice was loud and

threatening. His words could be heard now as clearly as the day he uttered them. "Stop this incessant drinking or I'll leave your sorry ass." The frightful scenario was repeated numerous times before his dad carried out the threat and abandoned both him and his mom on Allen's thirteenth birthday.

He was abandoned by his father as a teenager, and left emotionally scarred by his mother's withdrawal into alcoholism. Allen felt isolated and alone, now betrayed by his lover and loyal conspirator. He desperately needed a plan.

*   *   *

Zeta owned three Harley bike shops in California, one in Oakland and two in Los Angeles. He had hit pay dirt in the Harley market selling badass motorcycles to RUBs.—Rich Urban Bikers—middle-aged, upper-class, white males that made more money than they knew what to do with. Unlike traditional Harley dudes, these wealthy types, bankers, doctors, and lawyers, bought all the trimmings. These week end warriors were fond of heated handlebars, luggage racks, stereos, and cruise control, stuff that really jacked up the retail price of the bikes. Zeta's business mushroomed, and he soon found out that his wealth opened the door to lucrative investment opportunities. That was when he met Theta, an owner of several gun stores in both Northern and Southern California. His biggest financial success was a gun shop in Burbank, in the Valley over the hill from Santa Monica. He was the mirrored image of Zeta, only he made his financial bones in guns.

Their friendship flourished, especially after meeting The

Saint. They didn't know his true identity, and he didn't know Zeta and Theta's true names. They met at a secretive gentlemen's club where no one used their real names. A lucrative partnership in crime soon developed. In short time, they became enforcers for Fire Power, the strong arm of the NRA. The two burly entrepreneurs loved playing the part of enforcers, playing out their true natures, bad asses to the bone.

They had a new assignment; deliver a special message to Matt Tyson from the NRA, a message written in blood. The only qualifier was to stop just short of death. "We only want the bastard silenced, not killed," ordered The Saint.

Zeta and Theta were in luck. Matt Tyson was in Los Angeles on assignment for *The Socratic Rag*. And they located his temporary residence, a Holiday Inn in Santa Monica. They checked out the hotel and talked to the night clerk. They were about eight hours late. Zeta and Theta learned that Matt Tyson had checked out early in the morning. When they asked the clerk where he was headed, he shrugged his shoulders and said, "Don't know, not my business." They'd call *The Socratic Rag's* headquarters in the morning. Someone there would surely know his whereabouts.

Chapter Twenty-One

Matt Tyson needed a change of pace, so he switched hotels, swapping the Holiday Inn for the Double Tree, just three blocks from the Santa Monica Pier. His last blockbuster article earned him a generous bonus, so he wanted to splurge. Before dinner, he drove to Mulligans for a beer.

The Irish pub was humming; people were getting off work, and it was the middle of happy hour. Draft beer was two for the price of one. Bottled beer was more expensive, but if you bought two, the third was free. Matt took a seat at the bar and opted for a draft. Soon after his first sip, he felt a hand on his left shoulder. He looked back and saw Allen Carter; his eyes were bloodshot and his hair unruly. He had obviously forgotten to shave this morning.

"Want to join me? I'm at the back corner booth." He gave Matt a half smile and added, "Come on, I need to talk."

Matt slid from the bar and joined Allen at his corner booth. "You looked bushed," Matt said. He put his draft on the table and slid into the booth.

Next to an empty bottle of Guinness was a half full one.

Allen had a head start. He smiled and said, "No clients and court appearances today, just a lot of paperwork."

"Any plans for a costume party?" Matt wanted to start out on a good note. Their last phone conversation ended badly. He had pushed Allen for an interview with Jerry Rizzo.

"A matter of fact, that's what I want to talk about. We're planning one a week from this coming Saturday. Think you can make it?"

Matt's mind raced, searching for an appropriate response. Another party might get him closer to a story. He pretended that he wasn't eager for an invitation and said, "If I'm in town. I've got a story to write."

"I think I can help you with Jerry Rizzo." Allen took a tug on his beer, leaned back, and studied Matt.

"You got my attention." Matt added, "I know you and Jerry are tight."

"We have a professional relationship. But I have reason to believe he's connected with some big players." Allen took a sip of beer and then said, "Are you interested?"

Before Matt could answer, two burly bikers dressed in Levis and wearing leather vests approached the table. The taller of the two had heavily tattooed arms and a bushy, dark moustache. He gruffly asked, "Which one of you is Matt Tyson?"

Matt frowned and said, "Who's asking?"

"I've got a message for him," the other one said. "Stay clear of the NRA. No more nosing around and no more blogs and whining publications denouncing the Second Amendment." He was shorter, with a full beard, and was heavily inked. He sported a fire-breathing dragon on his right arm, inked in midnight black and blood red. On his left shoulder, visible because of the sleeveless shirt and vest, was the NRA spelled out in bold blood-red letters. A tattoo of a soaring eagle clutching crossed rifles in its talons was just below the bold letters.

The first biker slammed his fist on the table and declared, "You've been forewarned."

Then the bikers abruptly left Mulligans.

Matt shook his head and said, "I guess the NRA is on edge. I didn't think they were thugs. I guess I was wrong."

"This smells of a set up. You know these thugs?" Allen clenched his fists and drummed the table.

"No. You think I should call the cops?" Matt was half joking, but on edge nevertheless.

"Not yet. I'm your witness if things get out of hand. Where are you staying?" Allen looked genuinely concerned.

"At the Double Tree."

"I know the place. It's a couple of blocks from the pier." Allen frowned. "Why don't you stay with me? I don't think you should be alone. My house is gated, a veritable armed fortress." Allen smiled.

"Thanks, but I don't want to involve you in this." Matt attempted a smile. It was strained.

"Come on. Grab a few things at the hotel, and we're off." Allen stood, pulled twenty-five dollars from his wallet, and dropped it on the table.

Matt got up and said, "Okay, you win." It was a win-win situation. A little added protection and a chance to pick Allen's brain.

Matt got his rental car, and Allen followed him to the Double Tree in his Vette. Zeta and Theta, unknown to

Matt and Allen, tailed them discreetly in a black four-door Cadillac sedan.

Within a half-hour, Allen and Matt were speeding north on PCH toward Malibu. The Vette's convertible top was down allowing the sea breeze to whip their hair about. They both cheered as the sun sank into the Pacific.

The sleek Vette made a hard right on Las Flores Canyon Road and effortlessly climbed the steep grade, its deep-throated horse power rumbling, bringing a smile to Allen Carter. The Vette climbed to an elevation where the dying lights of the setting sun cast reddish hues across the Southern California sky. Allen and Matt pulled into the gated drive, both delighted with the exhilarating ride from Santa Monica. They entered Allen's estate through the garage, unaware of the Cadillac sedan parked a short distance down the hill.

*　*　*

Within five minutes, Zeta pulled the Cadillac up the hill and blocked the driveway. Zeta and Theta were not deterred. They had breached the security of homes, gated communities, and military compounds with impunity.

The enforcers of Fire Power got out of the Cadillac and opened the trunk. Inside was a treasure trove of equipment, everything from handguns and assault weapons to gas masks and sarin, a colorless and odorless chemical weapon. They retrieved a smartphone programed to open just about anything electronically controlled. They breached the security of the estate within five minutes, opened the garage door, and monitored the sounds and movement inside the home. They would wait to strike. They relished the element of surprise.

Zeta went outside, rounded the house on the south side, and spotted two figures on the upper deck. From his vantage point, he couldn't identify the figures, but the voices were definitely recognizable. It was Matt Tyson and his friend.

Back inside the garage, Zeta quietly said, "Tyson and his friend are out on the upper deck."

Theta nodded his head and said, "Let's storm the house and surprise them on the deck." Before leaving the garage, Theta spotted a set of golf clubs. He grabbed a nine iron and followed Zeta's lead.

The two enforcers from Fire Power stealthily entered the house from the garage and made it up the stairs to the main level. The kitchen was empty, and the sliding glass door wide open. With the stealth and agility of a big cat, they sprang onto the deck and hovered over Allen and Matt now seated at the table.

"Surprise! Did you think we'd go away?" Zeta waved a Smith and Wesson .38 special in Matt's face. "We need to continue our talk. But first, is there anybody else here?"

"No," Allen quickly answered.

"If you're lying, there will be trouble," Theta growled, waving the commandeered nine iron over Allen's head. "I like golf, but I don't hack away at Nike or Titleist. I prefer the human variety."

"And you, my friend, we need some answers." Zeta leaned over and tugged at the collar of Matt's shirt. "Theta, check out the premises. I'll keep our new *friends* company." Zeta motioned to the sliding door. "If you find anyone, escort them to our little party." Zeta laughed and waved the .38 special at his captives.

Theta, armed with a .44 Magnum, made a sweep of the house. He left the nine iron next to the sliding door on the deck. In the master bedroom, the last room checked in his sweep of the house, he found an attractive lady in the bathroom applying makeup.

When she caught the image of him in the mirror, she shrieked. She immediately whirled around, covered her upper body with her hands, and screamed, "Who are you?"

"I'm a new friend. There's a party downstairs. Come and join us." Theta grinned, looking the voluptuous woman up and down.

"What?" Her eyes were wide with fear.

Theta motioned for her to move with his gun. "Put on a robe. Come on, bitch, we haven't got all day."

She scurried past the intruder, grabbed a robe from the bed, and covered her partially clothed body. She wore only bikini panties and sandals. The short robe concealed her voluptuous breasts but did little to conceal her long, well-toned legs. On the way to the deck, Theta enjoyed her feminine charm. *Fucking hot chick*, he thought.

Out on the deck, Theta pulled out a chair and motioned for her to sit. "Look what I found upstairs."

"Nice addition to the party," Zeta gushed. "Quite a looker."

"Allen, what's going on?" she whimpered.

"It's a home invasion, Alexis. Just keep your cool." Tears appeared at the corner of her eyes, and her hands trembled.

"This is a summit meeting," Zeta said. "We're here to nail down an agreement. Matt Tyson must cease and desist."

Alexis looked at Matt and asked nervously, "Do you know these men?"

Matt shook his head and said, "They confronted us at Mulligans. Out of the blue, they started a NRA rant."

"Rant," Zeta barked. "We're here to put a stop to your fucking anti-NRA propaganda. We're here to deliver a message."

Theta, losing his patience said, "Let's get this over with."

"Agreed," Zeta said. "Take the broad to the garage and cuff her to a water pipe."

Theta approached Alexis, yanked her from the patio chair, and forcefully ushered her to the garage where he cuffed her securely. He didn't find an appropriate water pipe, but he did secure her to the front bumper of the Duesenberg. He looked down at the whimpering beauty, wishing he didn't have such high moral values. His honor code prohibited messing with helpless ladies. But his passions got the best of him. He yanked on her robe, exposing her breasts. They were full, blemish free, and beautifully shaped. He stopped himself from touching her, not wanting to violate his code. Before leaving the garage, he blurted out, "You're one fucking hot chick."

Back on the deck, Theta flew into action as Zeta watched with immense satisfaction. After ordering Matt and Allen to stand and lean against the side of the house, Theta wielded the nine iron like a young Tiger Woods. He hit the bull's eye, shattering the tibia of each man with lightning speed and accuracy. He had done this before and was quite accomplished at orthopedic mayhem. Both men cried out, filling the night with piercing screams that echoed off the nearby canyon walls.

"Message delivered. You don't want a replay." Zeta looked down at the fallen men. Matt and Allen writhed in pain.

Downstairs in the garage, Zeta and Theta said their good-byes. Zeta informed Alexis that her "friends" would eventually come downstairs to render assistance. "It might take a while." Theta laughed. "They're not moving well, but they'll eventually come."

Zeta and Theta collected their equipment and put it back into the trunk of the Cadillac. On the way down the hill, they argued over where to party. They settled on a biker bar in Van Nuys, not far from one of Zeta's Harley shops.

Chapter Twenty-Two

William St. George smiled broadly and said, "Mission accomplished. Armageddon is in full swing." He was alone at his desk at NRA headquarters. He had read the *L.A Times* article twice and relished every word. It reported the home invasion of Allen Carter, a prominent Santa Monica lawyer who represented many of Hollywood's best. He counseled the likes of Charlie Sheen and Sean Penn, as well as directors and producers. The article detailed the strong-arm tactics used by intruders who left both *The Socratic Rag* writer Matt Tyson and attorney Allen Carter with a fractured lower leg. Alexis Williams, Mr. Carter's longtime girlfriend, was physically unharmed but psychologically traumatized. She was found by the police handcuffed to a Duesenberg in the garage.

The Prince felt partially vindicated. The NRA had suffered vicious attacks lately, culminating in a rash of gun show bombings across the width and breadth of the country. But now the picture was coming clearer. The chain of command had solidified. He was now in the know. He knew the identity of Gemini, had been a guest at Shangri-La, and had seen the War Room. He was the important link in the chain of command, taking orders from Gemini and ensuring Fire Power carried them out. The Saint felt both pleased and empowered. A US senator and a Supreme Court justice had paid the price for standing in the way of the NRA. Now a mouthy writer for *The Socratic Rag* had been warned. *Might makes right*, he thought. He was on top of the world.

*   *   *

Allen Carter leaned his crutches against the end of his desk, glanced at the pile of unread documents, sighed loudly, and carefully sat down. The cast on his right leg was necessary but a drag. It had been three days since the home invasion, and the pain in his lower right leg dulled only with the heavy pain medication. The codeine and Tylenol combo made him feel mentally sluggish. But what really bugged him was the real reason he and Matt were singled out. The thugs leveled their threat directly at Matt Tyson for his anti-NRA publications. But he was plagued by the haunting question, *Why me? Do they know anything about Gotham City? Did they get to Alexis?* He was long on questions but short on answers. He dialed Bill Paxton, his favorite private eye.

"Hey, Bill, I guess you've heard the news." Allen Carter suspected he had. He had received two voicemail messages but hadn't had time to get back to him. He'd been too busy with hospitals, doctors, and demanding clients.

"What the hell really happened?" Bill asked.

"Just like the papers reported. We were first confronted

at Mulligans and then, unknown to us at the time, tailed home."

"They sounded like bad-ass dudes," Bill commented sympathetically.

"I'm puzzled about why they targeted me in addition to Matt Tyson. He's a high-profile writer critical of the NRA. But me, I just occasionally rant about their rigid stance on guns."

"The NRA is a tough bunch. They're acting like a cornered animal."

"You bet. Say, could you follow up on the thugs? I'll send you an e-mail detailing what I can remember about the bastards."

"You got it. I'll get right on it."

"Thanks, I need to get to the bottom of this." Bill Paxton had worked for Allen for years. He liked and respected him. Allen signed off and grabbed a legal brief from a pile on his desk. He was up to his ears with work.

* * *

Matt Tyson's lower leg throbbed, a constant reminder of the Malibu thugs, that's what he called them. He didn't think Malibu had such animals. He had no idea where they came from, only that they wanted him silenced. The pain killers had dulled his senses, but not his memory of the attack. He had trouble sleeping, but when he did, he was haunted by horrific nightmares of biker thugs wielding instruments of torture.

He was now home at his Washington D.C. condo, nursing his wounds. Doctor Jonathan Lee at Kaiser Hospital in Los Angeles expected a full recovery within three months. But of course, it all depended on circumstances, notably his health, unexpected complications, and fidelity to his doctors' orders. Dr. Lee cautioned that he'd have to religiously follow the formal medical guidelines for a speedy and safe recovery.

Matt's doctor here in Washington D.C., Dr. Julio Gonzales, pitched him the same advice. He had received a stable fracture to his lower right leg, and because the very same bones lined up, he wouldn't need surgery. First a cast and then a boot would follow. It looked like he would be a gimp for about three, maybe four months. That wouldn't stop him from writing. And it wouldn't curtail his obsession to get at the bottom of the attack. *Who are these thugs? Who do they work for? How can I find them?* He wouldn't rest until he had answers.

* * *

Despite Allen Carter's insistence that Alexis stop therapy, she found herself in the office of Dr. Emily Hollingsworth. She was driven to her therapist by pure desperation. The home invasion had pushed her over the edge. She was in a state of panic. Last night she had a frightening nightmare. The head in the black box spoke to her. It was clearly Motley Wag. His message was loud and clear. "You are a murderer, a cowardly princess, hiding behind a comic book character. Face your true self. You're a sociopath. Seek help."

Alexis began the session on a cautionary note. "Allen has laid down the law," she told her therapist. "All psychological counseling must end." Her voice cracked with tension just uttering the words.

Dr. Hollingsworth cleared her voice and said, "Why is he so insistent that you stop therapy?"

"He's afraid I'll reveal too much." Alexis looked down.

"Reveal too much? Our sessions are geared to bringing to consciousness those feelings that are harming you. We're trying to free you from inhibitions, distorted, and conflicting emotions."

"I know, but he's afraid I'll say something harmful." Alexis stopped, suddenly hamstrung, torn between needing help and crossing Allen.

"What is he afraid of?" Dr. Hollingsworth paused and then added, "Is it Allen who is afraid of something harming him?"

"Maybe, that's why I'm here. Two days ago, we suffered a home invasion. Allen's leg was broken. His friend was with him. He was attacked, and I was cuffed to Allen's car in the garage." Her eyes glazed over, and a tear trickled down her right cheek.

"I saw the report in the *L.A. Times*. I was waiting for you to bring it up. Is he in trouble?" Dr. Hollingsworth crossed her legs and leaned back in her chair.

"I don't know. It was awful. The men were brutes, bearded and tattooed thugs. Allen's friend is a writer. He's well-known." Alexis frowned and said, "He writes for *The Socratic Rag*."

"I know of him. He's a thorn in the side of the NRA." Dr. Hollingsworth stood and walked toward her desk. "Do you mind if I brighten the room?"

"Fine," Alexis said.

The therapist hit a button on her desk, and the blinds opened slightly, casting a soft light across the room. After adjusting the blinds, Dr. Hollingsworth took her seat and said, "Didn't you tell me that Allen hates the NRA?"

"We both do," Alexis bluntly answered.

"Why?" Dr. Hollingsworth's tone was sympathetic, non-confrontational.

"They flood the world with guns. Innocent people are needlessly slaughtered."

"But this is a policy issue. It's political. Why do you harbor such hatred?" Dr. Hollingsworth pressed on. "Who do you really hate?"

"The bullies, they're the ones who use force." Alexis's full lips curled into a vicious snarl.

"Who uses force?"

"The clown, the head in the black box, he torments me."

"Who is he?"

"He's with me night and day." Alexis clenched her hands, leaned forward, and blurted, "He makes me do it."

"Do what?"

"Dress in costumes, wear disguises, and fool people." Alexis's arms and hands trembled.

"Why?"

"It's our mission."

"What mission?"

Alexis shouted, "Gotham City!"

The room became silent. Dr. Hollingsworth waited for more. After a long pause, Alexis said, "We have a mission."

"What mission?"

"We must stop the bad guys." Alexis's eyes had glazed over.

"Who are the bad guys?"

"The NRA."

"And what about the clown in the black box?" Dr. Hollingsworth pressed.

"Him too! He's a bad guy."

"Is he hurting you?"

"Yes. He punishes me."

"How does he do that?"

"He slaps me, holds me down, and physically smothers me."

"Is that what he calls sex?" Dr. Hollingsworth asked.

"At first it was exciting, but now I feel like a prisoner."

"Do you want to be free?" Dr. Hollingsworth pressed on.

"Yes. I want to be free. I want to change the past."

"We can't change the past. We can only change how we feel about it."

"I have blood on my hands," Alexis blurted.

"Whose blood?"

"He made me do it." Alexis began to cry.

"Who made you do it?"

"The clown."

"Let's continue this next time." Dr. Hollingsworth walked toward her desk to get her appointment book.

"There's no next time." Alexis suddenly stood and fled the office.

PART TWO:
The Pen is Mightier than the Sword

Chapter Twenty-Three

Gemini was throwing a party. It was no ordinary affair. It was a celebratory event for the inner circle. David Berringer was hosting the event at his 740 Park Avenue address. Armageddon had so far been a roaring success. US Senator Elizabeth Huntington was put to final rest for her stubborn anti-gun advocacy, Supreme Court Justice Helena Bartoletti permanently silenced for her excessive leftist political stance, and Matt Tyson had been delivered a clear warning to stifle the rants he published in *The Socratic Rag*. David and his brother had a special proposal to pitch to the inner circle, so he opened his Park Avenue residence to the secretive group.

David emerged from his Mercedes and glanced up at his tenth-floor apartment. *Tonight's the night,* he thought. He was right at home in his nineteen-story art deco building, certainly New York City's best. It had thirty-one units, not too busy for the oil tycoon. He liked the expansive floor plans. Most residences featured formal dining rooms, libraries, living rooms the size of tennis courts, and spacious entrance halls known as "galleries." Jacqueline Onassis had lived there as a child. *If it was good enough for her, it was good enough for a special meeting of the inner circle*, David thought.

David was inordinately proud of his apartment. He had laid out seventeen million for the eighteen-room duplex and had spent a year renovating the place before moving in. He opted for dark oak wood paneling, hardwood floors, and oversized furniture that you could get lost in. The den was the home of prized wild animals he had bagged on safari in South Africa. He had used New York's best taxidermist to preserve the head of a male lion, Cape buffalo, and white rhino. He liked wild animals, but he loved them when they were stuffed, mounted, and *dead*. Tonight he and his brother Charles were about to kill off the old Armageddon; it would be replaced by a more genteel but deadly model.

All six members sat around a long, dark oak table at the center of David's library. The high-ceiling room was lined from floor to ceiling with books, everything from the classics to contemporary economic and political theory. He collected anything available on libertarian philosophy. In fact, he had read every one of them. Ayn Rand's *Atlas Shrugged* was dog-eared; he had read it more than a dozen times.

The only wall not covered by books featured a brick fireplace. On the mantle was an antique clock owned by his father. The clock was dedicated to David and Charles. The inscription read: *Take the bull by the horns.*

David and Charles had parlayed their generous inheritance into one of the wealthiest privately owned companies in the world. Tonight they had a plan that could significantly enhance that wealth.

It was not until every member of the inner circle was

on his second cocktail that the Berrigan brothers sensed the time was right. David, who sat at one end of the table while his brother sat at the other end, lightly struck his cocktail glass with a metal letter opener.

"Gentlemen, my brother and I have a surprise. We have a plan to alter the course and strategy of Armageddon. It's time to join the information age."

Charles spoke up and said, "We would do well to join the twenty-first century. The old war tactic of "might makes right" is counterproductive. It's not only out of style, but dangerous. It leaves a bloody trail."

"Are we becoming squeamish?" asked Carlos Grande. "Have we lost our balls? A little blood adds flavor to the meat."

"But there's a more effective way. Hear us out." David paused, looked each man in the eye, and said, "And, Carlos, you'll love our new approach. It's right down your alley."

"Let's hear it." Carlos leaned back in his chair, stroked his large, graying moustache, and said, "I'm all ears."

David cleared his voice and announced, "My brother and I have made the final arrangements to buy the Tribune Company's eight regional newspapers, including the *Los Angeles Times, Chicago Tribune, Baltimore Sun, Orlando Sentinel,* and *Hartford Courant.* It could cost us roughly 623 million dollars, but this is a bargain. It would provide the inner circle with a megaphone to shout our laissez-faire ideas across the land. The *L.A. Times* is the fourth largest paper in the country. And the *Tribune* comes in at number nine.'"

"Are you telling me we're going soft?" Jerry Rizzo leaned back and shook his head. "Besides, how are you going to control the message?"

Charles jumped in to defend his brother. "Look at Fox News. They've convinced a majority of their listeners to vote for candidates that propose policies that are antithetical to their own economic interests. So we're going to buy up the printed page and the airways to spread the good news. We will bit by bit shrink the size of government, deregulate the financial institutions, cut back on environmental regulations, and enshrine the Second Amendment. We'll convince the people that the Second Amendment should be part of the Ten Commandments and that the NRA has been blessed and sanctioned by God."

George Stinger shook his head and said, "You're sounding like an Evangelical Christian. We're in business of making money, not saving souls."

"We need to frame the debate and write the narrative. We believe the pen is mightier than the sword. We'll conduct a quiet revolution," David said.

William Stinger stood and asked, "Do you have evidence that our heavy-handed tactics have been found out? Have the bloodhounds picked up the scent?" He then turned and walked to a temporary bar set up near the fireplace and poured a fresh drink.

David stood to address the inner circle. "Look, Armageddon has been executed flawlessly. We have left nothing to chance. Fire Power has carried out our orders perfectly."

"I say we experiment and go hybrid," William Stinger suggested.

"Go hybrid? What do you have in mind?" Jerry Rizzo asked.

"We give David's proposal a go, but when it wanes and

lacks a punch, we go back to our proven ways." William Stinger paused and then added, "We have been very successful at silencing our adversaries."

"But we've pushed the envelope. There will inevitably be a backlash," David said.

As the drinking escalated, so did the debate. The Stinger brothers and Jerry Rizzo played the devil's advocate, probing and slicing up the proposal with an endless series of counterarguments. But little by little, the pieces fell into place, creating a compelling vision of the future. Carlos Grande sealed the deal. He was on board. After all, he had become a billionaire on the back of the communications industry. His holdings in Mexico were legendary.

Around midnight, Charles stood and said, "I move that we vote on David's plan."

"I second the motion," Jerry Rizzo said.

"All those in favor of putting down the sword and embracing the pen signify by saying yay." Charles looked around the room. Starting with David and ending with the Stinger brothers, the answer was yea. "It's unanimous," Charles announced. "The pen is mightier than the sword."

* * *

Yesterday afternoon, Matt Tyson received a surprise call from the FBI. Senior Special Agent Alex Martini had requested an interview. The Bureau wanted to know more about the Malibu home invasion. Last week, while on the West Coast, he had been interviewed by the Malibu Police Department and the LAPD. The phone conversation with the agent was brief but polite. Agent Martini said only that the FBI had an interest in the case.

Alex Martini felt like an old rag doll. First, he was investigating the deadly bombing of a gun show in San Francisco. He was yanked from that assignment and swiftly switched to the poisoning of the late Senator Elizabeth Huntington and the surreal assassination of Supreme Court Justice Helena Bartoletti. But that wasn't the end of the endless merry go round. He was now directed by FBI Director Tom Parker to look in on the high-profile writer for *The Socratic Rag*. There must be a pattern here. But he was clueless. When Alex questioned Director Parker on the latest assignment change, he barked, "I've got my reasons. Chop, chop, time's a wastin'." This reassignment derby was a first for the senior agent. Never before had he been jerked from one assignment and plopped down in the middle of another with no explanation.

It was eight in the morning when Agent Martini rang the doorbell at Matt Tyson's Washington D.C. third-floor condo. Alex had to ring three times before the door slowly opened. Matt Tyson leaned on his crutches and said, "Agent Martini, I presume."

"Your presumption is correct. May I come in?" Alex smiled, noting the youthful appearance of his new person of interest. Based on his aggressive writings in *The Socratic Rag*, he would have expected more of a bulldog look. But he had learned long ago that looks can be deceiving.

"Sure, but may I see some ID?" Matt asked. His tone was soft.

Alex produced ID and Matt, after a quick look, leaned on his right crutch and used his left crutch to motion to the living room sofa. "Make yourself comfortable, Senior Agent Martini," Matt said. "Care for some coffee?"

"No thanks, I've already surpassed my morning quota." Alex took a seat, retrieved his notebook from his coat pocket, and scribbled something down in his private shorthand.

Matt struggled briefly with his crutches. He leaned one against the side of the chair, and with one hand on the chair and the other on the single crutch, he settled awkwardly into the overstuffed chair. "So what brings you to my humble abode?"

"I have a few questions about the home invasion out in Malibu." Alex looked about the living room and thought the apartment nice but Spartan. This guy no doubt made big bucks.

"Fire away."

"By the way," Alex said, "I love your pieces in *The Socratic Rag*. I'm a regular reader. I'm not much into the music scene. But I like your biting investigative reporting, especially your take on Wall Street."

"Thanks, but they do get away with murder." Matt smiled.

Agent Martini looked down at his notes, studied them for a second, and said, "Tell me about the intruders."

"It's been covered in the papers. The *L.A. Times* had several pieces about our Malibu encounter and our run-in with the thugs at Mulligans." Matt leaned back in his chair and grimaced when he stretched out his cast-covered leg.

"Yes, tell me about Mulligans." Agent Martini again scribbled something in his notes.

"Allen Carter and I ran into each other at the bar the evening of the attack."

"How do you know Allen Carter?" Agent Martini cocked his head and looked intently at Matt with raised eyebrows.

Matt grinned and paused. "Sorry, but you remind me of someone. As a kid, I was taken with detective stories and TV detectives. Columbo was one of my favorites. I swear you're the spitting image of one of my childhood heroes."

"Thanks, but both my eyes are good." Agent Martini smiled.

"That's right; Peter Falk had a bad eye." Matt grinned and added, "I hope I didn't offend you."

"No offense taken. So, tell me about you and Allen Carter."

"An old college buddy of mine told me about this racquetball player who showed an open disdain for the NRA. He knew I was doing research on the NRA." Matt bent his knee a bit, allowing his right cast-covered leg to settle into a more comfortable position.

"Why him? Lots of people have trouble with the rigidity and callousness of the leadership of the NRA," Agent Martini said.

"After weekly games of racquetball, they would go out for beers at Mulligans. Allen Carter talked of inside information he had about the big money behind the NRA. Allen's a very successful lawyer and represents clients with close ties with the movie industry. Let's just say I had a hunch. And I checked it out." Matt opened up his hands and said, "I just followed my gut instincts."

"Tell me about the bikers. What did they look like? Any unique physical characteristics, hairstyle, beards, or tattoos?" Alex stretched his neck and glanced around the room. He noticed chess pieces set up on a small table at the end of the bookshelf. "You play chess?" he asked.

"I do. And back to your question, beside the beards and moustaches, both men were covered in ink."

"Anything stand out?" Agent Martini asked.

"Indeed. The shorter of the two had both arms covered in tattoos. His right arm had a fire-breathing dragon on his forearm. His left shoulder had NRA in bold red letters. Just below the letters was the image of an eagle with talons clinging to crossed rifles. The tattoo was hard to miss."

"How is it that you remember such details?" Alex said, jotting down notes.

"When you're held captive, terrorized, and then maimed, it's impossible to forget. You see before you their handiwork." Matt extended his cast toward the FBI agent.

"Good point. What about the other biker?"

"He was taller, heavily inked. He had a tattoo of a Madonna and child on his left shoulder."

"Was it of the religious variety?" probed Agent Martini.

"Yes, it was a classic Catholic depiction of mother and child."

"Like the virgin Mary?"

"That's it. I didn't sense anything spiritual about the guy. He was definitely old school," Matt said.

"What do you mean?"

"You know—a lot of hell fire and damnation plus a healthy dose of wailing and gnashing of teeth."

"It sounds real old school." Alex closed up his notes and put them away. He stood and said, "Thanks for the info. Here's my card. If anything comes up or you remember something, don't hesitate to call."

"Will do." Matt Tyson got his crutches and stood.

"I'll see my way out. Please don't hesitate to call me."

Agent Martini left feeling good about his visit. The bit about the tattoos resonated with what he already knew.

Chapter Twenty-Four

Special Agent Martini once again found himself on the West Coast. FBI Director Tom Parker wanted a closer look at Allen Carter and his girlfriend, Alexis Williams. Matt Tyson's description of the bikers, especially their tattoos, set off alarm bells at the Bureau. The FBI database had singled out several possible suspects with ink work honoring the NRA. The fiery dragon tattoo was another matter. Over five thousand dragon tattoos surfaced, most of them breathing fire.

After calling Allen Carter's secretary several times, both from Washington D.C. and when he arrived in Los Angeles, Agent Alex Martini was able to catch the busy Santa Monica attorney at 4:30 Wednesday afternoon. It was mid-July, and the weather was hot, but not muggy like D.C. Allen had been in court all morning and half of the afternoon. Agent Martini arrived five minutes early and chatted with Millie, the lawyer's secretary. They chatted about Italian cuisine and good Santa Monica Italian restaurants. Allen Carter's secretary didn't disappoint; she blurted, "My, you do favor the TV detective Columbo."

Alex Martini, always gracious, smiled and thanked her for the compliment.

The inner office door opened, and Allen Carter welcomed the agent with a quick smile. "Special Senior Agent Alex Martini, please come in. Good Italian name."

"Yes, sir. My grandfather was an immigrant from Sicily."

"I hope he wasn't part of the mob." Allen Carter grinned.

"No, sir. He was a baker."

The lawyer's lower leg was still in a cast, and he used a cane to get around his office. "Please take a seat. Would you care for some coffee?" Allen Carter carefully slid into his chair, bracing himself with his left hand on the desk.

"I'm good. But thanks. I see you play racquetball." Agent Martini checked out the trophies lining a back shelf.

"I did, but not lately. I miss it though. So how may I assist you?"

"It's about the home invasion. But first, how is it that you know Matt Tyson?"

"He looked me up. He's doing a piece for *The Socratic Rag* on the NRA." Allen shuffled some papers on his desk and leaned back in his chair.

"Tell me about the home invasion. Did the bikers have any unusual physical characteristics, body piercing, beards, or tattoos that might help the FBI in locating these guys?" Agent Martini grinned and impulsively commented, "You look a lot like Mel Gibson."

"Thanks for the compliment. He's a neighbor of mine. We don't hang out. I've seen him around town. But as to your question, the bikers were bearded and heavily inked."

"Tell me about the tattoos."

"Two tattoos were certainly memorable. The shorter thug had NRA prominently inked in red on his left shoulder. Under the bold letters was an eagle perched on crossed rifles. The taller one had a mother and child tattoo on his left shoulder."

"Was it a Madonna?"

"I think so. If it was, it didn't match his vicious nature." Allen was tired and found it difficult to focus. He needed a drink. "How about we finish this discussion over a beer? I know of a good Irish pub."

"I don't think my boss would approve. But I would like to question your girlfriend." Agent Martini looked down at his notes, cleared his voice, and said, "I believe her name is Alexis Williams."

"She's been ill lately. I would appreciate it if you would allow her some breathing room. It's only been a little over two weeks since the home invasion. She's still shaky."

"It wouldn't take long." Alex wouldn't be put off. He needed to talk to her. She might have noticed something missed by Matt and Allen. He knew she was a professor at Pepperdine University.

"You'll have to call her."

"May I have her phone number?"

"Sure, here's her cell number."

Agent Martini jotted down the number and stuffed his notebook in his coat pocket. He glanced at the back wall and remarked, "Say, you must be fond of airplanes. A friend of mind flies a Cessna."

"When I have the time, I fly. I'm most familiar with small planes, like a Cessna. But I've flown vintage by-planes and have been certified to fly a Lear Jet."

"Say, you're a talented guy. I'm envious." Agent Martini wrapped up the questioning and thanked Allen Carter.

* * *

Agent Martini decided not to phone Professor Alexis Williams. He opted to take her by surprise and drop by campus during her office hours. He wanted her fresh and unrehearsed. It was just after three on Thursday afternoon when Agent Martini entered the faculty offices on the Pepperdine campus. For mid-July, the weather was pleasant and the vistas spectacular. He'd seen many campuses on the East Coast, but none were as picturesque as Pepperdine. Tucked in amid the rolling hills of the Santa Monica Mountains, the sprawling campus looked more like an upscale country club than a university. From a second-floor window, Agent Martini had a spectacular view of the Pacific Ocean.

Halfway down the long corridor he spotted her name— Alexis Williams, Professor of Philosophy. Just below her nameplate was posted her class schedule and office hours. The door was closed, so he knocked.

"Come in," a soft voice answered from behind the closed door.

He opened the door and found a bespectacled woman, smartly dressed, leaning over her desk, reading a letter. "I'll be right with you," she said without looking up.

He stood for a couple of seconds before clearing his throat and introducing himself. "Professor Williams, I'm Special Senior Agent Alex Martini. May I have a few words with you?"

Alexis Williams looked up, frowned, and said, "Do you have an appointment?"

"No, ma'am, I just have a few questions concerning your recent home invasion. May I have a seat?"

"Yes, but may I see some ID?" She removed her glasses and cleaned them with a small cloth.

Agent Martini showed his credentials. While she looked them over, he studied her face. She wore no makeup, and her eyes were blood shot and puffy, and her high cheek bones and smooth, wrinkle-free complexion revealed a pretty but stressed young woman.

"How may I help you?" She put back on her glasses, crossed her legs, and folded her arms across her chest.

Alex took a seat across from the professor and said, "Tell me about the home invasion. Any details about the bikers' appearance and behavior would be helpful. Especially important are physical characteristics, beards, body piercings, tattoos, or scars."

The professor inhaled deeply, rolled her eyes upward, and exhaled. The room was silent for several moments before she spoke. Her description of the beards, moustaches, and tattoos matched those of Matt Tyson and Allen Carter. She told of being handcuffed to the Duesenberg in the garage. Finally she said, "The ordeal was humiliating. I felt degraded and defiled."

"Defiled, that's a strong word. Could you expand on that?" Agent Martini got out his notes and attempted to write something. His pen was out of ink. "Oh dear, my pen has failed me. Could I borrow a pen for a second?"

Alexis Williams reached across her desk and retrieved a pen. "Here you go," she said.

"Thanks. You were saying you felt defiled ..." Agent Martini spoke softly, sensing she was under duress.

"Yes." She paused, looked down, and said, "He leered at me. It was awful."

"He leered at you. Which biker did that?" Agent Martini scribbled something in his notes.

"It was the shorter of the two bikers, the bearded one, the one with the NRA tattoo and the dragon on his right arm." The professor shuddered, again clutching herself with crossed arms.

"Did he have a name?"

"The taller biker called him Theta."

Agent Martini jotted down the name in his notes and then asked, "Did he touch you?" Alex was making good use of the borrowed pen.

"Yes. When I was cuffed to the Duesenberg, he yanked on my robe and exposed my breasts. He stared at my breasts for the longest time. He moaned loudly and blurted something obscene."

"What did he say?"

"I can't repeat what he said. It was crude."

"I know you're under duress. But I need specifics. Please, what you tell me will remain confidential."

"He said, 'You're one fucking hot chick.' It was disgusting." The professor's eyes glazed over, and she began to tremble. "It was terrifying."

"I'm sorry to put you through this. I understand your grief, but just one more thing." Agent Martini put away his notes, stood, and returned the borrowed pen.

"Yes?"

"Besides escorting you to the basement and yanking at your robe, did the biker touch you?"

"No. But he raped me with his eyes." The professor closed her eyes and shuddered.

"Sorry to put you through this. Here's my card. If anything comes up or you remember something important, call me." Agent Martini thanked her again and quietly left the grieving professor. He felt there was more to the story. He sensed she was hiding something. But the physical descriptions given by the three victims matched. The boys at the Bureau already had several persons of interest for him to run down. His California stay was not over.

Chapter Twenty-Five

After hitting several gun stores in West Los Angeles, Agent Martini headed for the San Fernando Valley. It was Friday afternoon, the 405 Freeway was snarled with rush-hour traffic, and the temperature was quickly rising. It would soon get much hotter. He had landed a hot tip at the last gun shop; the owner of Gun World was a biker and heavily inked. When he finally pulled up in front of Gun World, he found no available parking. He pulled around the block and parked in a residential neighborhood. Agent Martini hoofed it a couple of blocks back to Gun World, working up a slight sweat. He missed the cool breeze of Malibu and Santa Monica. He'd rather be on the Pepperdine campus talking with Professor Williams.

The store was crowded. Several clerks worked the counters, while a middle-aged guy with full dark beard was on the phone in the next room. Agent Martini could easily see him through the large glass window that overlooked the showroom. The office was elevated about three feet above the showroom floor, providing a bird's-eye view of the shop.

The walls were lined with rifles and shotguns, while the

glass cabinets featured handguns ranging the gamut from derringers to .44 Magnum revolvers. He caught the attention of a clerk who had just finished with a customer and flashed his credentials. "I need to see the owner," said Agent Martini.

"Just a moment," he said. The tall, lanky salesman left the showroom and climbed a few stairs to the elevated office. Alex could see him talking with the owner through the glass window. After a few words with the boss, the salesman motioned for Agent Martini to come up.

The salesman returned to the showroom after Alex introduced himself to the owner. He explained that he was following up on a home invasion case in Malibu. Interviews with the three victims had led him here.

"Why here?" the bearded man said.

"We have confirmation from all three victims that the perpetrators were heavily inked. A tall man had a Madonna and child tattoo on his shoulder. A shorter man had an NRA tattoo on his left shoulder." Agent Martini stood before the seated owner and asked, "Do you know anyone with such tattoos?"

The owner grinned, his uneven teeth barely visible because of the shaggy beard. "Hey, lots of dudes have those tattoos. The Madonna thing is everywhere, and the NRA logo can be seen around town. I saw one last week at the Rock Store out on Mulholland Highway."

"Did the guy have NRA inked in blood red with an eagle clutching crossed rifles?" Alex sensed the owner was being defensive.

"Maybe, but I definitely saw the NRA spelled out in red. Those are sacred initials in this part of the world." The owner stood and started toward the door. "Sorry, I can't help you."

"I notice some ink work around your wrists. How about your arms and shoulders, are they inked?" Agent Martini gestured toward the owner's partially pulled up long-sleeve shirt.

"My arms are inked," the bearded owner said sternly.

"Could I have a look?" Agent Martini asked.

"Do you have a search warrant?"

"No."

"Well, if I haven't committed a crime and you have no search warrant, then you're out of luck." The owner started to push by Agent Martini, but he stood his ground and asked, "May I have your name?"

"It's public record who owns the shop." The owner brushed by the agent and started downstairs.

When he reached ground level, Agent Martini asked, "Are you Jeremiah Bates?"

"I'm known as Suicide Bates. But yes, I'm Jeremiah Bates."

"Why the suicide bit?"

"I ride my bike like I'm flirting with death."

Mr. Bates headed for the front of the store. Agent Martini caught up with him at the front door. "Say, does the handle Theta ring a bell?"

Suicide Bates stopped in his tracks. He looked at the agent and said, "You better fuck off. You're talking gibberish." He then stomped out of the store, his jack boots smacking the concrete sidewalk loudly.

Agent Martini had hit pay dirt.

*　　*　　*

Alexis Williams was distraught. All morning before leaving for the university, she had this uneasy feeling. The idea of dropping by the campus just didn't feel right. There was no compelling reason to go to her office, spring semester was over, and she wasn't teaching summer school. *Damn, I should listen to my inner voice*, she thought.

Allen had informed her this morning that he had to meet with a new client and wouldn't be home until eight. It was 4:30, CNN was filled with depressing news, and she wasn't hungry. All afternoon, she had been plagued by this inner voice. At first it was too faint to make out, but as they day wore on, the voice became audible and then built to a screaming pitch. She couldn't block it out. It had become a deafening roar. "Leave! You must escape the black box. Run from that clown."

The unexpected visit by that FBI agent dragged up unpleasant memories for Alexis. Adding to that was the emergence of that dreadful inner voice. She ran upstairs, threw some clothes and personal necessities into a small suitcase, and left a note on the kitchen counter. It was short and cryptic:

> *I'm in need of a break. The home invasion and unexpected visit by Agent Martini has pushed me over the edge. I don't know when I'll be back. Please keep this confidential. I need some space. Alexis.*

Long before the sun had set over the Pacific, Alexis was headed north on the 101 Freeway toward Santa Barbara. She had no idea where she was going. Her Lexus was full of gas, and she had plenty of cash and three credit cards. And she wasn't due back to work until the beginning of the fall semester.

*   *   *

Allen Carter was tired, and his leg hurt. He had put excessive stress on it much too quickly. He had avoided the crutches and overused the cane. His stubbornness had crossed him.

When he returned from his late-evening meeting, he entered the kitchen and spotted Alexis's note next to the countertop TV. He picked it up, read it, and said, "Fucking crazy *bitch*. She's going to get us fried." Allen limped to the fridge, grabbed a cold bottle of Guinness, and with his cane in one hand and beer in the other, hobbled out to the deck. There he was greeted by a rising full moon and the distant howls and yips of coyotes. Suddenly he was gripped by the bizarre notion of being a vampire equipped with formidable fangs, capable of sucking his adversaries dry. Black and white images of Bela Lugosi as Dracula flooded his mind. But he couldn't abandon Motley Wag.

Alexis had quickly become a new member on Allen's enemies list. She was possessed, tormented, and fooled by her twisted conscience. *But that's impossible*, he thought. *She has no conscience. But she's fucking crazy and dangerous.*

Allen's mind raced. Impulsively, he phoned Bill Paxton, his private eye. His instructions were terse. "Find and return her post-haste. Do not alert the authorities. I'll deal with her personally."

Chapter Twenty-Six

J eremiah Bates was in deep trouble. The feds were breathing down his neck. They had the biker cornered. And they knew too much. The two tattoos, the fiery dragon and the NRA Logo, were enough to put him behind bars. His only recourse was The Saint.

Jeremiah called a middle man who alerted The Saint. In turn, The Saint contacted the Berrigan brothers. They immediately arranged for Theta to disappear from the map. Within forty-eight hours, he had a new passport, driver's license, birth certificate, and appearance. Suicide Bates was now seated at a bar in Puerto Vallarta savoring a margarita. He had shaved his beard, and tomorrow he had an appointment with a tattoo artist. His NRA and soaring eagle atop crossed rifles was due for a facelift.

Jeremiah signaled the bartender for another margarita. His Spanish was limited, but he knew enough to keep him well supplied with tequila, beer, vodka, and chicken. He also knew enough Spanish to sweet talk a young lady into staying the night at his hotel. He needed to cultivate some new friends, especially female. This was his new home. He may never return to Gun World, let alone ride his Harley through the winding curves of the Santa Monica Mountains. He was a wanted man.

*   *   *

On Monday morning agent, Martini returned to Gun World, this time with a search warrant. The FBI and LAPD had enough evidence to convince a judge of the necessity for inspecting persons and property at Gun World. There was ample evidence that Jeremiah Bates had cooked the books, violated California gun laws, and skirted local ordinances..

He entered the shop and immediately cornered the same lanky salesman that helped him last Friday, demanding to see the owner.

"Mr. Bates is on vacation." The salesman smiled and added, "He needed a break. It had been two years since his last real holiday."

"Where did he go?" Agent Martini glanced at a customer next to him fondly cradling an AR-15.

"Not sure." The salesman shrugged. "I didn't want to be nosy."

"Do you have his cell phone number?" Agent Martini took out his notes.

"Yes, but it won't help you."

"What?" Agent Martini snapped.

"He said he needed a complete break from the business." Another employee approached and asked the salesman a question about the pricing of magazines for the AR-15.

Agent Martini took out the search warrant and showed it to the salesman. "We need to inspect the premises, especially the business records of Gun World, including the personal correspondences of Jeremiah Bates."

The salesman took the warrant in hand and studied it, asking Agent Martini for clarification on several points. When his queries were satisfactorily answered, he allowed Agent Martini, another FBI agent, and a LAPD detective access to Gun World, Jeremiah's office, and all business records, file cabinets, and computer. The hunt was on.

* * *

Alexis felt a temporary reprieve from the taunting of her inner voice. It no longer screamed and ranted the command to flee the black box and the hideous clown. Instead, it praised her for fleeing. She had classical music on the CD as her Lexus cruised passed the cities of Ventura and Santa Barbara. She spotted the Solvang turn off and made a hard right just as Stravinsky's "Rite of Spring" reached its finale. She felt suddenly energized. She headed east toward the Danish community. But then the idea of hassling with tourists and quaint souvenir shops struck her as ghastly. So she headed north for the nearby town of Los Olivos. There she could unwind and regroup. It was a small town, more like a country village that specialized in wineries and bustling tasting rooms. The tiny community was known for peace, quiet, and wine tasting.

Alexis checked into the Fess Parker Wine Country Inn. It was eight thirty, and she was wired. Stravinsky had ignited her, charging her passions. She showered, put on makeup, and chose a short black skirt, heals, and low-cut powder blue blouse. Alexis noticed some split ends in her dyed hair. She had recently decided on a brunette look; it flattered her eyes. She retrieved a pair of tapered scissors from her makeup kit and trimmed the frayed ends. She placed the pointed shears on the end table next to the king-size bed and checked out her appearance in the bathroom mirror. She was satisfied.

Tonight there would be no eyeglasses, conservative business attire, or loose-fitting clothes. She felt the need to let go. She needed to express herself. She was, for a while, free of the black box and the controlling clown.

The Country Inn had a bar and lounge. It was Thursday night, and the only entertainment was an aging female vocalist belting out old torch songs. She took a seat at the bar and ordered a house Chardonnay. There were three elderly couples seated at the tables and booths, and two middle-aged guys at the bar. After the vocalist finished a set of oldies from the thirties, the taller of the two men approached her. He had a trimmed beard, slicked back hair, and a slight accent. He reminded her of the guy on the Dos Equis commercial, a slightly younger version of The Most Interesting Man in the World.

"May I join you?" he asked, smiling.

"Certainly, be my guest." She liked his eyes. They were engaging but not threatening.

"May I buy you a drink?" He waved over the bartender.

"I never turn down a free drink." She liked his accent. It sounded European, maybe Italian.

"I'm Manual Romano." He paid for the drinks and asked, "May I ask your name?"

"Alexis." She didn't offer a last name.

By the time they reached their third drink, the conversation became livelier and more personal.

"Are you married?" Manual asked.

Alexis flashed him a wicked smile and lied. "I am. My husband is on a fishing trip. So I decided to take a trip of my own." Lying and hiding behind a false persona was liberating. It took her away from her fears and smothering obsessions.

"What would he think of you drinking and laughing with a stranger?" Manual reached over and lightly touched her left hand.

"He's far out at sea with his drunken buddies. What he doesn't know won't hurt him." Alexis responded by warmly rubbing his right hand. She leaned closer to him, offering a generous view of her half-exposed breasts. "Like what you see, Manual?"

"You are an incredibly beautiful woman."

The flirting escalated, and soon after the vocalist wrapped up her last song, the tipsy couple headed for Alexis's hotel suite. As soon as the door closed behind them, Alexis and Manual were in a full embrace. They kissed and groped each other with mounting fervor. In less than ten minutes, they had shed their clothes and were eagerly enjoying the thrills of foreplay. As the passion escalated, Alexis made it clear that she enjoyed more than tender, romantic sex. Manual upped the ante and became more physical and demanding. He held her down, bit down on her neck, and grabbed her derriere with the intensity of a MMA fighter.

Manual leaned back and gazed at Alexis beneath him. Her eyes glazed over, and her moans morphed into gentle cries of forbidden passion. But it wasn't sexual delight she was experiencing. When she looked up into Manual's lust contorted face, she saw the clown in the black box. Its face alarmed her. It was the face of the clown. The inner voice returned, deafening, shrieking orders of "Kill, kill, kill." Alexis screamed, impulsively reached for the sharp scissors on the end table, and thrust them upward into Manual's neck. Her strength and resolve stunned her. He howled from the impact, and his enlarged eyes nearly popped from their sockets. Blood instantly spurted from his neck, and his head, bobbing erratically, plopped down with a thud on her breasts. She could hear the gurgling sounds of blood pooling in his mouth and throat.

She lay in bed for a long time, paralyzed by her violent attack on the stranger. Slowly and with considerable effort, she managed to push him aside and then roll out of bed. She went to the bathroom and checked herself out in the mirror. Blood was splattered on her dark hair, and more had run down her face and splashed her breasts. Her nipples, completely covered with the stranger's blood, dripped his vital fluids on the bathroom counter.

While Manual lay lifeless in bed, Alexis took a shower, a vain attempt to wash away the sins of her act. The voice returned, consoling her. *It is self-defense. The clown in the black box, the one with the hideous smile, is out to harm you. You are right, justified, and should be lauded for your act. The clown is evil. He has been put in his rightful place, back in the black box.*

Chapter Twenty-Seven

Allen Carter tossed and turned Thursday night, unable to sleep. Alexis had mysteriously disappeared, had left no hint of her destination, and was emotionally distraught. What if she cracked? He feared that she would talk. And that would bring down Gotham City.

Allen battled through Friday, made two morning court appearances, and then met with clients in the afternoon. Upon returning home after a day of legal drudgery, he grabbed a Guinness from the fridge and turned on the news. After ten minutes of the latest in the sports world, he was hit square in the face with coverage of a grisly murder scene at a Los Olivos resort. A middle-aged man was found dead in a suite at the Fess Parker Wine Country Inn. Police investigation was in the preliminary stages, but officials were saying he likely bled to death. His carotid artery had been severed. At this time, no weapon was found at the scene. The suite was registered in the name of an unidentified woman.

Allen's heart skipped a beat. Could it be? Alexis was on the lam. He had no idea where she had gone. All he knew was that her Lexus was not in the garage, her makeup kit was nowhere in sight, and a small piece of luggage and a backpack were missing. He immediately phoned Bill Paxton.

Luckily he picked up. "Hey, Allen," he answered.

"I'm calling about Alexis. Anything new?"

"Not yet. I have an assistant on it full-time."

"Did you see the news from Los Olivos?"

"No. What's up?" Bill was calm, perhaps too calm for Allen.

"A guy was murdered at an Inn in Los Olivos. Preliminary investigation suggests he bled to death." Allen was nearly breathless.

"You think Alexis has something to do with this?" Bill's voice showed immediate concern.

"I don't know why, I just have this feeling. Maybe my mind is playing tricks. Could you check it out? I'm worried sick about her welfare."

"I'll be right on it." Bill signed off with the assurance he'd be personally involved in the investigation.

As soon as Allen put down his cell phone, it chirped. He checked, and it was Matt Tyson. "Hey Matt, what's up?"

"I thought I'd check up on the latest with the home invasion. Anything new?" Matt sounded cheerful.

"Not really, but I have some troubling news," he blurted.

"Don't tell me that you're having problems with your leg," Matt ribbed him. After all, they both had their lower leg shattered.

"Some discomfort, but that's not the worst of it. Alexis has flown the coop. I came home from work Thursday evening and found a note on the kitchen counter. It said she needed space and didn't know when she would be back."

"Wow, that's a shocker," Matt said.

"I'm worried for her safety." Allen's tone was serious.

"Has she sought help, maybe some counseling? She was put through quite an ordeal."

"No," Allen lied.

"How can I help?"

"I don't know. You're an investigative reporter. Maybe you have some insights on how to find her."

"I dig for stories, but they're more about the scandals on Wall Street." Matt paused, and then added, "But I have contacts. I'll nose around and see if I can come up with something."

"Thanks. I appreciate that," Allen said.

Allen said good-bye and headed upstairs for a shower. He thought about driving up north and checking out the Fess Parker Inn. But he rejected the notion. He'd let Bill Paxton do the legwork.

*   *   *

Alexis's inner voice was her only consolation. Images of the scissors piercing his neck, his eyes bulging, and blood spurting from his neck made her shiver. Her hands trembled to the point she had to slow down and pull off the highway. Her inner voice had softened in tone and now lavished praise on her gallant behavior. *You stood up to evil. You put the clown in his place.*

The professor headed north on Highway 101, the CD cranked up to the sounds of Wagner. She arrived in San Francisco late Friday afternoon. The traffic brought the Lexus to a crawl. She toughed it out, crossed the Golden Gate Bridge, and turned off the highway in Sausalito. Tired, she checked in to the Casa Madrona Hotel and Spa. She registered as Monique Monet, paid cash, and gave a fake license plate number. She was pleased with her third-story room. It had a great view of the San Francisco skyline across the bay.

After showering, shaving her legs, and drying her hair, she turned on the TV. She channeled surfed, checking out Fox, MSNBC, and CNN. She then switched to a local station and was stunned. As the reporter rattled on about the grisly killing at the Fess Parker Inn, images of the killing scene once again flooded her mind. She turned off the TV and ran to the bathroom where she threw up. She then lay down on the bed but couldn't rest. She went to the bathroom, used mouth wash, brushed her teeth, and then studied her reflection in the mirror. Her face disgusted her, so she spent twenty minutes applying makeup. Satisfied, she dressed for a night out. Again she chose a short black skirt and heels. It was too cold for a skimpy blouse, so she opted for a tight sweater and light leather jacket. She needed to blow off some steam.

* * *

Agent Martini had supervised a team of FBI agents in the search and scrutiny of the sales, e-mails, FAX, and phone records at Gun World. He was about to leave for lunch when his cell chirped.

"Agent Martini," he said mechanically.

"Hey, this is Matt Tyson."

"Matt, what's up?"

"I just got off the phone with Allen Carter. He's in a panic."

"What's his problem?" Agent Martini assumed it had something to do with the home invasion.

"Alexis Williams has gone AWOL."

"What?"

"She left Allen Carter a terse note. Said she needed some space."

"Where did she go?" Agent Martini was suddenly very interested.

"He hasn't a clue."

"That doesn't sound good. I'll give him a call." Agent Martini was about to sign off when Matt made a request.

"Say, Senior Special Agent Martini, could you do me a favor?"

"What's that?" Alex sensed he was being stroked. The use of Senior Special Agent had a good ring to it, but in this circumstance, it was over the top.

"Don't tell Allen Carter I alerted you. I just sense that something is out of whack here. He asked for my help, but I doubt that meant getting the FBI involved."

"I'll try to be diplomatic." Agent Martini signed off and immediately phoned Allen Carter. He reached him on the third ring.

"Allen Carter, how can I help you?" He apparently thought it was a client.

"This is Agent Martini. I'm just checking in to see if everything's okay. How's your leg holding up?"

"It's a bit sore. I think I've abused it. I still use the cane."

"Well, at least that's progress. Has there been progress with anything else? Anything new turn up?" Agent Martini said.

"It's not the leg that's really bothering me." Allen paused. "Something happened to Alexis."

"What's happened?" Agent Martini said. "I just saw her the other day."

"She's gone AWOL ..." Allen rattled off the latest on Alexis. The rapid delivery left him nearly breathless.

"Do you think she's in any danger?" Agent Martini's mind raced. *Could Jeremiah Bates have something to do with this?*

"I don't know. I'm worried."

"What make and color of car is she driving?"

"She has a silver 2012 Lexus."

"Do you have the plate numbers?"

Allen Carter supplied him with the info and informed him about her credit cards. He was conflicted. He wanted her home but feared she'd talk. He hoped he could have intimate access to her before the feds probed too deeply. His mind raced, conjuring up one scary scenario after another.

Chapter Twenty-Eight

Alexis skipped dinner and hit a couple of bars in downtown Sausalito. She eventually settled in at Smitty's Bar. It was a local's hotspot and featured four pool tables, a dart board, and jukebox. She befriended a couple of twenty-something young ladies, played some pool, shot darts, and drank too much. A couple of guys hit on her, but they were either too young, too old, or not her type. She ended the evening with two cups of coffee and cautiously drove back to the hotel without incident.

As she approached her third-floor room, she stopped in her tracks. A tall guy wearing jeans and a sweatshirt was knocking on her door. Alexis was at the far end of the outdoor walkway, concealed in the midnight shadows. She immediately retreated, hurried down the stairs to the parking lot, and got into her Lexus. She peered up at the third floor. She wasn't positive, but it looked like one of the younger guys that hit on her at Smitty's. He had tried to pick her up, but she said no thanks. When he persisted, she said that he looked like one of her college students. He shook his head and said, "I never had a professor as sexy as you." He slurred his words and said, "I'd give anything to have you."

She had gone back to playing pool but noticed that he never took his eyes off her. When she left Smitty's, she didn't notice anyone following her. She had taken a roundabout way back to the hotel, making a couple of wrong turns. *How did he know what room I'm in?* she thought. Then it donned on her. It was at Smitty's Bar she had drunkenly slipped and told him her fake name and where she staying. He must have worked the desk clerk for her room number.

Within five minutes the tall guy was gone, so she cautiously climbed the steps to the third floor and entered her room. He was gone, so she thought. She brushed her teeth and relieved herself.

She was about to undress when she heard a knock at the door. She froze. Again she heard several taps, then a louder series of knocks. Not liking the racket and wanting to end this charade, she slowly opened the door.

Greeting her at the door was the young guy from Smitty's Bar. He smiled and said, "May I come in?" He looked her up and down, obviously liking what he saw.

"It's late," Alexis said. She tried to close the door on him, but he pushed his way through, knocking her back into the room. She stumbled and fell back on the bed, causing her skirt to bunch up around her upper thighs and hips. It gave the intruder a lot of flawless flesh to feast his eyes on.

"Do you have something to drink," he asked, looking about the room for some booze.

"No! So why don't you go play somewhere else." For some odd reason, she was finding out that her predicament was not unwanted. In fact, she was aroused. Her inner voice returned, uttering repeatedly, "You need to blow off steam. You need to blow off steam."

"Well, I have some grass. Let's party." He pulled out a joint and lighter from the front pocket of his jeans and swiftly lit it. He inhaled deeply, blowing a giant smoke ring toward the ceiling. He plopped down on the bed next to Alexis and offered her the joint.

"I haven't smoked in years," she lied. Allen Carter smoked regularly, and she often joined him. It did wonders for their sex life, enhancing the sensuality of their foreplay.

"Come on, let's be friends." He was charming. He was probably mid-twenties, had the beginnings of a beard, a definite five o'clock shadow, and thick, unruly, dark brown hair.

Alexis took the joint and stared at it. She rolled it in her hand, raised it to her full red lips, and inhaled deeply. She instantly felt a rush. The tension she had felt all day suddenly vanished. Alexis took another long hit on the half-smoked joint and sent a smoke ring floating toward her new friend. She handed the burning joint to him and said, "What's your name? You told me at Smitty's, but I can't remember." She felt herself slipping into a dreamlike state. Her lungs burned a bit from the marijuana, but her senses were fully alive. She was aroused.

"Alex. The name's Alex. I mentioned it to you several times." He took another hit and handed it back to Alexis. "Do you have any music?"

"No. There's an FM radio on the nightstand." Alexis scooted back on the bed, propped herself up on pillows, and leaned against the headboard. She tried to lower her skirt but gave up. He had already had a good look.

Alex got up, walked around the bed, and fiddled with the small clock radio. He found a rock station, an oldies but goodies late-night affair. He pulled off his sweatshirt and threw it on a nearby chair. Underneath he had on a tight black short-sleeved T-shirt. He obviously pumped iron. His broad shoulders, flat stomach, and tattooed arms rippled with muscle.

He arrogantly asked, "Have you been with a younger man?"

"Not lately." She scooted down in the bed, causing her short black skirt to bunch up around her hips. She rolled halfway over on her right side and gazed up into his dark brown eyes. "What do you have in mind?"

He dropped down on the bed, leaned over her, and said, "This for starters." He slowly lowered his head and kissed her tenderly on the lips. The soft sensual kisses rapidly morphed into unbridled passion. The lovemaking was romantic and playful at first but soon turned into rough sex. Alexis gave into the attack, her twisted lust building to an intense orgasm. Her second orgasm mirrored his, leaving the sweat-drenched couple breathless.

After long moments of heavy breathing, Alexis pushed herself up and leaned against the headboard. When she looked at Alex, his face had transformed into that of a clown. Not some ordinary clown. It was Motley Wag. He was back.

She jumped up and ran for the bathroom. There she washed her face with cold water. She peeked out from the slightly opened bathroom door and looked at Alex. He was gone. In bed was Motley Wag, his wide mouth, painted red. He was laughing, taunting her to come back to bed. "Come back and finish what you started," said Motley Wag.

She closed the bathroom door and stared at her reflection in the mirror. Two bloodshot eyes, glazed over by rage and fear, gazed back at her. She looked like a Salem witch with her pasty white face and full lips gorged with blood. Her eyes fell upon the scissors lying next to her makeup kit, the metal blades shining brightly from the overhead lighting. She grabbed them, hid them behind her back with her right hand, and returned to bed. She mounted the reclining clown and straddled his hips.

Motley Wag laughed loudly, shaking his head. "Why don't you finish me," he taunted. She leaned down for a closer look. His lips were not moving. All she could see were the scars, smeared red lipstick, and pasty white skin. He definitely wasn't speaking. It was her inner voice. "Now's the time, lash out, kill the bastard." The words reverberated in her skull like the chiming of a cathedral bell. It was deafening. The hideous smile, alive but hauntingly petrified, terrified her, causing her to lurch forward and drive the pointed scissors deep into Motley Wag's neck.

*   *   *

It was three in the morning when Alexis pulled into a Denny's coffee shop just north of Sausalito on the 101. She had changed into a navy blue sweat suit and wore a Yankee baseball cap that she found in her backpack. She hadn't eaten for more than twenty-four hours, and the marijuana had given her the munchies. She ordered a vegetarian omelet, rye toast, and black coffee. She was headed north toward the Oregon border. Alexis had no final destination, but she sensed that her life as a college professor was over.

There was no way she could once again teach a course in ethics. Or could she? Time would tell, but now she needed a plan. As she ate, she entertained various escape plans. The only way she could beat the system was to leave the country. Her passport was filed away at her faculty office at Pepperdine University, her considerable funds tied up in a CD and checking account at two Santa Monica banks, but these facts didn't tell her what to do. Her emotions were raw and her thinking chaotic.

By the time she left Denny's and got into her car, the breakfast had kicked in. With the enhanced brain power, Alexis suddenly seized on a plan. She'd return to Malibu by way of I-5, retrieve her passport from Pepperdine, withdraw cash from both her CD and checking account, and book a flight to Puerto Vallarta. She just loved margaritas.

Alexis turned her Lexus south, hooked up with the I-5 outside of Oakland, and headed for Malibu. By noon, she should be at Pepperdine.

Chapter Twenty-Nine

lexis Williams hadn't slept in two days. But her energy and will were strong. Her demonic inner voice had calmed, now occasionally whispering words of encouragement.

With the university pass displayed on the driver's side window of her Lexus, she breezed past campus security and parked. In less than fifteen minutes, she had found her passport in her office. While there, she used the campus phone to book a five o'clock flight to Puerto Vallarta. Time was of the essence; she had four hours to visit two banks and check in at LAX.

She managed to skirt through campus unnoticed. A history professor walked by her but probably wouldn't recognize her. She had never stooped to wearing sweats and a baseball cap on campus. Besides, as he was accustomed to do, he had his nose buried in a book.

She arrived at the airport at three, left the Lexus in long-term parking, and cleared security check with thirty minutes to spare. She had her boarding pass, ten thousand dollars in cash, and a hankering for a margarita. The transactions at

US Bank and Wells Fargo went smoothly, and the security check at LAX was a walk in the park. No one gave her a second look. By the time the United Airline Flight 76 was airborne, Alexis was sound asleep.

*   *   *

It was Saturday morning. Alexis had been missing for three days. Allen Carter had finished breakfast and checked his gym bag. All was in order. He had a racquetball tournament this afternoon; he needed to blow off steam.

He turned on CNN and saw that a young man had been found dead in a Sausalito hotel, his neck punctured. He had bled to death. The room was registered to an unidentified woman. His suspicions deepened, and his mind raced, conjuring up a slew of ghastly scenarios.

His cell chirped, wrenching him from his paranoid ruminations. He checked caller ID. It was his private eye, Bill Paxton.

"Good morning, Bill. What's up?" Allen was hoping for some good news.

"Hey, Allen, I wanted to check in. I just returned from Los Olivos late last night." Bill's tone was grave.

"Is it bad news?"

"I'm not sure. I talked with the night clerk that worked the desk the evening of the murder." Bill took a deep breath.

"What did you dig up?"

"He checked in the woman in question. She registered as Samantha White, had dark hair, great body, and brown eyes that were puffy and bloodshot. He added that she was, in his words, a looker."

"Fuck, it's got to be her." Allen felt sick. It was her.

"Hold on. The license plate numbers provided by Samantha White don't match Alexis's car."

"She could have lied," Allen said. "She's good at that."

"Do you want me to check out the Sausalito case?" Bill asked.

"Yes, right away. Money's not an issue. You need to *find her*."

"I'll leave immediately." Bill signed off.

Allen Carter decided to take his frustrations out on the racquetball courts.

*   *   *

Agent Martini got an urgent call from the Sausalito Police Department. Sergeant Adams reported that surveillance cameras at the Madrona Hotel and Spa recorded the license plate of a late-model Lexus. It matched the plates of a Lexus registered to Alexis Williams. The address listed on the California registration was an address on Los Flores Canyon Road, Malibu, California.

He immediately put out an all-points bulletin. She needed to be questioned. Reports from officers on the scene reported that the night clerk checked in a dark-haired woman, relatively young, and very attractive. "She was a babe," the clerk said when interviewed by police.

*   *   *

Alexis had slept a straight twenty-four hours since arriving at the Villa Premiere Hotel and Spa in Puerto

Vallarta. After a long soak in the Jacuzzi, she visited the hotel's full-service health spa for an hour massage. Her muscles, mainly in her neck and shoulders, were tense, sore, and tight. The massage did wonders for her, body and soul; she was now ready to celebrate her new life. In her suite, she dressed casually, choosing a brightly colored summer dress and high-heel sandals. She asked the concierge for a cantina that had good fresh fish tacos and served delicious frozen margaritas. He suggested the Blanca y Negro.

She called a cab and was seated at a crowded bar in less than fifteen minutes. It was Sunday night, but the cantina was jumping. The bar was full, but she was lucky and got the last available barstool. An ensemble of four musicians entertained the revelers, mostly tourists, with a montage of popular Mexican folk songs. The vocalists pandered to the crowd while violins and guitars filled the air with a lively Latin beat.

On her left were two middle-aged ladies celebrating a birthday. On her right was a middle-age guy that looked vaguely familiar. They struck up a conversation and shared several drinks. He had on a sleeveless top that revealed a tattoo on his left shoulder that spelled out NBA. Underneath was a basketball. It featured an eagle clutching crossed swords. The tattoo intrigued her to the point that she asked the guy what it signified. He laughed and said, "When I was much younger, I was a diehard basketball junkie." She smiled and dropped the subject.

After another drink, she began to feel tipsy. She politely excused herself and said, "I need to eat before I get drunk." Before she left the bar, the guy asked where she was staying and gave Alexis his cell number. He said, laughing, "Just call me Gerry."

As she left the bar, she said, "You can call me Maria."

*   *   *

Agent Martini decided to phone Allen Carter. Maybe Alexis had returned home. His expectations of that were slim, but he needed to check all bases. It was about nine Sunday morning when he placed the call.

Allen answered on the fourth ring. "Hello," he said sleepily.

"I hope I didn't wake you. This is Agent Martini."

"Oh, I was just thinking of you. I was hoping you had some answers about the whereabouts of Alexis." Allen paused and then said, "I'm worried sick."

"Well, I think we have evidence of where she was."

"What did you find out?"

"Surveillance cameras at the Casa Madrona Hotel and Spa recorded her license plate in the parking lot."

"Oh shit. Are you positive?"

"The plates matched the registration of a Lexus owned by Alexis Williams residing at Los Flores Canyon Road in Malibu." Agent martini's tone was matter of fact.

"Oh God, help me." There was a long silence, and then Allen said, "What happens now?

"I put out an all-points bulletin. We need to talk with her. The recording of the Lexus is not by itself incriminating. But we need to investigate. We need to know what business brought her to the Sausalito hotel."

"How can I help?" Allen said.

"Let me know immediately if she shows. I've got to go."

"Of course."

Chapter Thirty

Charles and David Berrigan summoned the inner circle for a weekend retreat at Shangri-La. It was a time for business and pleasure. After dinner and drinks, they met in the War Room where the Berrigan brothers had prepared a short video. When the members were seated, Charles activated a sixty-inch monitor and announced, "Let the show begin."

While the video began with a full-screen picture of the American flag waving proudly over the Capitol Dome in Washington D.C., the sound system belted out strains of Richard Rodgers's "Victory at Sea." The next scene featured the crux of Dwight Eisenhower's famous "Military-Industrial Complex" speech in 1961. The prediction of the thirty-fourth president of the United States had come true. His warning had now become reality. A close-up of President Eisenhower delivering his televised farewell speech from the Oval Office flashed on the big screen. The camera closed in on Ike; his spoken words, enhanced by the wonders of modern technology, echoed loudly in the War Room:

"We have been compelled to create a permanent armaments industry of vast proportions ... we must not fail to comprehend its grave implications. In the councils of government, we must guard against the acquisition of unwarranted influence, whether sought or unsought, by the military-industrial complex. The potential for the disastrous rise of misplaced power exists and will persist."

The voice of Charles Berrigan followed Ike's prophetic words. The elder Berrigan brother said with great pride and satisfaction, "Gentlemen of the inner circle, we have cashed in on the great president's prediction. We have become major players in the inner workings of the military-industrial complex. We are at the center of corporate power and war profiteering."

Images of the pentagon appeared on the screen while Charles Berrigan provided an inspirational narrative eliciting a hearty round of cheers and cat calls. "We have our hands in the deep pockets of five private contractors," he said. "We control 20 percent of Lockheed Martin, 25 percent of Boeing, 20 percent of Northrop Grumman, and just over 30 percent of both Raytheon and General Dynamics. That's over one-third of all Pentagon contracts." The War Room erupted in applause.

Images of helicopters flying over Iraq and Afghanistan filled the screen. "We have profited from the wars in Iraq and Afghanistan and are looking to expand our influence in Syria. There are 400 billion dollars of contracts now on the table, and we are involved in more than 25 percent of them.

"And our last victory," said Charles," thanks to the inner circle, especially Carlos Grande, we have successfully purchased the Tribune Company's eight regional papers, including the *L.A. Times, Chicago Tribune, Baltimore Sun, Orlando Sentinel*, and the *Hartford Courant*." Again there was a round of applause. "The Tribune is a seven-billion-dollar media company that owns twenty-three television stations. We now control the narrative. We control the flow of money and words that fuels the war industry."

"And last but not least," said David, "we control the NRA. Long live anything that goes bang." The room erupted with loud proclamations.

There were rounds of high fives. Before they left the War Room, Carlos Grande asked, "Are we any closer to finding the bastards that bombed the gun shows?"

Charles answered, "We have some promising leads. Members of Fire Power are working on the problem as we speak."

"What's the latest on Theta? Has he been replaced?" asked Jerry Rizzo.

"We have an operative in mind. We'll discuss that tomorrow. But now we celebrate."

The War Room once again erupted with cheers and obscene words. The men had women of the evening waiting out on the deck. The Cloak brothers had hired enough female companionship for two ladies per gentlemen. "We can't let the ladies wait," said Charles.

* * *

Alexis had downsized. She had checked out of the Villa Premiere Hotel and Spa and settled for the quaint, but cheaper, Hotel Encino. She had to watch her funds. Her original ten thousand dollars would not last indefinitely. Eventually she might have to land a job, but she had no visa and only a passing knowledge of Spanish.

Yesterday she had scored some sleeping pills at a local pharmacy. Alexis had sweet talked the pharmacist. His English was better than her Spanish. This sealed the deal, and she got her drug prescription. The pharmacist knew that she was an American tourist, so she had no local connections and couldn't blow the whistle on him. He was quite adept at working the black market.

The prescription Ambien had allowed her to sleep soundly last night, so her mood was good. Her inner voice had calmed, but it became restless when she consumed more than two drinks. It was hard for her to refuse that third margarita.

It was two in the afternoon when she stopped for coffee at a second-story seaside cantina with a great ocean view. Outside on the patio, she had found a shaded corner table where she enjoyed watching the colorful parade of people walking on the strand below. The ocean air felt cool and refreshing, comfortable for a July afternoon. She smiled as she watched the colorful sailboats as they made lazy circles across the bay. The scene was truly mesmerizing.

As Alexis nursed her coffee, her mind revisited her escape from Allen Carter. She was caught up in a vortex of sights and sounds, violent images of bulging eyes shocked with surprise, piercing screams, and the eerie sounds of gurgling blood. She had felt rage when she committed the acts. But now she was bewildered by her psychotic outbursts.

She had always thought of herself as above the fray, in control, able to carry out the bombing of a gun show where scores of people were maimed and traumatized. But now she had lost her grip on reality. How ironic it was for a person who lived in her head, an intellectual, a professor of philosophy who taught ethics and knew about the workings of the rational mind. She had excelled at logic, problem solving, and conceptual analysis, and she relished the challenge of a complex philosophical argument. But now she was held hostage by another master, a force that didn't follow the rules of logic. She was drowning in a sea of emotions and didn't know how to keep her head above water. But Alexis knew one thing for sure: she had dirty hands.

"Hey, stranger," came a distant voice. Alexis blinked several times and then squinted through her sunglasses at the guy she had met several nights ago at Blanca y Negro. He was standing over her, a beer in hand. "May I join you?"

"Why not? The day is young. I remember you … Gerry, the man in love with the NBA."

"That's me. And I remember you, Maria with the sexy eyes." Gerry took a seat next to her and smiled. "So," he said, "have you settled into Puerto Vallarta?"

"I'm not sure. I've only been here three days." Alexis smiled. "What about you?"

"I've been here about ten days." He tugged on his draft beer. "I know I've seen you before."

Alexis laughed. "That's an old line."

"Oh, no," he said, "I don't forget a face." He looked her up and down. "Everything about you is memorable."

"There are plenty of beautiful women in the world." Alexis took a sip of coffee and then said, "But thanks for the compliment."

"If I could see you naked, I'd know for sure if I've seen you before." He grinned and then laughed.

"Well, that's a new one. I never had a guy say he'd recognize me if I was nude." Alexis laughed. "Your comment makes me feel like a porn star."

Gerry said, "You're more beautiful than any porn star I've laid eyes on."

"It sounds like you've seen a few."

"Oh, you bet," he said, laughing. "I'm from the San Fernando Valley, the porn capital of the world."

"I read in the *L.A. Times* that Los Angeles requires the use of condoms." Alexis had read several articles on the issue, and one of her male students at Pepperdine had raised the condom requirement in one of her ethics classes.

"Where are you from?" Gerry asked.

"Malibu," she said. As soon as the word was out of her mouth, she regretted saying it.

"Malibu, that's the playground of the rich and famous."

"I'm neither rich nor famous."

"Well anyway, we're practically neighbors." Gerry motioned for the waiter to bring another draft. "How about joining me for a cold draft beer?"

"No, it's too early. Besides, I've got an appointment, and I'm late," she lied. She got up and thanked Gerry for the offer.

"Wait, where are you staying?"

"I told you before. I've got to go." She turned quickly and dashed downstairs without paying for her coffee. She had talked far too much. They both knew that they had met before. It finally donned on Alexis that Gerry was one of the bearded intruders involved in the Malibu home invasion.

Chapter Thirty-One

Zeta of Fire Power got hold of Theta through a prearranged contact point in Mexico. The message was sent to Theta's P.O. box in Puerto Vallarta. It read:

> *The inner circle has confirmed that Alexis Williams, the woman handcuffed to the Mercedes in Malibu, was tied to the bombings at the San Francisco gun show. Take her out.*

Jeremiah Bates, known in Fire Power as Theta, relished the idea of taking out the lovely Malibu beauty queen. Beauty only ran skin deep in her case. *She's a mass murderer, an anti-gun and anti-NRA bitch that's crossed paths with the wrong dude*, he thought. *Justice will be done.*

Jeremiah had struck up a casual friendship with several drinking buddies since his relocation in Puerto Vallarta. He now needed their assistance in running down Maria, alias Alexis Williams, gun show bomber and NRA hater. He wasn't aware that she had recently morphed into a vicious serial killer.

* * *

Soon after the chance meeting with Gerry, Alexis's inner voice stirred, urging her to defend herself at all cost. "Beware," the voice repeated again and again, "of the tattooed man. He hurt you once, and he'll hurt you again." It was true. The tattooed thug had invaded her home, cuffed her, and raped her with his sinister eyes. His evil actions had pushed her over the edge and drove her from her beloved professorship at Pepperdine University. "Beware, beware," the voice repeated incessantly. "He is evil."

A plan, a plan, I need a plan, Alexis thought. "Use your feminine charm," suggested her inner voice. "Lure him as a black widow lures its prey."

It had been more than twenty-four hours since she had seen Gerry. But the night was young, it was party time, and above all, Alexis had a plan. She once again opted for a margarita at the Blanco y Negro Bar and Café. It was 9:30, the crowd rowdy and the music loud. Her attire reflected her mood. She chose a short black skirt and black blouse, set off with a delicate gold chain and black heels. The black widow had spun her web.

Her wait was short. Before she had finished her first margarita, she felt a soft tap on her left shoulder. She looked up and saw Gerry grinning from ear to ear.

"Mind if I join you?" he asked. He didn't wait for a response. He slid into the seat on her left and motioned to the bartender in one continuous motion. "We cross paths once again. It must be destiny."

"You're not a bit bashful." Alexis smiled. "Be careful what you wish for."

"What does that mean?" He narrowed his eyes and then erupted in a full-throated laugh.

"Is it destiny or choice?" Alexis stared at him. He looked like he had lost weight in his face. Of course it was hard to tell. With no beard and threatening snarl, he seemed kinder and gentler. His stocky and muscular build exuded a quiet but confident strength. His polo shirt concealed his NBA tattoo but failed to hide his thick, powerful build. But back in Malibu, when she was handcuffed, the biker thug was definitely intimidating. His dark eyes had devoured her partially nude body. He had raped and defiled her with his eyes.

"I believe a real man takes charge. I have a code: live for today, party hard, and die with your boots on." He tugged on his beer.

"What about a real woman?" Alexis had finished her first margarita and ordered a second.

"Man or woman, it's all the same." Gerry paid for her margarita and ordered another beer.

The two were a match. They bobbed and weaved like heavyweight boxers, throwing and blocking punches. As the night progressed, so did their drinking. By the fourth margarita, Alexis had become tipsy. Their conversation was less combative and more flirtatious. Alexis said she needed some fresh air, so they left the bar and took a stroll along the waterfront. The full moon lit up the evening sky, and its rays shimmered brightly on the calm surf.

"How about we top off the evening with a nightcap at my place? It's only two blocks from here?"

"Is that a proposition?" Alexis said.

"I've wanted you since the first time I laid eyes on you." His tone was confident, perhaps a bit cocky.

"Let's see what you're made of," Alexis said, feeling nervous for the first time this evening.

Gerry's boutique bungalow was small, but his second-floor room had a great ocean view. The open shutters flooded the room with intense moonlight. Within five minutes, they were rolling around the bed, both eagerly peeling away the other's clothing. When Alexis was stripped naked, Gerry moaned "fucking sexy bitch and you're mine."

The foreplay was tender and sensual, each pleasuring the other with the skill of an experienced lover. The passion they felt could not be controlled and soon exploded into intense physical coupling. They lost control at the same time and yelled out, completely in the grips of carnal desire. After a series of sexy epithets, Gerry groaned and then rolled off Alexis, breathing heavily.

Alexis whispered, "You sure know how to rock a woman's world." She then grabbed her purse and walked gingerly on wobbly legs to the bathroom. After washing up and brushing her hair, she regained her strength. She took a deep breath and then removed a six-inch hunting knife from her purse. Alexis had bought the knife not more than eight hours ago from a street vendor. The elderly man with snow-white hair and trimmed beard insisted the knife was good. He said in broken English, "It will slice right through the neck of a chicken." After another deep breath, she turned off the bathroom lights, peeked out from the shadows, and focused on her adversary. Gerry was flat on his back, arms outstretched, and the moonlight glistening on his sweat-covered chest. He looked like a man ready to be nailed to the cross.

Still nude, she slowly moved toward the king-size bed. Her right arm was behind her, concealing the hunting knife. Alexis slowly but seductively eased her body on top of her prey and straddled his hips. While in the bathroom, her inner voice had started up again. Now it had increased to a deafening roar. Trying to stay calm, she scooted back a bit onto his upper legs and hips and then reached down with her left hand and slowly stroked his manhood. After a minute of manipulation, his penis, gorged with blood, came alive.

He moaned, and said, "Are you ready for big daddy?" He folded his muscular arms behind his head and gently arched his hips. The moonlight lit up the NBA tattoo.

She grimaced, and said, "Are you ready for big momma?"

Before Gerry could answer, she twisted her hips slightly to the right, dug her bare feet into the softness of the mattress, and with her left hand gripping his staff for added leverage, thrust her right arm in a wide arc toward her target. Half of the six-inch blade disappeared into the biker's neck. Warm blood squirted up, hitting her in the eye. Alexis reloaded and thrust the knife again and again. Soon her heaving breasts were soaked with his vital fluids. He bucked up, and she hung onto his staff like a rodeo cowboy hanging onto the horn of a saddle. She blinked but didn't see Gerry. She lowered her head for a better look. Bouncing wildly on the flailing biker, she only caught glimpses of his face. But it wasn't Gerry staring back; it was Motley Wag.

His muscular body thrashed and twitched violently,

driving her up and down like a cowboy riding a wild bull. Her left hand gripped his manhood, a vain attempt to ride out the bucking biker. She held on for a few seconds before his violent thrusts sent her tumbling to the floor. The knife flew from her hand and landed on the soft carpet, smack dab in the bright moonlight filtering through the open window. She lay on the floor, her heart pounding, and savored the cool ocean breeze bathing her blood-drenched body. Sounds of gurgling blood and twitching muscles ruffling the bed sheets filled the room. Her inner voice had the last words: "Motley Wag is back in the black box. You are safe now."

* * *

Alexis slept in, exhausted from the late hours and heavy drinking. It was noon before she showered, fixed her hair, and finished her makeup. She turned on CNN and was confronted with the horrifying reality that she was now an international serial killer. Details of an American tourist being stabbed to death in his hotel room immediately raised questions about a disputed drug deal. But in this case, no drugs were found at the scene. There was no evidence of a robbery either. The unidentified man's wallet contained more than six thousand Mexican pesos.

Alexis dropped to the bed and cried. She was terrified. She had no plan and no one to help her.

Chapter Thirty-Two

Agent Martini had taken up temporary residence in Los Angeles. He had his hands full with the fallout of the Malibu home invasion. He'd been in contact with Matt Tyson, Allen Carter, and Alexis Williams. Alexis had now become the center of attention. His phone chirped before he had finished his morning coffee.

"Special Agent Martini," he answered, folding up the *L.A. Times.*

"This is Donald Driver, the manager at Hertz."

"Mr. Driver, yes the manager at Hertz Rental Car at the San Francisco Airport." Agent Martini could picture Donald Driver as they spoke. He was the spitting image of his freshman-year English professor at university. His college buddies back in the day immaturely tossed around disparaging labels like weasel and toad when referring to the professor.

"Yes, sir, we had a nice chat a few weeks back," Donald said.

"I remember well. You're a gun enthusiast."

"I've got some big news."

"Hit me. Give me what you got." Agent Martini was still smiling.

"The couple that rented the car from me, the guy who looked like Mel Gibson and his hot babe, well I saw a picture of her on the local evening news. A surveillance camera in the hotel parking lot caught her on camera."

"What?" Donald Driver got the FBI agent's undivided attention.

"The woman who drives a Lexus, the one with the all-points bulletin, I've seen her. She's the one who had the bags with NRA plastered on them."

"How do you know about the all-points bulletin?"

Donald Driver cleared his voice and said, "I have a police scanner."

"You have a police scanner?" Agent Martini was glad but not surprised.

"Yes, sir. I have a Droid. It's an app," he said.

"Are you positive it's her?"

"Absolutely. I wouldn't forget her." His tone was strong, full of confidence.

"Would you testify to that in court?"

"Name the date and time," Donald Driver answered emphatically.

"What about her friend, the guy who looks like Mel Gibson? Could you identify him?"

"Without a doubt."

"I'm going to send an agent over to talk to you in person."

"One more thing," Donald said. "A private eye questioned me yesterday. He wanted to know the whereabouts of Alexis."

"Did he give you a name?"

"He did. Brad Smith, that's the name he gave me."

"Did he give you a business card?"

"No."

"Did he show you his credentials?"

"He flashed them at me. I didn't get a good look. That's why I'm calling you. Something didn't seem right with the guy."

"I'll be in touch." Agent Martini signed off.

Agent Martini contacted major airports in California. He zeroed in on Oakland, San Francisco, John Wayne, Burbank, and LAX. If she had fled the country, she'd need a valid passport and ID. She most likely used her real name. He immediately put together a three-agent task force. *Donald Driver better be right*, he thought.

* * *

Allen Carter had another restless night. He had trouble getting to sleep, and when he was finally able to, he was haunted by nightmares. Last night he suffered through a doozy. Alexis had been arrested, interrogated, and confessed to the gun show bombings. She had exposed the inner workings of Gotham City. His name was plastered all over the front page of every major newspaper. Images of Motley Wag saturated cable news, the major networks, and the print media.

His cell phone rang. It was the feds. "Good morning," Allen said.

Agent Martini identified himself and said, "I've some alarming news."

"What's happened?"

"We have confirmed that Alexis was at the Casa Madrona Hotel and Spa the night of the Sausalito killing. We have surveillance camera video of her license number and a few frames of her face."

"Oh, I can't believe it." Allen paused and then said, "Perhaps there's a misidentification."

"I've seen the surveillance tapes. There's little doubt."

"Do you know her whereabouts?" Allen's voice cracked with tension.

"No. That's why I'm calling you." Agent Martini paused, cleared his voice, and asked, "Have you heard anything?"

"Absolutely nothing. I'm completely in the dark." It was true; he was completely in the dark when it came to Alexis. But the secrets he sat on would have sent Agent Martini reeling.

"Well, we've increased the size of the task force. Keep in touch. I'm on the case full-time." Agent Martini signed off.

*　*　*

Matt Tyson had banged away at the keyboard all morning, crafting another article for *The Socratic Rag*. He was primarily interested in the NRA and gun violence in America, but he was requested to do a short piece on the "Stand Your Ground Law" in Florida. There were twenty-two states that officially recognized a version of the controversial law.

Just as he took a break for lunch, his cell rang.

"Matt here, what's up?"

"Hi, Matt, this is Agent Martini. Have you heard the latest on the Malibu home invasion case?"

"No, I've been cooped up in my study trying to make a living. What's the latest?"

"Alexis Williams is on the lam."

"What?"

"We have video surveillance of her near a murder scene. She's been AWOL for days. We have an all-points bulletin out for her as we speak."

"That's shocking. I've attended parties with her, even danced with her. We were the victims of a vicious home invasion. It doesn't ring true." Matt was breathless. "This can't be true."

"We'll know more when we catch up to her. We need to interview her. She has a lot of explaining to do. If you hear anything, let me know immediately."

After the FBI agent signed off, Matt surfed the Internet for anything related to Alexis Williams. Her name popped up in several places, including her professional affiliations, academic papers, teacher evaluations, and a recent slew of articles on the Malibu home invasion. Her notoriety had grown exponentially. Matt smelled a story. He packed his bags and was on a plane for Los Angeles before the sun set in Washington D.C.

* * *

Agent Martini's dragnet had paid off. FBI investigators confirmed that Alexis Williams boarded a plane for Puerto Vallarta Saturday evening, July 28. Perhaps it was coincidence that an American tourist was stabbed to death six days later, but Agent Martini had his doubts. *A distinctive pattern has definitely emerged*, he thought.

He had just gotten off the phone with Mexican authorities when Donald Driver showed up at the FBI Field Office in West L.A. He was there to ID Allen Carter. Allen had been questioned at his Malibu residence and requested to come to the FBI Field Office. The Santa Monica lawyer was under the impression that his services were needed to locate Alexis Williams. That was partially true. What he didn't know was that Mr. Driver, the Hertz Rental Car manager, was at the field office to ID the lawyer.

Within in an hour, Allen Carter's worst nightmare had come true. He was interrogated by Senior Special Agent Alex Martini. The questioning centered on driving his corvette to the San Francisco Airport, renting a car, and carrying bags emblazoned with NRA. Agent Martini repeatedly asked why he drove to San Francisco instead of flying. "You're a pilot. Why not fly?" Agent Martini pressed, sensing he was lying.

"We were on a road trip. I love my Vette."

He wasn't charged with a crime, but was released with the caution, "Don't leave town." Agent Martini told Allen Carter that they were close to apprehending Alexis. They insisted that Alexis would crack and reveal all.

Chapter Thirty-Three

Alexis stared at the TV in disbelief. Her mug showed up everywhere, from local coverage in Puerto Vallarta to CNN, MSNBC, and Fox News. Commentators reported that she had departed LAX and landed in Puerto Vallarta Saturday, July 28. Alexis Williams had become a person of interest in two separate California killings, and the grisly stabbing of an American tourist last night at a Puerto Vallarta hotel.

She felt trapped with no plan. She threw herself on the bed and cried, feeling isolated and alone. After falling asleep for a short nap, she was awakened by her inner voice. "Don't panic. Pack your backpack with essentials and leave the suitcase behind. Defend yourself. Don't let Motley Wag win." The name "Motley Wag" reverberated in her mind, echoing in her skull. It was loud, authoritative, and repetitive. "Don't let Motley Wag win," became a mantra. The inner voice was her only friend. It was her master, protector, and soul mate. It was her true self.

Time was of the essence. She immediately departed her charming residence near the sea and caught a bus for Mexico

City. Dressed in jeans, a plain, off-white cotton blouse, no makeup, and head scarf, she blended in with the locals. The clerk at the bus station was a doll. When her Spanish failed, he accommodated her and spoke English. He had a pleasant laugh and was very helpful. She blew him a kiss and hopped on the bus within twenty minutes. Alexis opted for the back of the bus, took off her backpack, popped an Ambien, and slept half the eight-hour ride to the heart of Mexico City. When she arrived, she made a dash to the restroom. Her bladder was about to explode.

She felt tired and disoriented. Within an hour, she had registered and secured a room at the Hotel Del Principado in Mexico City's Zona Rosa, a popular tourist and business district. The highly popular location featured art galleries, restaurants, nightclubs, boutiques, and theaters. She spoke to the desk clerk in Spanish, provided a bogus name, and signed the registry. Alexis provided the hotel with a bogus home address in Mazatlan. She stuttered, so as to conceal her limited Spanish. The conversation wasn't eloquent, but it worked.

After a quick bite to eat at the hotel café, Alexis returned to her room. She felt grimy, so she shaved her legs, showered, and popped another Ambien. *Tomorrow I'll explore my new world as Maria Morales*, she thought. She was fast asleep within five minutes.

* * *

Charles and David had just finished dinner at David's Park Avenue residence and retired to the study for a cognac. The topic was the death of Theta, the Malibu home invasion,

Alexis Williams, Allen Carter, and *The Socratic Rag* agitator. The twins had both talked to the NRA front man, William St. George, and convinced him that the new philosophy of "the pen being mightier than the sword" was paying double dividends. Violent assassinations were a thing of the past.

"The wheel has turned," Charles said. He savored the cognac with glee. It was Hennessy XO (Extra Old) cognac. The six-year-old Hennessy was David's favorite.

"Yes indeed, my brother. We got the feds on our side. Let them do the legwork and bring the anti-gun thugs to their knees." David removed two Cuban cigars from a sturdy, hand-carved oak box on the coffee table and offered one to his brother. They clipped the ends and had them lit before they spoke again.

"Alexis Williams is a loose cannon. It isn't guns she hates. It's men," Charles said, blowing a giant smoke ring above David's head.

"The killings in California were tragic. But the vicious attack on Theta crosses the line. It's personal now." David countered and blew a smoke ring over Charles's head.

"Guns don't kill people, but scissors and knives sure do." Charles glanced at his brother and grinned. They both laughed uncontrollably. When they calmed down, the twins shared boyhood stories of rafting the Missouri River.

David listened intently as Charles retold the story of their first rafting adventure down the Missouri River. After Charles finished with the latest embellished version, he said, "I remember our first encounter with Ayn Rand. I think it was the summer between our junior and senior year of high school."

"Oh, yes. We both finished reading *Atlas Shrugged*. She

became our mentor, guru, and philosopher," Charles said. He admitted to rereading it just last summer.

David motioned to the bookshelf and said, "My dog-eared edition of *Atlas Shrugged* is just over there." David got out of his deep leather chair and retrieved the book. He thumbed through it and found what he was looking for. He read, *"I started my life with a single absolute: that the world was mine to shape in the image of my highest values and never to be given up to a lesser standard, no matter how long or hard the struggle."*

"Very good, David," Charles said. He then quoted *Atlas Shrugged* from memory, *"Let me give you a tip on a clue to men's characters: the man who damns money has obtained it dishonestly; the man who respects it has earned it."*

The twins ended the evening paying homage to their favorite philosopher. They both agreed that the essence of *Atlas Shrugged* could be boiled down to this: there were two kinds of people in the world, creators and leeches. The twins knew damn well who they were.

* * *

Allen Carter had received numerous calls from the other members of Gotham City. He had put them off for weeks, insisting that secrecy and caution should be their guide. He finally agreed to meet with Mikhail Medved at Mulligans in Santa Monica. He was the owner of a Cadillac dealership in West L.A., avid racquetball player, and long-time L.A. Laker fan. He had orchestrated the gun show bombing in Carson City, Nevada. He also had a cousin in the Russian mafia.

It was happy hour on a Friday night. Allen and Mikhail

were tucked away in a corner booth and had just finished their first Guinness. Another round had just arrived. The two conspirators were tense, paranoid, and worried sick about Alexis.

Allen shocked Mikhail when he said, "I'm concerned more about what she says than what happens to her."

"Are you serious?" Mikhail asked in disbelief.

Allen knew his words were harsh, but they were honest. He feared that the game was about over. He studied Mikhail's face. When happy, he looked like Jack Nicholson at a Laker game. When worried, he looked like Jack from *The Shining*. "Serious as serious can be," Allen said. "It sad to say, but if the authorities get a hold of Alexis before we do, we're toast."

"Are you afraid she'll talk?" Mikhail sipped his Guinness, feeling conflicted. He adored Alexis but feared for his life. "What can we do?"

"She has to be silenced." Allen said.

Allen words sent shivers through Mikhail. He was visibly shaken. He took several tugs on his beer before he could speak. He finally said, "What are you going to do?"

"I'm staying put. The feds are following my every move. I want you to go to Mexico and find Alexis. I want her silenced."

"I can't do that." Mikhail was shocked at the dreadful tone of their talk.

"Then hire someone who can. Money is not an issue. I'll pay top dollar to have her rubbed out." Allen stared at Mikhail and said "Capisce?"

"I'm at a loss for words," Mikhail said.

"If you don't act now, you'll be at a loss for life." Allen

got up from the corner booth, leaned over, and whispered, "I'll have fifty thousand dollars in your hands by tomorrow morning. I'll leave it in your mail box at 10 a.m. Make sure you're nearby. Take the cash and do what has to be done. If need be, get hold of your cousin."

Chapter Thirty-Four

Maria Morales, Alexis's new persona, dressed down, wearing sandals, blue jeans, and a black gypsy peasant blouse. The plain cotton blouse was trimmed in delicate red and green embroidery around the sleeves and neck. She had purchased it from a street vendor this morning. It was early evening now, and the streets were buzzing with a blend of locals and tourists looking for entertainment. There were good pickings because of the plethora of boutiques, theaters, restaurants, and bars. She felt alone and in need of companionship but recently discovered that the Zona Rosa was dominated by gays during the evening hours. That wasn't the type of companionship she craved. She was irresistibly drawn to domineering men who could make the pain go away.

Her inner voice had calmed, assuring her that she was safe and had made prudent choices. She now led her life in the shadows, rubbing elbows with the unsavory. She no longer had good standing with the good guys. She now navigated the troubled waters of the unknown as Maria Morales. She'd be careful. Her inner voice had her back. She was adept at reading people.

This morning after breakfast Alexis accessed her hotel's Internet and read an account of the arrest of a Mexican drug lord just two days ago. He was apprehended in an after-hours club in the Zona Rosa district. She would definitely stay away from illegal drugs. But she had her eye on the legal variety. Maria Morales craved a margarita. Nothing had changed; she had the same tastes and proclivities as Alexis.

She tried two sports bars, had a margarita in the first one, and settled for a coke in the second. She quickly tired of the rowdy sports crowd. The franchise sports bars were overrun with American and European tourists. She needed to blend in and practice her Spanish. The third bar catered to locals. It had a jukebox, a couple of pool tables, and a mixture of gay and straight patrons. She settled in at one end of the bar and ordered a margarita. She nursed her drink, not wanting to get drunk and do something stupid. She was, after all, a wanted woman.

After several songs on the jukebox played, a dark-haired man with a trimmed beard slid onto the barstool next to her and ordered a beer. He chatted briefly with the bartender about football. Maria understood bits and pieces of their banter. He turned and introduced himself.

"I'm Jose," he said. He had sad eyes but a brilliant smile. His brown skin contrasted well with his wide smile.

Alexis spoke in Spanish. "I'm Maria."

Jose smiled and asked, "Where are you from?"

"Mazatlan," Maria answered.

After about ten minutes of labored Spanish, Jose switched to English. He complimented her on her attempt to communicate in Spanish and asked her where she was really from. Maria smiled, held back the real story, and told him that she was on holiday and was trying to experience Mexico City from the inside, not as a gawking tourist.

Jose challenged her to a game of pool and found out that Maria could hold her own. After another margarita and a second game of pool, he invited her to check out a lively bar that offered dancing, better music, and far better margaritas. The cantina was definitely an upgrade, and the patrons, live band, and dancing put Maria in a partying mood. A bit after midnight, Maria's inner voice cautioned her, and said, "Flee the scene. There are too many unknowns."

She thanked Jose for a wonderful evening. He gave her his business card and said, "Don't hesitate to call. I can introduce you to more hidden marvels of Zona Rosa."

Maria Morales was new to this world. She'd take it slow and keep a low profile.

* * *

Mikhail Medved struck a deal with his cousin. "It will take one hundred thousand dollars for the hit on Alexis Williams, fifty thousand up front, and the remainder when her body's returned to the US. Official ID by US authorities seals the deal," Mikhail said. His cousin was sworn to secrecy.

He said bluntly, "The Russian Mafia guarantees their work."

After the deal was sealed, Mikhail met Allen Carter at Mulligans with the news. They left the Irish pub after one Guinness. Allen Carter's eyes glazed over after Mikhail filled him on the deal. Allen still loved Alexis in his twisted way.

* * *

Director Thomas Parker had Agent Alex Martini on the road again. The latest assignment had the FBI agent in Puerto Vallarta two days after the brutal stabbing of Jeremiah Bates. The past six months had been one for the ages. From the East Coast to the West Coast, and now south of the border, his frequent flyer miles had set a new FBI travel record.

He checked in to the Sol y Luna, phoned the FBI legal attaché, contacted local authorities, and got permission to examine the remains of Jeremiah Bates. After a shower and a bite to eat, he caught a taxi to the Puerto Vallarta Morgue. The taxi driver loved his horn, had the pedal to the metal, and squealed his tires on every turn, nearly hitting a bicycle rider a block from the morgue. When the cab pulled up to the entrance, Agent Martini thought he was in for a medieval experience. The morgue was housed in an aging building with colorful, mural-covered adobe walls and a red tile roof dating back to the early twentieth century. But once inside, he discovered a well-run department with the latest medical equipment.

A uniformed officer greeted Agent Martini in the medical examiner's outer office and politely told him to take a seat. He was informed that the doctor was on the phone and would be available in a few minutes. Alex Martini glanced about the office, impressed by the vintage photos ringing the reception area. It was a visual history of Puerto Vallarta. True to the officer that greeted the FBI agent, Medical Examiner Juan Perez emerged from his office with a big smile and warm greeting. He wore a white lab coat, was short, overweight, and sported a bushy, graying moustache. After questions about the FBI agent's trip, he peppered Agent Martini with questions about the victim. His English was impeccable. Agent Martini later learned that he had studied medicine at UCLA.

After some routine shop talk, Dr. Juan Perez led Agent Martini down a long, brightly lit corridor. They entered the last door on the right. It was a large room containing several dozen stainless-steel refrigeration units. The overhead fluorescent lights flooded the morgue with intense light. The medical examiner approached a four-drawer unit and effortlessly slid back the top right-hand drawer.

"Be prepared for the worst," Dr. Perez said. He then slowly pulled back a gray cover and revealed the corpse. The ashen biker looked far less intimidating stripped of his beard and defiant attitude. But his stocky build and tattoos remained intact. Agent Martini had not seen the original NRA tattoo, but he saw how it was possible to convert it to the NBA spelled out over a basketball. His right arm bore the tattoo of a fire-breathing dragon. But beard or no beard, it was Jeremiah Bates. The brutish biker had met his match.

Dr. Perez took out a small bottle of Vicks Vapor Rub from the pocket of his lab coat, applied a dab to his upper lip, pasting some on his moustache, and passed it to Agent Martini. Since the senior FBI agent had an acute sense of smell, he gladly followed the medical examiner's lead.

Using a blue laser pointer, he highlighted what was left of the dead biker's neck. "The attack was savage," began Dr. Perez. The laser pointer traced a path from under the chin to the Adam's apple. "Here the trachea is completely severed. As you know, the trachea is a tube that connects the pharynx and larynx to the lungs."

"Could a woman have the power to do that?" Agent Martini had seen many corpses, but this was more personal. He had questioned the uncooperative biker at Gun World and visited the alleged killer at Pepperdine. She was a sweet college professor that liked to dress up as a comic book character.

"She must have straddled him, pinned him to the bed, and dug her feet in for added leverage," the medical examiner said. "That's not all. The muscles that moved the neck, the sternocleidomastoid, were nearly cut in half, and the common carotid artery, internal and external jugular vein, and transverse cervical artery were punctured. The knife struck and sliced into the seventh cervical vertebrae."

"How many times was the deceased knifed?" Agent Martini cocked his head and studied the right side of Jeremiah's neck.

"I have distinct evidence of five entry wounds. I also have sufficient evidence that the assailant was right handed and would have been face to face with the victim."

"Gutsy killing," Agent Martini said.

"Crazed killing might be more accurate." Dr. Perez shook his head and added, "This looks like a mauling by a crazed animal."

"What was the cause of death?" Agent Martini shook his head and added, "Puerto Vallarta police on the scene reported that the bed was a bloody mess."

Dr. Perez's answer was terse and clinical. "The heart was not compromised and pumped blood out the severed arteries for a minute, maybe two. The heart was pumping at a rapid beat. It appears that the savage attack occurred during sex."

Agent Martini thanked Dr. Perez, called a taxi, and

headed for the police station. He skipped lunch. He had suddenly lost his appetite.

*   *   *

After a long, cooperative talk with local police, Agent Martini checked several hotels and cantinas before he hit upon Blanco y Negro. It was midafternoon, and with the bar nearly empty, the bartender and barmaid had time for Agent Martini's many questions. He produced his FBI credentials and briefly explained that he was investigating a murder. He showed several photos of Alexis to the bartender. The young, dark-haired bartender with large, inquisitive eyes was sure she was here a couple of nights last week. She was at the bar with a stocky guy with tattoos. He recalled commenting on the man's NBA tattoo. The barmaid corroborated his recollection and added that the couple carried on an animated conversation. When Agent Martini pressed for more info, he hit a brick wall.

He then checked out two local taxi companies, a rental car outlet, and the main bus station. It was at the bus station that he got his first hot tip. An elderly, balding clerk at the ticket counter carefully examined the photos of Alexis. He said her hair was covered by a scarf, but the eyes and high cheek bones looked familiar. He also said the woman spoke with a heavy accent. Her Spanish was limited, and she groped for words. When he spoke to her in English, he said with a slight chuckle, her mood picked up dramatically. She thanked him, and when she left with her ticket, she blew him a kiss. Agent Martini asked him her destination. "Mexico City," he said with a broad smile. "She was a looker," he added, and said the kiss made his day.

That night around 9:30, Agent Martini was on a flight to Mexico City. The chase was on. The prospects of finding her in Mexico City were daunting. Even though the Mexican police were cooperative, the odds of finding her in such a vast metropolis were next to nil. He only hoped he could apprehend her before she struck again.

* * *

Unknown to Agent Martini, he had been followed. A tall guy dressed in beige cargo shorts, sandals, an L.A. Dodger's baseball cap, and a Hawaiian shirt adorned with hula dancers had overheard his conversation with the bartender and barmaid at Blanco y Negro. When Agent Martini left the bar, the stranger talked briefly to the barmaid. He flashed her a phony Mexican Police ID and asked in fluent Spanish why the American was interested in the ongoing murder investigation. She said he was an FBI agent trying to locate an American woman. She and the bartender checked out some photos and agreed the woman was here last week on at least two occasions. The tall stranger dashed out of the cantina. He caught sight of Agent Martini getting in a Honda Civic in the Blanco y Negro parking lot.

The tall stranger hustled to his Ford Taurus and jumped in. He got lucky and caught Agent Martini at a red light. He tailed him to two taxi companies, a rental car outlet, and the bus station. He got lucky at the bus station. Again using phony Mexican Police credentials and his own photos of

Alexis Williams, the stranger ascertained that the American woman had just last week purchased a one-way ticket to Mexico City. It wasn't much, but the tall stranger in the Dodger baseball cap wearing the goofy Hawaiian shirt had his first clue.

Chapter Thirty-Five

Matt Tyson read everything he could get his hands on about Alexis Williams. She was linked to the killings in Los Olivos and Sausalito. News reports had her as a person of interest for the grisly killing of an American tourist in Puerto Vallarta. The latest killing hit home. Agent Martini left a message on his voicemail last night. It was big news. He said, "The man found brutally stabbed to death at a Puerto Vallarta hotel was Jeremiah Bates. He's the biker who shattered your lower leg with a nine iron. Alexis may be heading for Mexico City. How's your leg holding up? Keep this under your hat. This is strictly off the record."

Matt appreciated the heads up. The biker thug had left him hobbling about with the help of a cane. *Maybe it was karma*, he thought. *The biker thug sure had it coming to him.*

Matt was perplexed. The home invasion didn't begin and end with the bikers. They were operatives, the grunts in the trenches. Someone else was calling the shots. Who had Allen Carter and Matt Tyson crossed? Matt's investigative reporting had raised the ire of many. But who would retaliate with such heavy-handed tactics?

He had surely crossed the Berrigan brothers. But they were far too sophisticated for such thuggish behavior. That sort of behavior would be expected of the mob. But his instincts urged him to dig deeper into the biggest shot callers he could think of. He had to flush them out from the shadows. *But how? Another inflammatory article might get my other leg broken.*

*   *   *

Agent Martini considered his first day in Mexico City a winner. By noon of the day of his arrival, he was at a meeting with two detectives at the Ministry of Internal Security. Agent John Gardner, FBI attaché in Mexico City, joined the group. Detectives Manual Garcia and Javier Macias of Internal Security shared the latest on Alexis Williams with the FBI agents. Because the detectives spoke fluent English, there were no communication snags.

Since Agent Gardner had worked with Detectives Macias and Garcia as a legal attaché on previous cases, he chaired the meeting. After a humorous session of insider shop talk, including the latest on the restructuring of the agency, Agent Martini filled in the others on some specifics about his personal contacts with Alexis Williams, especially her penchant for dressing as her favorite comic book heroine and her professorial side.

Detective Javier Macias, a lean and balding man, slid a folder across his desk. "Please, take a look," he said. "There you will find a copy of the photo taken by Manny Ortega from our mounted police unit. It was taken two days ago."

Agent Martini opened the folder and immediately recognized Alexis. "That's her," he said.

Detective Macias turned his attention to his desktop monitor where three photos of Alexis Williams had been enlarged. "We agree. My photos match the officer's cell phone picture."

"Where was the officer when he snapped the photo?" Agent Martini suddenly felt encouraged.

Detective Manual Garcia cleared his voice and said, "He was in the heart of the Zona Rosa District. Officer Ortega was on horseback when he observed a woman bargaining with a street vender. He was first amused by the scene as the tourist negotiated for the best price. He was close by and could hear her broken Spanish. She seemed familiar, so he took a picture of her with his cell phone."

Detective Macias broke in and said, "Officer Ortega got a decent shot of her. The woman was only twenty feet from where he had stopped to allow two young boys to pat the head of his horse."

"Can we target the Zona Rosa District for extra surveillance?" Agent Martini was ready to hit the streets.

"No sooner said than done," snapped Detective Garcia.

FBI Agent Martini and legal attaché Gardner left the Ministry of Internal Security in an upbeat mood. Agent Gardner gave Agent Martini a lift to the Zona Rosa District. Before they parted, legal attaché Gardner said, "If you have any problems or questions, you can get me any hour on my cell number."

"Thanks for the ride. I'll need all the help I can get," Agent Martini answered.

Agent Martini quickly found a Starbucks. He was in

desperate need of a jolt of java. His head hurt, and he was troubled. At the back of his mind were disturbing reports he had read about the Federales. Corruption and inefficiency plagued the Mexican Police. Agent Martini recalled reading a survey a couple of years ago that claimed that 90 percent of the respondents had little or no trust in the police. He also recalled that nationwide, only 12 percent of the population had any confidence in the police.

Agent Martini shoved his skepticism aside and plunged into an exploration of the Zona Rosa District.

*   *   *

The tall stranger with phony Mexican Police ID got a hot tip. His gut instincts had paid off. With connections with Mexico's Internal Security and some cash, he had located Agent Martini. He learned long ago that the right amount of pesos could get you anything you wanted. First he wanted to follow the FBI agent; next he wanted Alexis Williams. Her death would gross him 100,000 dollars. Twenty-five thousand dollars got kicked back to the Russian mafia.

The tall stranger, known to his comrades as Serge, had found a shady spot on the stairs leading to the Ministry building. With one eye on a newspaper, and the other on people entering and leaving the building, he patiently waited for his mark. After twenty minutes of surveillance, he got lucky. He spotted Agent Martini leaving with another man.

Serge followed them to the parking garage, took note of the car they got in, and hustled to the exit. There he hailed a cab and tailed the FBI agent to the Zona Rosa District. He had the cab driver pull over abruptly when Agent Martini stopped at the corner across from a Starbucks. He paid the cab driver and watched as Agent Martini entered the popular coffee house. He kept his distance, went into a bookstore across the street from Starbucks, and watched the agent from the front window. He pretended to shop for a magazine, but his eyes were glued on the famed coffee house.

Serge was a patient man, never lost his temper, and never failed to close out an assignment. His only close call with death occurred when he got caught in the middle of a late-night bar fight in Moscow. He was only nineteen, but he had already earned the reputation as a mean brawler, a man to be treated with caution and respect. On a late winter's night, a fight broke out between two drunks from rival gangs. Broken vodka bottles and knives flashed about the dimly lit bar. A good friend of Serge's got caught up in the conflict, so he dove in to protect him. His efforts were successful, leaving two other men dead.

Unfortunately, he was not unharmed. He escaped the scene and was never apprehended for his involvement in the deadly brawl. But his face still bore witness to the effects of his participation in the mayhem. His handsome features had been altered by a scar that ran from just below his right eye, across his cheek, to the middle of his jawbone. He now had the looks of a rugged but distinguished war veteran. His youthful good looks were gone, but his smile and mannerism gave him an aura of mystery and intrigue. Women were irresistibly drawn to his beguiling charm. He could woo them in five languages. English and Spanish were two of his best, but his French and German got him what he wanted and needed.

Serge threw down a sports magazine, hustled out the front door, and followed Agent Martini. Serge dogged the FBI agent for two days, catching some intermittent shut eye, changing his clothes only once. He had located the agent's temporary residence, found a cheap hotel across the street, and watched his movements night and day.

It was on the third day of this tedious cat and mouse chase that Serge got his first big break. It was noon, and Agent Martini was seated at an outdoor café on Genova Street. The street, closed off to cars, was a tree-lined pedestrian thoroughfare lined with restaurants, bars, boutiques, and theaters. The agent suddenly jumped up, threw down some money on the table, and hustled out of the café, nearly knocking over a chair as he brushed by an incoming patron.

Serge hustled after the agent who had stopped at a corner traffic light. There the agent took out his smartphone and took several pictures of a woman wearing a black peasant blouse trimmed in red and green. She turned toward the agent, and he quickly snapped another picture. He tried to follow her but dropped back into the surging crowd of pedestrians.

Serge's interest was piqued. He ran across the street against a red light, nearly getting hit by an oncoming taxi. Horns blared, a taxi driver cursed him, and a fellow pedestrian yelled out in Spanish, *"Hombre loco."* His foolhardiness paid off. The mystery woman ducked into a side-street bar. Serge looked about, but no FBI agent. He entered and found a small, dimly lit bar, half empty, a jukebox playing, and mostly elderly men drinking beer. It was a working-class bar for the lonely, those unlucky souls condemned by misfortune and unfulfilled dreams to live out their lives in quiet desperation. Their dearest companion came ready made in a bottle. There were many such places in Moscow. Serge had seen his father succumb to such a life.

The mystery girl was nowhere in sight. Serge walked to the jukebox and checked out the tunes. When his eyes adjusted to the darkness, he studied the patrons. Only one woman and a dozen men packed the bar. The half-dozen wooden tables scattered about the joint were empty. He turned his gaze from the bar and caught sight of the woman in the black peasant blouse leaving the woman's restroom. She found an open space at the end of the bar, took a seat, and ordered a margarita. Serge seized the opportunity and took the only seat open at that end of the bar. He was in luck. It was to the mystery girl's immediate left.

"May I join you?" he said in fluent Spanish.

"Of course. It's a free country." Alexis smiled.

The bartender appeared with the mystery woman's margarita. Serge said, "I'll have one of those." He paid the bartender for both drinks and said in English, "Cheers. Here's to a new friendship."

"You speak English," said Alexis.

"Yes, and so do you. Where are you from?" Serge smiled and added, "I'm on holiday. I'm a football fan. I'm here to see some football. It's what you call soccer."

"I'm also on holiday. But soccer, football, or whatever, is not my sport."

"What is your sport?" Serge took a slow sip of his margarita, checking her out over the rim of his broad-rimmed glass. The mystery woman was the spitting image of the woman in the photos he got from the Russian mafia.

"I'm not a sports fan. I do like working out, mostly

aerobic dance. But since I've been on holiday, I've been remiss about exercise."

"It's good for the soul to break with routine. But I do miss working out. I used to train." Serge smiled and took another sip of his drink.

"What kind of training?"

"I like to box and wrestle. I used to do it on the amateur level."

"You look fit. And you're so tall. How tall are you?"

"I'm about six foot five, give or take a centimeter. I think I'm getting shorter with age." Serge laughed.

"Gravity does have a way with our body." Alexis smiled and took a sip of her margarita.

"It hasn't done anything to harm your good looks." Serge sensed that the mystery woman liked him. But if she was Alexis Williams, she was definitely armed and dangerous. He'd already suffered one monumental knifing. He was in no way looking for another.

"You're kind. But the blouse and jeans hide all my flaws." Alexis smiled and asked, "What's your name?"

"Serge," he answered. "And you?"

"Maria."

Chapter Thirty-Six

A gent Martini checked the photos he had taken with his smartphone. There was no doubt. The woman he saw and snapped pictures of was Alexis Williams. He notified the Mexican Police. Within an hour, the Federales swarmed the Zona Rosa District. He needed their assistance. The FBI needed the Mexican authorities to make a legal arrest.

Within two hours of Agent Martini's citing of Alexis Williams, he was walking Genova Street with Detective Javier Macias of Internal Security. The street was crowded with late-afternoon shoppers, tourists, street venders, hawkers, panhandlers, and business people carrying on their busy lives. His eyes were peeled for a woman in a black peasant blouse trimmed with the red and green embroidery. The energy of the district added to his mounting apprehension. Alexis was within arm's distance. He couldn't and wouldn't let her slip through his hands.

A uniformed officer approached Detective Macias and showed him his smartphone. He had taken the picture less than five minutes ago. The officer saw the woman enter the Mestizo Lounge accompanied with a tall blond man wearing a Mexico football jersey.

Agent Martini, Detective Javier Macias, and three uniformed police officers from Internal Security converged on Mestizo Lounge. The side and back doors were covered. A uniformed officer stayed at the front entrance while Agent Martini and Detective Macias entered the bar. They quickly scanned the interior and found the bar crowded. All but one table and booth were taken. It was happy hour, and the crowd was lively and jovial. Agent Martini spotted the woman in the black peasant blouse at the bar sipping a drink. The stool to her left was vacant, but there was a full drink on the bar.

Detective Javier approached on her left while Agent Martini held back and stood three feet off to her right. The detective from Internal Security tapped her on the shoulder and showed his credentials. He said, "Are you Alexis Williams?"

"No," the woman answered in Spanish. "I'm Maria Morales."

Agent Martini tapped her on the right shoulder. When she turned her head, Agent Martini said, "I know who you are. You're Alexis Williams. You're the professor from Pepperdine University. You live with Allen Carter in Malibu."

Her face turned white as a ghost. She teetered on the barstool and then fainted. As she collapsed on the bar top, she knocked over her unfinished margarita. The crowded bar suddenly became quiet.

Standing twenty feet away was Serge. He was stunned. His finely honed instincts were on high alert. He grabbed a baseball cap lying unattended on a nearby table and dashed to the restroom where he turned his football jersey inside out. He put the baseball cap on backward and left the Mestizo Lounge in the midst of a group of stunned but boisterous young partygoers. He didn't look back. He had been beat to the punch.

* * *

At the headquarters of Internal Security, Alexis was fingerprinted, mug shots were taken, and she was briefly questioned by Agent Martini and Javier Macias. The buzz was gone, her head hurt, and her inner voice admonished her. "Your cavalier ways have come back to bite you. You need a plan. The day is not over."

Later in her holding cell, she fell asleep. But she got no rest. Alexis thrashed about the hard, unforgiving jail mattress, tormented by a nightmare. She was in court testifying against Motley Wag. He sat next to his lawyer, decked out in a purple top coat, green vest, orange shirt, and flowing green bowtie. A broad-brimmed black hat shadowed his hideous and distorted features. She knew them well, the wide mouth, painted red, distorted by scars into a permanent smile. She had to put him back in the black box.

* * *

Allen Carter stared at the kitchen TV in horror. His darkest nightmare had come true. CNN had reported that Alexis Williams had been apprehended by the FBI and Mexican authorities. She was now in custody at Internal Security Headquarters in Mexico City.

His mind raced, searching for a grip on his spinning reality. He was already fifty thousand dollars in the hole to the Russian mafia. He'd gladly spend another fifty thousand for proof of her death. But now she was in custody, protected by the feds, susceptible to talking and telling all.

CNN's Anderson Cooper, in the middle of a story on gun violence, broke in with a news flash from Mexico City. He reported that Alexis Williams, while being transported from headquarters at Internal Security to Benito Juarez International Airport in Mexico City, was shot by an unknown assassin. She was immediately rushed to a nearby hospital and was in intensive care. "No more details are available at this time," reported Anderson Cooper.

Allen's grip on reality suddenly took hold. Alexis was in intensive care. Was she near death? Was she conscious? Would she talk while heavily medicated? He prayed for her death.

Allen's phoned chirped. He checked caller ID. It was Mikhail Medved.

"Hey Mikhail, I just heard the news," Allen said.

"I just got confirmation from my cousin. All is well. That's all I can say now. Let's meet later this afternoon at Mulligans for more updates."

"See you at 5:30." Allen signed off, knowing his phone could be bugged. The less he said the better.

*   *   *

Agent Martini and Detective Javier Macias stood near the bedside of Alexis Williams waiting for the attending doctor. Nurses cautioned not to go in, but they couldn't resist. They needed a peek.

Alex was informed by Mexican authorities that Alexis had been rushed to Hospital General de Mexico, a medical facility operated by the federal government. Alexis had been shot, they informed him, while leaving the Headquarters of Internal Security. A van transporting her to the airport was stopped at a red light one block from the Internal Affairs' building. A shot rang out, according to the van driver, just as the traffic light turned green.

The hospital room door opened, and a tall, gray-haired man waved the investigators out to the corridor. "I'm Doctor Hernandez. I was working the emergency room when Alexis Williams arrived." His English was impeccable.

Detective Macias cleared his voice and asked, "What was the cause of her injury?"

"We don't have the bullet because it passed right through her brain," said Dr. Hernandez.

"What's her chance of recovering?" Agent Martini asked.

"It's too early to tell for sure. But from what I've seen so far, she was hit by a high-speed bullet. In essence, the heavier the bullet and the faster it moves the more damage it can potentially cause. What I can say now is that the bullet didn't explode when it passed through the left side of her brain. It entered from the back and exited through the front of her head. She was responsive to voice commands and was taken to the operating room within thirty minutes."

"Is it possible to talk to the neurosurgeon that operated on Alexis?" asked Detective Macias.

"He's in surgery. I'll keep you informed."

Dr. Hernandez began to leave but was politely stopped by Agent Martini. "When can we talk to her?"

"She is unconscious and sedated. I'll keep you posted."

Agent Martini and Detective Macias assigned an officer to guard Alexis's room. They left, unfortunately, with more uncertainty than they liked.

Chapter Thirty-Seven

Matt Tyson was stunned by the latest on Alexis Williams. Immediately upon hearing the news, he phoned Allen Carter. He got through by the third ring.

"Hey, Allen, I just heard about Alexis."

"It's tragic. I'm in shock," Allen said.

"Do you have any inside information?" He was always digging for a story.

"No." Allen paused and then added, "Agent Martini informed me that she was in Mexico. That's all I know."

"Listen," Matt said, "I've got a hunch I'd like to check out. Remember when you told me about the guy over at Universal Studios?"

"You mean Jerry Rizzo?"

"That's the guy. Do you know anyone else that he hangs with? Can you hook me up with somebody he's close to? Preferably connect me with somebody who's privy to his inside business practices?" Matt was awkwardly fishing for some way to come up with a connection to the Berrigan brothers.

"There's one guy, an independent film maker that made a documentary on the Berrigan brothers."

"What guy?"

"His name is Larry Alexander. He produced a documentary called *Citizen Berrigan*. The documentary was slated to air on PBS. It got yanked because the Berrigan brothers were deeply offended by its critical tone."

"I'll check it out. But back to Jerry Rizzo, can you think of anyone who could shed light on his relationship with the Berrigan brothers?"

"I think Rizzo is intimately involved with the Berrigan brothers. But it's hearsay. It's just some scuttlebutt I've heard."

"Oh, by the way, how's your leg holding up?" Matt asked.

"I use a cane, but only sparingly." Allen's voice dropped off.

"Same here. Okay, keep me posted." Matt signed off. He was going to hit some leads he had recently come across on the Berrigan brothers. Larry Alexander and *Citizen Berrigan* were now at the top of his list. He smelled a story.

* * *

Larry Alexander was in Hollywood promoting his documentary *Citizen Berrigan*. The film was about money in politics. It documented how the US Supreme Court's *Citizen United* decision gave carte blanche for billionaires like the Berrigan brothers to spend unlimited funds on politics. Alexander's award-winning documentary had drawn the ire of David and Charles Berrigan and moved them to pressure PBS into yanking the documentary. The billionaire industrialists had recently donated 23 million dollars to PBS. Money talks, so the Berrigan brothers got their way.

Matt Tyson's articles for *The Socratic Rag* were not wasted on Larry Alexander. He could use the publicity to fight corporate censorship. So he agreed to meet Matt Tyson for drinks around 5:00 at the Beverly Hills Hotel. Pink was his wife's favorite color. So, there was no better place for an interview than the famous Pink Lady.

The Beverly Hills Hotel's Polo Lounge was buzzing with gossiping Hollywood insiders, high-level corporate types, celebrity lawyers, and tourists gawking at movie stars. The bar was full, but Matt Tyson had reserved a center table. It was their first meeting.

Matt stood and shook hands with Larry Alexander. "I'm Matt Tyson. Thanks for meeting with me."

"I'm honored," Larry said. "I'm a big fan. I follow your blogs and never miss one of your exposés in *The Socratic Rag*."

"And I'm impressed with your latest big hit. *Citizen Berrigan* is a winner." Matt smiled broadly and added, "I want to hear the inside story."

They both opted for wine, a fine cabernet for Matt and a merlot for Larry. Larry was a seasoned documentarian, known for his hard-hitting interviews. He was a fearless investigator.

Matt sized up his new friend. Larry was tall, maybe six foot four, with broad shoulders, a thick barrel chest, and a full belly laugh; he was physically imposing. He also had a dark brown beard, untrimmed. *He'd make a hell of a mountain man*, Matt thought.

Matt started the ball rolling by asking questions about the making of *Citizen Berrigan*. "Were you able to sit down and have a conversation with the Berrigan brothers?"

"At first they were cooperative," Larry admitted. "That

is until I started hard balling them. As soon as I challenged them, they clammed up. They have sensitive skin."

"I had the same experience. In fact, I had a short sit down with them right here at the Pink Lady. They quickly tired of me and kicked me out."

"Are you serious?" Larry looked amused.

"We had a brief sit down in one of the bungalows. It didn't go well."

"Join the club. I've been there. Either you kiss ass or you hit the road. They're control freaks. And they've got connections, big bucks, and man power. With their recent purchase of the Tribune papers, they look a hell of a lot more like Fox News and the *New York Post*. They use their wealth to wield influence with elected officials. It's gotten out of hand."

"You're preaching to the choir," said Matt Tyson. He took a sip of wine and added, "They've attacked limits on campaign finance, promoted discriminatory voter ID, and exacerbated income inequality."

The two hardnosed investigative reporters exchanged war stories, agreed on most political issues, and laughed at their failed attempts at getting closer to the Berrigan brothers. Matt finally admitted he was desperate for an inside look at David and Charles Berrigan. "Larry, do you have any connections, clues, or leads that could get me closer to the inner workings of this dynamic duo?"

"Good luck. But there is a possible avenue," Larry said. He paused and added, "I suspect that William St. George over at the NRA has an inside track to their operation."

"What?" Matt's jaw dropped. "Say that again."

"William St. George is involved."

"How do you know?" Matt hung on every word.

"I'm close with William Bossley. He did the Park Avenue documentary. We've compared notes. St. George has been seen at the 740 Park Avenue address several times. David Berrigan is a prominent resident of the exclusive address."

"Could be a coincidence," Matt said. He'd had his crack at the NRA top guy.

"There's more." Larry paused and added, "I have some fairly reliable evidence that the Berrigan brothers have a secret compound out west. A pilot friend of mine knows a fellow pilot who has flown St. George to Bozeman, Montana. He also knows a helicopter pilot who's flown St. George to a place somewhere near the Bitterroot Mountains in western Montana."

"Is this mere conjecture or hard evidence?" Matt scooted forward toward the edge of his chair.

Larry cleared his voice and said, "This is off the record. I don't want to see me quoted in *The Socratic Rag*. St. George's involvement with the Berrigan twins is more likely than not. I hate and fear those guys. They've already had me censored. *Citizen Berrigan* got bumped from PBS. They'd like to silence me. Hell, they might try to buy me out."

"We're on the same page. I'll keep a low profile. But could I have your pilot friend's name and number? I'd like to talk to him."

"Sure, why not. But again, I don't want see my name plastered all over *The Socratic Rag*."

After a second drink, they had dinner, exchanged more journalistic war stories, and then called it a night. It was a great night for Matt Tyson.

Chapter Thirty-Eight

Neurosurgeon Dr. Anthony Gomez motioned for Agent Martini and Detective Javier Macias to enter the conference room. "Please come in, gentlemen. I've only ten minutes before I'm due in surgery." He was relatively young and thin, with dark hair and wire-rim glasses. He looked a bit like John Lennon.

"Good morning," Detective Macias said. "Thanks for the opportunity to speak with you."

"Please be seated. Here's what I have." Dr. Gomez motioned for the investigators to gather round him. He opened his laptop and retrieved his notes on Alexis Williams. "I've summarized my findings here."

Agent Martini squinted, pulled out his reading glasses, and leaned closer to the monitor. "That's better," he said. "Either the print's too small or I'm getting older." The doctor laughed, and Detective Macias merely shook his head and chuckled.

"This is where we stand. The bullet entered the back of the left side of Williams's head, grazed the left hemisphere of her brain, and exited through the front of her skull—near but missing her left eye socket." Dr. Gomez paused and looked up from the laptop.

"Was her eye damaged?" asked Agent Martini.

"Fortunately the bullet missed her eye by several centimeters. At this time, there's no evidence of trauma to the eye." Dr. Gomez looked back at his computer screen and continued the briefing. "Since the bullet only grazed the left hemisphere of the brain, there will be less swelling than if the bullet penetrated the complex central area where the two halves of the brain communicate. We looked for hematomas, pockets of blood that follow the trajectory of the bullet. Also there was some debris, parts of the scalp and hair that had been swept in by the bullet. We removed the debris because of the chance of infection. "

"Will she be able to speak?" Agent martini questioned.

"Alexis Williams was communicating with doctors, when not deeply sedated, by squeezing their hand. But now she's in an induced coma. Since the bullet only grazed the surface of the brain, vital brain functions were missed. If Miss Williams had been struck mid-brain, say the brainstem or basal ganglia, she would be unable to control things like body temperature, hormones, heart rate, and breathing." Dr. Gomez looked back at the laptop and continued. "I removed a portion of William's skull, allowing the brain to swell without being crushed in the skull. This procedure is crucial. If the brain swells within that confined space, it could lead to death."

"When can we see her?" said Detective Macias.

"Not now. As I mentioned, she's in an induced coma. She'll be unconscious for several days." Dr. Gomez stood and said, "Please excuse me. I'm needed in surgery."

"Just a heads up," said Agent Martini. "Detective Macias has assigned around-the-clock security. Additional arm guards will be stationed at the door to her room."

"I saw one this morning." Dr. Gomez smiled and hurried out of the conference room.

Agent Martini and Detective Macias could do nothing but wait. Security concerned both men. After all, Alexis Williams was the victim of an assassination attempt.

*   *   *

Serge had a backup plan. He knew from news reports that Alexis Williams was in the Hospital Central de Mexico. He bought some scrubs, a surgical mask, a small cooler, a hypodermic syringe loaded with potassium chloride, and a clipboard. The potassium chloride took some enterprising work and cost him more pesos than he liked.

He waited for a nursing shift change and then entered the ground level of the hospital. He approached the information desk and asked a volunteer for the room number of Alexis Williams. Within thirty seconds, he had the information, took the elevator to the third floor, and headed for intensive care. He approached the guard, flashed some phony credentials, and explained in fluent Spanish that he had important medication in the cooler. The guard swallowed the story, opened the door for Serge, and allowed him to enter.

Once inside, he removed the hypodermic syringe, aspirated it, and was about to insert it in her IV tube when the door opened. A nurse ran to the side of the bed and reached for the syringe. Serge whirled around striking the nurse across the face, knocking her to the ground. Her scream alerted the guard, who burst through the door, pulled his gun, and yelled in Spanish, "Drop it."

Serge hurled the hypodermic syringe, hitting the uniformed officer in his right hand, causing him to drop the revolver. Serge rushed passed the officer, knocking him to the floor. He ran down the hallway, took the stairs to the ground level, and escaped into the crowded streets. He ditched the cooler, clipboard, and mask in an alley trash bend, bought a cheap sweatshirt from a street vender, and disappeared. Plan two was a bust. But Serge was a patient man.

*   *   *

Detective Macias and Agent Martini were livid. How could the assailant get by the guard? The two detectives pulled the guard into a conference room and questioned him for thirty minutes. Juan Mendoza, the officer on duty, was adamant in his answers.

"Did the assailant show you credentials?" asked Detective Macias.

"Yes," replied the guard.

"Were they valid?" Detective Macias persisted.

"Yes. I checked for the seal, date issued, and distinguishing marks. Everything was in order." Officer Mendoza shook his head in frustration. "I followed proper protocol."

"Did you ask him what was in the cooler?" Agent Martini asked.

"Yes. He said it was medication." The officer looked down at the floor, averting the investigators' eyes.

"Was he wearing a badge?" Detective Macias pressed.

"Yes. The name matched the credentials he showed me."

"What did he look like?" Agent Martini asked.

"He was very tall, maybe six foot four, blond hair, and broad shoulders. He was a big man." Juan Mendoza looked up at the investigators and said, "I followed orders. I feel bad. Am I in trouble?"

"We'll leave that to Internal Security. You are relieved of your duties," Detective Macias said. He and agent Martini turned and abruptly left the conference room.

Officer Juan Mendoza sat staring out the conference room window. His wife was pregnant; he loved his job—and now this. Tears streamed down his cheeks.

*　　*　　*

Serge was holed up in his room, the third hotel since he arrived in Mexico City. He had always been a patient man, in control of his emotions, cool and calculating in both his personal and professional life. "Life is like a game of chess," he often said to his friends. "Impulsive and emotional responses can lead to no good." Cold, calculating logic was his master. A fellow countryman, Vasily Smyslov, had it right when he said, "In chess as in life, a man is his own most dangerous opponent."

He turned on CNN looking for an update on Alexis Williams. He was not disappointed. The American serial killer's exploits were well covered. The assassin who put her in the hospital with a serious gunshot wound to the brain had struck again. An assailant, most likely the same person who shot her while being transported to the airport from the

National Security facility in Mexico City, bypassed security at the Hospital Central de Mexico and attempted to kill her while she lay unconscious in bed. Authorities were looking for a tall, blond man with a prominent facial scar. During the hospital attack, the man was wearing hospital scrubs and was carrying a small cooler and clipboard.

Serge turned off the TV and headed for the bathroom, deciding on his new disguise.

Chapter Thirty-Nine

Matt Tyson had thoroughly enjoyed *Citizen Berrigan*; he had seen the documentary twice. But what excited him more was the bit about William St. George's frequent visits to 740 Park Avenue and the pilots who shuttled the NRA's top dog to the Berrigan brothers' Montana compound. Since David Berrigan resided at the prestigious 740 Park Avenue address, he decided to hop a plane to New York and do some digging.

Twenty-four hours after having dinner with Larry Alexander at the Pink Lady, Matt Tyson was standing outside 740 Park Avenue talking to the doorman. The uniformed doorman instantly recognized Matt, greeted him as sir, and asked who he was there to see.

"I'm here to see you." Matt grinned, taking in the stately looking doorman. He was dressed in black jacket and trousers, black cap with gold trim, white shirt and gloves, and a gray bowtie.

"I beg your pardon, sir." His tone was formal but courteous.

"As you know, I write for *The Socratic Rag*," Matt said.

"Yes, sir. I've read most of your work. I'm a big fan." He politely turned toward an approaching resident, addressed her, and opened the door. After greeting the tenant, the wife of a prominent hedge fund manager, he leaned over close to Matt and said in a hushed tone, "My favorite quote, and I can't say it too loud here, is where you refer to Goldman Sachs as a 'great vampire squid wrapped around the face of humanity.' It's hilarious but *ooohhh* so true."

"Thanks, I've gotten a lot of mileage out of that reference. But I'm writing a new article. Could we meet when you get off duty? I'll buy you a drink."

"I'm off duty in an hour," said the doorman.

Matt glanced at the nametag on his custom tailored jacket. "Michael Moore" was scripted in black on a gold background. "Okay, Michael. Let's meet at the Office Lounge. It's less than a mile from here. Do you have wheels?"

"No, but I can hoof it in twenty minutes. I'll be there."

Matt thanked Michael and headed for the parking garage. He made a few phone calls, including one to his managing editor and a call to one of the pilots Larry Alexander mentioned.

* * *

The Office Lounge was a lively Upper Manhattan bar featuring live music and dancing. It was Friday, happy hour, and the bar was full. Matt grabbed a booth, checked his cell phone messages, and made a call to a friend in the publishing business. Just as he put his cell away, Michael Moore showed up. Matt caught his eye and waved him over.

"Have a seat," Matt said. "What are you drinking?"

"I'm not a big drinker. But I'll have a light beer." Michael looked around.

"I'm working on an article about the NRA. I'm especially interested in William St. George. Have you seen him at 740 Park Avenue?"

"Before we get into details, I'd like to establish a few ground rules," Michael said.

"I respect that. What are they?" Matt asked.

"I want anonymity. My job is at stake. Please, no photos, no names, or incriminating descriptions of who I am." The beers arrived, and Michael took a drink.

"As you wish. I'm only interested in David Berrigan and his connection with William St. George." Matt smiled. He sensed that Michael had cold feet.

"The residents are a quirky bunch. They're billionaires who play by a different set of rules. They're high tempered, and you need thick skin to work there. They bark orders, seldom smile, and become livid if you make the wrong move. I have to know their preference, who likes their door opened, whether they sit in the passenger side of the front seat or the backseat. Most have chauffeurs, but some insist on driving. One mishap and I'm fired." Michael shook his head and frowned.

"Money has a way of distancing a person from humanity." Matt sipped his beer. He'd go easy and let Michael get comfortable.

"So I'm walking on thin ice here. I have to be careful. I certainly don't want to be quoted in *The Socratic Rag*."

"I give you my word. No names, no direct quotes, no hints of your identity." Matt smiled and studied Michael's appearance. He was tall and lean, had reddish brown hair and brown eyes. He looked like a typical thirty-something out on the town. He had on dark slacks and a blue and green polo shirt. He looked less imposing than when in uniform. At 740 Park Avenue he looked regal. A man in a dark tailored suit, stylish cap with gold trim, white gloves, and a gray bowtie creates a dignified image. *Perhaps clothes do make the man*, Matt thought.

"I've seen William St. George twice in the last three months. A fellow doorman has seen him once," Michael said.

"Did you see anything out of the ordinary?" asked Matt.

"Not really. But on one occasion, David's brother, Charles Berrigan, visited. He was with William St. George." Michael took a sip of beer and looked around as if someone nearby could overhear their conversation.

"Do you know much about the Berrigan brothers?" Matt asked.

"They're billionaires, big players in liquor industry, own a major chain of distilleries, oil refineries and pipelines, and got a head start in life. Their old man made a great deal of money in Russia. He had something to do with refining oil." Michael finished his beer. He seemed more relaxed.

"Were the Berrigan brothers friendly?" Matt dusted off his beer and ordered a second round.

"Decidedly not. David Berrigan was curt, didn't mince words, and would anger easily. He was a poor tipper. Many a time, I've loaded up two vans with luggage for their weekly trip to the Hamptons. And not one word of thanks. The only tip I saw from him was a fifty-dollar bonus check at Christmas."

"Not exactly nice people to work for," Matt said. He shook his head and frowned.

"Do you recall anything else about St. George and David Berrigan? Did you notice anything out of the ordinary?"

"There's nothing ordinary about this crowd. They live by a different set of rules." Michael thanked Matt for the beers and said he had a date with his girlfriend.

Matt said good-bye and again promised anonymity. He checked his voicemail and noticed an important call. It was from the pilot he had left a message with.

*   *   *

It was Saturday afternoon. Matt caught an early morning flight and was once again at home in his Washington D.C. apartment. His phone rang before he unpacked his bags.

"Matt Tyson," he answered as he tossed his dirty clothes in the laundry hamper.

"Bill First. You called earlier."

"Yes, Bill, thanks for returning my call. I'm doing an article on the NRA for *The Socratic Rag*," Matt said.

"How can I help you?" Bill's tone was friendly.

"We have a friend in common. Larry Alexander and I met couple days ago in Los Angeles. In our discussion of his documentary, your name came up." Matt paused, waiting to see if he'd be cooperative.

"Oh yes, Larry's a good client. I've worked with him for several years. *Citizen Berrigan* is a real eye opener."

"Larry said you know a fellow pilot who has personally flown the Berrigan brothers," Matt said.

"Actually, that pilot is me. Larry Alexander gave me a heads up. He was cautious and gave me a way out," Bill said.

"I appreciate your willingness to help. I'm interested in William St George's business relationship with the Berrigan brothers."

"I'm not privy to their business dealings, but they have flown with me on several occasions. I've flown them from New York to Bozeman, and I've flown St. George from Washington D.C. to Bozeman and back," Bill First answered.

Matt cleared his voice and said, "Did anything stand out, something special about the flights?"

"Well, there was a special request. Since I also have a helicopter's license, they wanted me to fly them to the compound in the Bitterroot Mountains. It's quite a spread. There's a heliport, a huge log structure with an American, Montana, and NRA flag out front," Bill said. He paused and then added, "I don't want my name appearing in *The Socratic Rag*. I'm letting you in on some confidential information. I'm doing it for Larry. The Berrigan brothers have done Larry Alexander wrong. The bastards censored him. They forced PBS to boycott his documentary."

Matt thanked him and asked a favor. "If I get to Bozeman, would you fly me by helicopter to the Berrigan brothers' compound?"

"I'll fly you over the compound. I can't land there without their permission. Any uninvited guests would be shot on the spot. That's private property, and they're armed."

"Gotcha. How about we take a flight over the compound next week?" Matt asked.

"I'll be there next Wednesday at noon. I'm free that afternoon."

"Book it," Matt said.

After they had finished working out the details for next Wednesday's flight, Matt signed off. He wanted more than a fly over. He had to come up with a plan.

Chapter Forty

Serge admired himself in the mirror. The dark full-collar shirt, white linen band attached, and ankle-length cassock stirred his soul. As a child, he aspired to be a priest. Now he would play one. The spiritual transformation gave him a divine sense of mission. He paid the clerk at the costume store and bragged how he would win best dressed at the company's costume party.

Serge strode out of the shop with a feeling of other-worldly power. The Russian mafia's best hit man was styling. He looked more the part of a man of the cloth than an assassin. The only hint to his dark side was the scar running from his right eye to his chin. In two hours, he'd make another visit to the General de Mexico Hospital.

Back at his hotel, he assembled his kit. He had a Bible, rosary, and his handgun of choice, a .44 Magnum with suppressor and laser sight. Being a member of the Russian mafia had its perks.

He had earlier confirmed that the hospital had a change of shift at 3:30. Serge entered the front entrance and took the elevator to the third floor. As he got off, he bumped into a nurse carrying a potted plant. He excused himself, smiled, and said, "Bless you, my dear." Today he had no cooler or clipboard. His spiritual arsenal was tucked out of sight in a large black briefcase.

Three doors from Alexis Williams's room, he paused and watched the changing of the guard. A uniformed guard exchanged brief words with his replacement before leaving. Serge approached the new guard, showing his credentials and a fake letter from Internal Security. The guard studied the letter, questioned Serge, and then opened the door.

Serge thanked the guard, blessed him, and moved quickly inside. One bed was unoccupied, and the other had a curtain drawn for privacy. He quickly removed his .44 Magnum, attached the suppressor, and released the safety. When he pulled back the curtain, he found an empty bed. He blurted an expletive in Russian. He then turned quickly, cursing in both English and Spanish. He put his .44 Magnum back in his bag and slowly opened the hospital room door. His eyes ballooned with surprise when he was greeted by three uniformed guards with weapons drawn.

Serge instinctively threw his bag in the face of the police officer to his left and whirled around with a flying leg kick, knocking the other two officers to the floor. The officer who got hit with the briefcase recovered and discharged one shot. It barely missed Serge's head, piercing a hole in an adjoining room door.

Serge sprinted down the corridor, darting and weaving amidst doctors, nurses, and visitors, and descended three flights of stairs. He took a side door, ripped off his Cassock and collar, and bolted into a back street. After several blocks, he turned the corner and quickly vanished into a local bizarre. There he bought another sweatshirt and cap.

Serge was a patient man, but his patience had worn thin. He had never embraced defeat, but today's failure left him doubting his skills. His rationality had shown cracks, his plans were not foolproof, and his will had been tested and shaken. If this was a game of chess, he was indeed his worst enemy. In chess, checkmate brings finality to the game. In the life of a hit man, death is the defining moment. From a very early age, Serge had thought of himself as a grandmaster, an invincible force played out on the game board of crime and intrigue. He was known by his friends and enemies as a finisher, the master of endgames. But for the first time, he had encountered doubt. His instincts and logic had been challenged. *I've confronted the enemy, and the enemy is me*, he thought.

* * *

It was scorching hot in Bozeman, Montana. The airport thermometer read 102 degrees, and it wasn't quite noon. Sweat beaded up on Matt Tyson's upper lip as he checked his voicemail. Allen Carter had left a message, asking if Matt had any news about Alexis.

Bill First spotted Matt, likely recognizing him from his numerous TV appearances and photos in *The Socratic Rag*.

"Matt Tyson, pleased to meet you," Bill said.

Matt stood without the use of a cane and shook Bill's hand. His lower leg was on the mend. "Thanks for making time. I'd like to get a firsthand look at the Berrigan brothers' compound."

"Everything's a go. I've got some paperwork to complete, and we'll be off in about fifteen minutes." After some pleasantries, Bill excused himself for some last-minute preparations.

Within a half hour, Bill and Matt headed west toward the Bitterroot Mountains. The helicopter tracked a spider-web-like network of creeks and rivers that meandered through the forested hillsides and grassy valleys. Snowcapped mountains reflected the bright summer sun. Bill gave Matt a combination history and geology lesson as they soared above the valleys and streams.

"Get ready for a treat," exclaimed Bill First. The Eurocopter EC120 descended to an altitude of a thousand feet, banked left, and crested a forest-covered hill. Looming ahead was the compound. The heliport, log fortress, flagpole, and backyard pond came into view. "That's a hell of a billionaire's getaway."

"Can we get a closer look?" Matt asked.

"I don't want to alarm the residents," Bill said.

"Is anyone home? The Berrigan brothers aren't there. You'd have flown them if they were there, right?"

"The brothers have often bragged about the elaborate electronic surveillance. It's as secure as Fort Knox."

"Make several low passes. I want to take pictures," Matt said as he took his Canon digital camera from the backpack.

"You're acting like a paparazzi," Bill First scolded.

"Whatever it takes," Matt said. For the next ten minutes, he fired off nearly fifty shots.

Matt Tyson was excited and impatient. He wanted access to the compound. Bill First was not the gatekeeper.

He needed someone with the knowhow and audacity to breach the compound's security. Before saying good-bye to Bill, he asked if he knew anyone who would go where no one else had gone before. Did he know someone who'd fly him to the compound, land, and take a look inside? After ten minutes of probing questions, Matt came away with a name.

"Max Milner," Bill First said, nodding his head. "He's a former Navy Seal who has turned private eye. He despises 1-percenters, billionaires who pay little taxes and make money off of other people's misfortunes. He might help you."

"Thanks," Matt said.

Not more than five minutes after saying good-bye to Bill First, he was on the phone with Max Milner. He landed an appointment at his downtown Bozeman office in one hour.

Matt drove his rental car to downtown Bozeman, grabbed a cup of coffee at a Starbucks, and was now seated in Max's outer office, looking at pictures he had taken of the compound. Mr. Milner's secretary, a plump, gum-chewing, middle-aged woman with black hair announced in a southern twang, "Mr. Milner will see ya now." She stood and waddled to the inner office door and opened it.

Matt stepped into an office with walls dominated with pictures from around the world. Most were of combat buddies in uniform celebrating both good times and challenging times. Max stood, walked around his desk, and gave Matt a hardy handshake and big hello.

"I know you. You're my favorite journalistic pit bull. You've got guts and style," Max said with a big smile. His dark leathery skin, strong build, and white teeth gave him a mature version of the All-American boy. He looked to be about six three and 230 pounds of muscle. His square jaw line and chiseled facial features reminded Matt of a comic book character from years past. *He'd make a hell of a Dick Tracy*, Matt thought.

Matt filled Max in on his mission. He was doing a piece on the NRA, had interviewed William St. George and the Berrigan brothers, but got stonewalled. He strongly suspected that the Berrigan twins controlled far more than the NRA. But he needed proof.

"I want a firsthand look of the compound. I want inside." Mat sat back and studied Max's reaction.

Max grinned and said, "You want to break in? That's trespassing, my friend."

"I'm willing to take the risk. In this case, the ends do justify the means," Matt said confidently.

"What about the heavy security, surveillance cameras, and guard dogs? People here in Montana shoot first and ask questions later." Max rolled his eyes and said, "But I *do like* a real challenge."

Matt smiled and said, "I'll pay well. I'd love to discover some dirt."

"And I despise the 1-percenters. This country is ruled by the rich. And half of them are at best thieves and scoundrels. It irks me to think that I served my country as a proud Navy Seal to protect their sorry asses."

Matt took out his camera and removed the digital memory card. "Download these photos. I took them today."

Max took the card and within minutes displayed a series of close-up photos of the Berrigan brothers' compound.

"Great pictures! The telephoto did a hell of a job. Let me study these. Can we meet tomorrow morning around nine? Maybe I can come up with something."

"That's perfect. I'll see you at nine." Matt stood, shook Max's hand, and said, "I really need to get these guys."

Chapter Forty-One

Matt Tyson was early for his nine o'clock appointment with Max Milner. He had downed two Starbucks, black, fired off three e-mails, and studied the photos taken of the compound. The plump, gum-chewing secretary had greeted Matt with a quick shout out as she left the office. "Max will be right with ya. I'm off to the post office."

As soon as she waddled out of the office, Max burst through the door. "Come on in. Let's get started," he exclaimed. His enthusiasm was palpable.

Matt settled in across the desk from the ex-Navy Seal. He once again checked out the photos ringing the office walls. The pictures ranged from guys in scuba gear to combat camouflage gear with black face paint. "Did the photos of the compound help?"

Matt's boyish looks and unbounded enthusiasm reminded Max of his days as a kid plotting the latest caper of the summer. "I have a few preliminary observations. First, a helicopter invasion will draw too much attention."

Matt frowned and said, "I thought a chopper would land us at the front door for easy access."

"Use of a chopper would be a convenient approach, but way too flashy. Our landing would create a commotion. We need stealth."

"How's that work?" The coffee and challenge at hand made Matt jittery. He tapped his foot and nervously clicked a ballpoint pen.

"We mount a land invasion. I propose a four-wheel vehicle, a Jeep, and drive near the outer walls of the compound. I noticed a trail just off the main entrance that leads to the rear of the property. With backpacks, rope, and simple climbing gear, we scale the high walls. They look to be only eight feet in height."

"We're going to scale an *eight-foot wall*?" Matt instantly wondered if his lower leg was ready for such acrobatics.

"It's a piece of cake for the right guy with the right equipment. I spotted the electrical panel at the back of the compound. The telephoto worked well. We disable it and then disable the gasoline generator. I spotted that next to a tool shed. Breaking in will be easy. The surveillance cameras won't operate without electricity."

"What about the guard dogs?" Matt asked.

"I didn't detect any dogs. I'll have treats and pepper spray just in case."

"When do we launch the land invasion?" Matt's foot tapping and pen clicking escalated.

"Tomorrow night is good for me. We launch our attack under the cover of darkness," Max said. "Are you up for it?"

"I think so. But there's a critical skill I'm lacking." Matt paused. "Are you good with computers?"

"I was trained by the very best. When serving for Uncle Sam, I excelled in I.T. There's not a computer I can't hack."

"Where do we meet?" Matt was in too deep to back out.

"I'll pick you up in my Honda Accord. We'll go to a prearranged place to transfer to the Jeep. I'll have everything in place."

*　*　*

Max was calm and committed. He hadn't had such a challenge since his time with the Navy Seals. He liked being a private eye, but his investigations were often routine and uninspiring. This one lit his fire.

Max was fed up with the US Justice Department's failure to prosecute the fat cats on Wall Street. Attorney General Hornsby had recently stated that the Justice Department couldn't indict too-big-to-fail banks because it would endanger the nation's, and possibly the world's, economy. Why did the attorney general back down? When Max was angry, he called the failure to prosecute the big banks *bullshit*. When in a cerebral mood, he called it *misdirection*.

*　*　*

Max eased the Jeep down the side road with the lights off. With assistance from a full moon, Max pulled under a pine tree, cut the engine, and pulled the gear out of the backseat. Keeping to the shadows, the two men crept to the wall where Max pitched a rope with an anchor. The first two attempts failed but the anchor caught snuggly to the interior side of the redwood log barrier on the third try.

With backpack and gear, he pulled himself up, assisted Matt with his assent, repositioned the rope, and descended into the compound. With backpack and newly mended leg, Matt repelled cautiously; they were both in. Matt's lower leg had passed the test.

Max searched two sides of the log structure in an attempt to locate the electrical panel. No luck. But on the north side he hit pay dirt. He opened the electrical panel, shut off the man switch, and quickly moved to the gasoline generator and disabled it. Any remaining surveillance cameras would be battery operated. They tried two windows, but they were locked. Max tried the side garage door, but it was locked. He banged it with his left shoulder, and to his amazement, on the third hit the latch gave. They were inside within five minutes. With flashlights, they did a thorough sweep of the log structure. It took another twenty minutes before they found the study and the secret door. Max struggled with the security lock. He flashed on a military operation conducted years ago during military training. He searched his backpack, retrieved a stethoscope, and with acute manual dexterity, cracked the code on the lock.

As Max and Matt explored the War Room with flash lights, they uttered words of amazement. "We've got to fire this thing up," Max said. "Wait here. I'll be right back. He returned to the electrical panel, threw the main switch, and turned off everything but the War Room. The label on the electrical panel simply read, "Inner Study."

Within five minutes, Max had the computers buzzing and all the monitors on. The room jumped to life with cable news, and live feed from sources abroad. Within twenty minutes, Max hit pay dirt. He found a profile on the

Inner Circle. Jerry Rizzo, the C.E.O. of Universal Studios Hollywood topped the list. Carlos Grande, the richest man in the world, George and William Stinger, hedge fund gurus, and the master minds, Charles and David Berrigan.

A complete dossier on William St. George at the NRA rounded out the find. Matt howled when he discovered the members of Fire Power. He immediately recognized the dead biker from Gun World. It was Jeremiah Bates, the bastard that broke his leg.

Max said, "Let's get the hell out of here."

Max and Matt downloaded the confidential material on Matt's laptop and fled the compound within five minutes. Before leaving, the electrical panel and emergency gasoline generator were back on line. They kept quiet until they were once again back on the main road.

"Do you think surveillance cameras found us?" Matt was shaking. He'd never pulled off anything like this.

"No way! The main panel was off at critical times. We kept out of range when the electrical panel was activated."

*   *   *

After two weeks, Alexis Williams's condition had stabilized. After a month, she had regained some strength and could walk, but communication was limited to hand squeezing and nodding. So far, she had cooperated with basic requests. Agent Martini had orders to fly her back to Los Angeles tonight. Director Tom Parker had worked out extradition with the Mexican authorities. Jeremiah Bates, the man murdered in Puerto Vallarta, was an American tourist. The other two men, one from Los Olivos, and the other from Sausalito, were California residents.

An Internal Security van waited outside the emergency room where Agent Martini, Detective Javier Macias, and three uniformed guards assembled.

Serge had intercepted communication calls between Agent Martini and Javier Macias. He had rented a Ford Focus and was parked across from the hospital entrance. Thirty days of waiting had been agonizing, but he had one more card up his sleeve.

The last rays of the setting sun disappeared behind the General de Mexico Hospital when the Internal Security van pulled out onto the street, followed by three officers on motorcycles. Lights on the motorcycles blinked, but no sirens were used. Serge kept his distance, preferring to stay three cars back.

A half mile from the airport, Serge pulled passed the Federales on motorcycles and glanced over at the van. Alexis was on the passenger side in the backseat. Her head was bandaged. Suddenly she turned and looked out the window. Her mouth opened wide, and she appeared to scream. Serge couldn't hear the scream, but he saw fear in her eyes. He moved ahead of the van and tracked its progress through the rear and side-view mirrors of the compact Ford.

Before entering the airport, he allowed the van and motorcycles to pass. He ducked behind the procession waiting for a clear view of Alexis. The three officers on motorcycles smothered the van, making it difficult to get a clear shot. The van suddenly veered off to the right and approached a private security gate for officials only. The sign said, "No Public Access." As the van stopped at the security gate, the three officers swung their motorcycles around, surrounded the Ford Focus, and drew their firearms.

The Ford Focus lurched forward. Serge spun the car around and floored it, nearly hitting one of the officers. All three officers fired shots at the fleeing vehicle, taking out the rear tires. Serge pressed on, but with deflated rear tires, he clunked along. The officers soon overtook him. They fired shots, flattening the front tires, and then shot out the windshield on the passenger side. Serge fired off a round from his Magnum, hitting an officer in the arm. The other two officers fired, simultaneously hitting Serge in the neck and head. His head slumped down, and blood spurted up onto the shattered windshield.

It was Serge's last stand. He had challenged the wrong person. Even while incapacitated by a brain trauma, Alexis ironically had the last word. She couldn't speak, but she could scream and respond to danger. Checkmate.

Agent Martini had communicated with Alexis by asking relevant questions, and she had responded by nodding and squeezing his hand.

Chapter Forty-Two

Allen Carter stared at the headlines of the *L.A Times*: "Serial Killer Alexis Williams is Coming Home." Allen's world was in a death spiral. The former Pepperdine University philosophy professor's health had improved, the FBI had arranged for her extradition, and she had been cooperative with US and Mexican authorities.

Allen jumped when his phone rang. He checked caller ID. It was Mikhail Medved. He picked up. "I just saw the news," Allen said.

"It doesn't look good. Do you want to talk?" Mikhail was purposely vague. Their phone, text, and e-mail may have been tapped.

"Let's meet at Mulligans at 2:00." Allen needed answers.

"See you there." Mikhail signed off.

It was Sunday, a day of leisure and recreation. Not today. He had to come up with a plan. The other members of Gotham City were restless. They wanted answers. Everybody wanted answers—his pushy clients, the feds, his comrades, Matt Tyson, and especially Agent Martini.

Allen had a couple of hours before heading over to

Mulligans. His monkey brain babbled incessantly, scolding him for his emotional weakness. He longed to once again dress up as Motley Wag, take back Gotham City, and manage his world with calculating logic and controlled passion. Images of Moody Muse, the Black Widow, Electra, Wonder Woman, and Bat Girl throwing caution to the wind took hold of him. The costume parties were more than just fun. They were artistic expression of pure passion, controlled passion, unadulterated by the tasteless norms of conventional society.

But now he had to get a grip, stabilize his raw emotions, and move on. Emotional fragility was for the weak. Controlled passion molded by a strong will was for the masters of the world.

He showered, shaved, and fired up his two-toned candy apple red and robust maroon 1935 Duesenberg. The SJ La Grand, Dual-Cowl Phaeton responded with a mellow rumble. *A short spin in the Santa Monica Mountains might be the drug of choice*, he thought. The vintage car responded well, easily handling sharp hair pin turns and steep grades. He descended to the beach and motored PCH, turning heads as he passed by. The classic roadster was a work of art. When questioned why he invested so much money in an automobile, he simply said, "It's functional art."

After a forty-five-minute joyride, he garaged the Duesenberg and returned to his workday car, the sleek and modern Corvette. The roar of the Blue Devil ZR-1 engine momentarily calmed his tormented soul. He arrived at Mulligans ten minutes early, ordered a round of Guinness, and nervously anticipated Mikhail's arrival.

It was early in the afternoon, and Mulligans was only

half full, so Allen easily spotted Mikhail as entered the Irish pub. He waved him over.

"The Guinness hits the spot." Allen raised his glass and said, "Get comfortable. We got a lot to talk about." Mikhail slid into the corner booth.

"Things are tight," Mikhail said. "I got a call from a concerned source. He verified that my cousin is dead. The Federales ambushed him. There was a fire fight. Serge took a round to the neck and head."

"Sorry to hear that." Allen paused briefly and then asked, "Do they have a backup plan?" Allen took a sip of his brew and absentmindedly drummed his fingers on the table.

"They offered their services. But there has been a slight change. The contract has doubled. The source said this is typical. The cost of the contract is based on the difficulty of the hit. Alexis is under heavy guard."

"Doubled! Christ, this is going to cost me a pretty penny." Allen shook his head in disbelief.

"It could cost us a lot more," Mikhail said. "If we don't silence her, the game is over. Do we act or end up on death row?"

"Do you need more money upfront?" Allen's finger-drumming of the table escalated.

"They need another fifty thousand."

"I'll have it tomorrow morning at ten. I'll deliver it to you, same place and same method of exchange."

The two comrades had another round of Guinness and called it a day. They were in no mood to party.

* * *

Matt Tyson had returned to his Washington D.C.'s condo with a laptop full downloads that could change the face of contemporary politics. Max Milner had performed a miracle. He had in his hands information that could cripple the NRA, bankrupt the Berrigan brothers, and most likely put them behind bars. He had the identity of the shot callers of Wall Street, the key players of the inner circle, and possible ties to the people responsible for the deaths of Senator Elizabeth Huntington and Supreme Court Justice Helena Bartoletti. He needed to prove that the Berrigan brothers were behind the Ricin that killed Senator Elizabeth Huntington and compromised computer program that monitored Justice Helena Bartoletti's insulin pump.

Matt had been sitting on explosive documents for weeks, downloaded material from the evil twins, diabolical men capable of almost anything. He was antsy. Sitting on a ticking time bomb made him jittery. He hadn't yet digested the enormity of his discovery. And he didn't know if he had been monitored. Maybe the Berrigan brothers had surveillance images of him and Max breaking and entering. *Maybe they're tracking me now,* he thought. *If they can bump off a US senator and a Supreme Court justice, they can easily rub me out.*

PART THREE:
Karma: What Goes Around Comes Around

Chapter Forty-Three

Alexis Williams had a new home. She had taken up residence on the fourth floor of the medical unit of the Twin Towers jail facility in downtown Los Angeles. It had been six months since she suffered a bullet to the brain. Physically, she had miraculously rebounded from the brain trauma, regaining her speech and amazing her doctors, court-appointed lawyers, and attending medical personnel. Physically, she was nearly 90 percent recovered. Psychologically, she was a blank tablet. She remembered nothing before being shot in the brain by Serge, a Russian mafia operative. She remembered nothing prior to being shot in the brain six months ago in Mexico City. So she said. Agent Martini had his doubts.

Agent Martini gazed into Alexis's eyes. He was puzzled and skeptical. *What's really going on inside her beautiful head?* he thought. She looked as good as she did when he first met her a little over six months ago in her faculty office at Pepperdine University. Her hair had grown out since the surgery, her speech was back, and her demeanor was friendly and cooperative. Alexis, however, remembered nothing about Malibu, Allen Carter, and being a professor of philosophy. She knew only that she was being held on three counts of murder. She had been indicted by the grand jury and charged with the murders at Los Olivos, Sausalito, and the brutal stabbing of Jeremiah Bates in Puerto Vallarta. Not only had she been accused of being a serial killer, but she had also been linked to the infamous gun show bombing at Candlestick Park in San Francisco.

"Alexis, I hope you remember me." Agent Martini smiled and took a seat across the table from Alexis Williams. They were in a small conference room adjacent to the fourth-floor medical facility. "Your trial date has been put off until April."

"That's three months from now. Does that mean I'm staying here?" Alexis's tone was soft, almost sensual.

"I'm afraid so. The L.A. District Attorney's office wants further psychiatric evaluation." Agent Martini opened his notebook and flipped a few pages. "You're scheduled for psychiatric evaluation this Thursday and Friday."

"How many more times do we do this? They've interviewed, questioned, and interrogated me. I have no answers. I remember only hospitals, doctors, nurses, and police of every stripe asking endless questions. I have no answers." Alexis looked down, shook her head, and said, "What do they want from me?"

"They want the truth." Agent Martini leaned back in his chair. Forensically, they had the goods on Alexis. Surveillance tape, license plates numbers, blood type, and fingerprints all pointed to the woman sitting before him. They had everything but a motive. The beautiful woman admitted to knowing nothing. Yet Agent Martini sensed that Alexis was hiding something. There was more to the story; there had to be. He'd bet his last dollar that a cold-blooded killer lay silently beneath her cool exterior, coiled and ready to strike. He sensed that the psychiatrists were being worked.

"I've been honest and cooperative. I can do no more." Alexis stood and said, "I want to go back to my cell."

"In good time, but first, the psychiatric nurse wants to see you. After that, you have a meeting with a counselor. I'll be back on Friday to check up on you." Agent Martini said good-bye and watched as a nurse escorted Alexis out the conference room door.

Later that evening, Alex tossed and turned, unable to fall asleep. His mind raced, reliving his encounters with Alexis Williams. *What makes her tick?* he asked again and again. *How do you get into another person's mind?* He wasn't a philosopher or psychologist, but he had been haunted by the question of other minds since childhood. As a teen, he had wondered what his girlfriend really thought of him. When married, he'd been thrown many a curve balls by his wife. *What is she really thinking?* Now he was endlessly baffled by criminals. He wanted to crack the interior of Alexis's mind, but how? *How does a person shed his ego and become another person. Hell, if you did, you would be that person and not you.* This mental knot paralyzed his brain, shutting it down. He finally let go of his mental obsession and drifted off into a welcomed sleep.

*   *   *

Allen Carter returned home from another day of legal headaches. His clients were as demanding as ever. But that wasn't his only problem. Agent Martini wanted to meet him at the West Los Angeles FBI Field office tomorrow at noon. He felt trapped. Alexis was in custody at the Twin Towers. He was certain she'd talk. And now he feared that the feds were on to Gotham City. His days, it seemed, were numbered.

Allen grabbed a Guinness from the fridge and slumped into a chair at the kitchen counter. He hastily switched on the TV and tuned into CNN. Anderson Cooper broke into a news commentary with breaking news. "Alexis Williams," he sternly announced, "has escaped the Twin Towers jail in downtown Los Angeles. A nurse was found gagged and bound near a medical station on the fourth floor of the Twin Towers. She had been stripped of her nursing attire, security badge, and personal belongings. The nurse had been preparing to leave for home. While administering a blood pressure test, she was attacked by Alexis Williams. She was knocked unconscious by a blow to the head."

Allen's jaw dropped. "Fucking bitch." He repeated the epithet again and again. Later commentary revealed that the maintenance crew making repairs earlier that day had inadvertently left a hammer on the nursing station counter. Authorities believed that Alexis Williams bludgeoned the nurse and escaped during the evening shift change.

* * *

Agent Alex Martini was livid. "How in the hell did she slip out undetected!" he yelled at FBI Agent Rob Johnson and L.A. County Sheriff Andrew Barton. "I need answers!"

Agent Martini quickly headed up an investigation team

that questioned everyone on duty the previous night. By day's end, he had a shaky picture of what went down. He addressed six members of the investigation team in the conference room on the fourth floor of the Twin Towers.

"This is what we've determined," Agent Martini said after distributing a time line of yesterday evening's events. "Alexis Williams said she accidentally dropped two of her meds down the sink in her cell. She requested two more Ambien, so Nurse Elizabeth Harris called Dr. Manual Espinoza and received permission for the additional meds. Alexis also requested that the nurse on duty take her blood pressure. The nurse said Alexis was insistent, so she let her out of her cell and brought her to the nurses' station. While the nurse cuffed her for the blood pressure test, Alexis grabbed the hammer inadvertently left on the counter by workman and bludgeoned her. She then dragged her into the locker room where she stripped her, took her nurses outfit, purse, security ID, and opportunistically escaped during shift change."

"How did she get through multiple security checks?" Agent Rob Johnson asked.

"Alexis had the same hairstyle and color, and was about the same height and weight as the attending nurse. It's not the first time inmates have escaped from the Twin Towers. Kevin Jerome Pullum walked out of the Twin Towers jail after being charged with attempted murder in a Van Nuys courtroom back in July 2001. He evaded police for sixteen days. Hell, Pullum used a fake ID with actor Eddie Murphy's picture."

"Anybody there notice anything unusual last night?" Sheriff Deputy Barton asked.

"Nothing. Alexis walked out with a group during the evening shift change," Agent Martini answered. "She took Nurse Elizabeth Harris's purse, including driver's license, credit cards, and L.A. County Sheriff's ID and badge. We have a serial killer feigning amnesia on the lam. I've ordered an all-points bulletin. She's smart, cunning, and very dangerous." Agent Martini left the meeting and went downstairs to a news conference. He dreaded answering questions from the news media.

Chapter Forty-Four

The nurse's purse Alexis had stolen had four hundred bucks in cash. Alexis Williams hurriedly walked from the Twin Towers jail to Sunset and Figueroa Street where she boarded a Metro Bus for Santa Monica. Breathless from a lack of exercise, she collapsed into a seat at the rear of the bus. Her physical abilities had not been compromised from her gunshot wound to the head. She agreed with her doctors; her rehabilitation had been indeed miraculous.

The bus was crowded with weary commuters eager to get home after a long day's work. No one paid her a bit of attention. Alexis blended in with the largely Hispanic riders. When an elderly lady asked her the time, she answered in Spanish. She got off the bus at Santa Monica Boulevard and Third Street, where she hailed a cab for Las Flores Canyon Road in Malibu. She had a score to settle.

During the thirty-minute ride, her inner voice gained strength, becoming a loud chant by the time the cab reached Las Flores Canyon Road and started the steep climb to Allen Carter's Malibu estate. "Motley Wag's time has come.

Motley Wag's time has come." The incessant chant was followed by the refrain, "That hideous clown will be put in his place, back in the black box." The refrain, "Back in the black box," echoed in her ears.

Alexis felt whole again. Her inner voice had returned. She would make the world right. As the cab approached the gated driveway, she searched the grounds looking to see if anyone was home. It was early in the evening, the sun had set, and the garage and driveway lights were on.

She paid the cab driver, tipped him well, and entered the gated drive after punching in the code. Her memory was spot on. Her brain injury had left it intact. Alexis found the spare key hidden under a potted plant near the side garage door entrance. She entered the garage, passed by the vintage Duesenberg, and listened for sounds coming from inside the house. Nothing. The place was as quiet as a cemetery at midnight.

Alexis cautiously opened the door leading from the garage to the kitchen. There was no sign of life, so she sprang upstairs, feeling giddy for the first time sense her gunshot wound to the brain.

She went directly to Allen's master closet and found what she'd dreamed about for the last six months. She gathered the costume and laid it out on the king-size bed. She grimaced as she smoothed out the wrinkles in the green blazer. She neatly organized the green vest, blue-collared shirt, funky orange tie, and gray and purple striped slacks.

In the bathroom, before dressing, Alexis tinted her hair green and applied the appropriate makeup. She had watched Allen fastidiously go through this drill many times. Alexis carefully added the final touches, putting red lipstick around her mouth and cheeks, molding wax for the scar, and putting black liner around her eyes.

Alexis stood transfixed before her reflection in the bathroom mirror. Motley Wag stared back, the same hideous face, the same wide mouth, painted red, distorted by scars into a permanent smile.

Back in the bedroom, she put on the baggy clothes. She rolled up the pant legs and tightened the belt to prevent the slacks from falling off her feminine hips. When all was in place, she checked her reflection in the full-length mirror next to the bedroom door. She was the spitting image of Morgan Watt's portrayal of Motley Wag in the blockbuster thriller *Dead Space*. Before going downstairs, she located Allen's .44 Magnum, loaded it, and stuffed it in her baggy trousers. *Yes, the bastard actually owns a gun,* she thought. *He hated the idea of gun ownership, but he was the exception. We will play that out tonight,* screamed her inner voice.

Downstairs, she grabbed a Guinness from the fridge and waited in the darkness of the living room. Tonight was homecoming, and the calls for the enemy's head were deafening. Her inner voice echoed loudly in her vengeful mind, "Back in the black box, back where you belong." But this chant was followed by the refrain, "If Motley Wag dies, where do you go? He is all you have. You are alone, alienated from others, stripped of your professorship, on the lam, and wanted by the authorities. You are only a stone's throw from death row." Alexis William's soul was fractured. She was hammered by contradictory feelings. She wanted both revenge and help. But who could help her? Motley Wag was the only one who could make the pain go away. But she hated him.

Alexis jumped, alerted by the sound of the garage door opening. She made out the rumbling sound of Allen's Corvette entering the garage. He'd be in the kitchen in a matter of moments. The inner door leading from the garage opened and slammed shut. The overhead lights in the kitchen flashed on, faintly illuminating the back half of the large living room. She leaned up against the adjoining wall, staying out of sight. She peeked into the kitchen and saw Allen remove a Guinness from the fridge. She leaned back out of sight, removed the .44 Magnum from her baggy trousers, and took a deep breath.

Sounds of the Sony TV filled the kitchen with local news. She took another deep breath, barged into the kitchen, wagging the .44 Magnum, saying, "Surprise. Your favorite person is at your service."

Allen Carter dropped the Guinness, sending beer splashing onto the counter and kitchen floor. His eyes bulged as he yelled out, "What the fuck!"

"It's time you're put in your place, back in the black box." Alexis's heavy breathing, pounding heart, and adrenalin-charged body spurred her on. "Any last words?"

When Allen attempted to stand, Alexis fired the .44 Magnum. She sent a bullet past his right ear, hitting and shattering a glass cabinet door. Allen froze.

"Has the cat got your tongue?" Alexis narrowed her eyes. "Sit down. We need to talk." Her hands trembled. The loud blast of the Magnum scared her. The reality of what just happened stunned her, adding confusion to her chaotic mind.

Allen slumped down in his chair. He stared helplessly at the Magnum as it wagged dangerously back and forth.

Alexis slumped against the far wall. The tables had turned. Alexis was Motley Wag, and he was at her mercy. "Please, Alexis," he said in a strained, high-pitched voice. "Please put down the gun."

Alexis ignored his desperate request and said, "Why didn't you help me? You abandoned me and set the forces of evil after me."

"What?"

"You tormented me, wormed your way into my brain, and poisoned my thoughts." Alexis waved the Magnum about, her emotions escalating. Her inner voice began its incessant chant, *Back in the black box, put Motley Wag back in the box.*

"Please, Alexis, we need each other. The FBI is breathing down our necks. We can team up, escape, and put all this behind us."

"I can't trust you." Alexis waved the gun back and forth and then aimed it at Allen's head.

"Please, Alexis, put the gun away. Let's talk. All we have is each other. Together we can escape, start a new life."

"Fat chance. We'd be caught in a minute." Alexis leaned back against the kitchen wall and lowered the Magnum to her side.

"No, I have a plan." Allen stood slowly and reached out for his former lover. "Please, it's our only chance."

Alexis took a small step toward Allen, both cheeks now moistened by tears. The Magnum now hung lifelessly at her side.

Allen slowly approached her and gently took her in his arms. "We'll pack up some things and once again hit the road in the Corvette. I've got a road trip in mind."

"Road trip?" Alexis was drained. She no longer had the energy or anger to fight back.

"I've dreamed about this for months. We'll make a last stand against the NRA and the Berrigan brothers." Allen pulled her to him and hugged her lovingly.

"What's up with the NRA and the Berrigan brothers?" Alexis said. Her voice was barely audible. She was drained, and her inner voice had quieted.

"Everything! I think we can have the last word." Allen stroked her hair and held her close. The Magnum dropped to the floor.

"I have something for you." Allen opened a kitchen drawer and took out a rolled joint. They went out onto the deck where they shared the joint and drank Guinness beer. A distant Coyote howled, as if signaling the appearance of the rising moon. After two joints and several beers, Allen took Alexis upstairs where they showered together. He washed the green dye from her hair and the makeup from her face. Then they both needed a fix. Two hours later, they fled the Malibu estate with bags packed, both armed, and with a suitcase full of cash.

Chapter Forty-Five

Matt Tyson had holed up in his Washington D.C. condo for months, writing articles for *The Socratic Rag* and digesting the downloaded documents from Shangri-La. It was an extraordinary catalogue of political and economic power amassed by the Berrigan brothers.

Matt hadn't yet decided on the best way to deal with the explosive material. He poured a glass of Cabernet and switched on his TV.

Anderson Cooper was in the middle of a CNN news alert. "Alexis has escaped from the Twin Towers jail in downtown Los Angeles. It is believed by the FBI that Alexis went to Allen Carter's home in Malibu before the two of them disappeared, possibly in Carter's late-model Corvette. The FBI sent out an all-points bulletin. The bulletin warned that the couple is armed and dangerous."

Matt was stunned. He had partied with Alexis and Allen. He had attended a costume party dressed as Hypnos, his favorite comic book character. He had shared Guinness beer with Motley Wag and danced with Moody Muse. The world had turned upside down. He was for the first time in his career lost for words.

Matt's phone chirped, wrenching him back to the present moment. He hesitated, picked up his cell phone, and checked caller ID. He was about to put the phone down, nervous and conflicted, when he impulsively answered. "Matt Tyson here," he said.

"Good evening. This is David Berrigan." Without giving Matt a chance to respond, he continued, "My brother and I would like to make a good will overture. We'd like to invite you to my place Friday night for a friendly interview. We have a story to tell. Please come to 740 Park Avenue this Friday night at 7:30 for cocktails." *Click.*

Matt poured another glass of Cabernet and downed it in three gulps. The third glass knocked him out. He wasn't a big drinker.

* * *

Matt caught a late-evening flight from Washington D.C. to New York and checked into the New York City Mid-town Holiday Inn just before midnight. He was more than a little apprehensive about tomorrow night's interview with the Berrigan brothers. Did they know of his break-in at Shangri-La? Had they retrieved surveillance images of Max Milner and him cavorting through their Montana compound? Had he been found out? Was this a setup? Was there really a story, or was *he* the story? Matt's mind buzzed throughout most of the night, making sleep elusive.

A few hours before hailing a cab for 740 Park Avenue, he phoned Max Milner. He informed him of the meeting.

Max was stunned. Matt's only request was that if he didn't hear from him tomorrow, assume the worst. "Please follow up on my abduction," he told Max over the phone. "There may well be foul play."

The doorman's eyes widened when he recognized Matt Tyson. He played it cool, however, and didn't let on that the two of them had shared a drink at a local bar several months ago. Matt took an elevator to David Berrigan's eighteen-room duplex where he was greeted by the butler at the front door. He was immediately ushered into the study where David and Charles were enjoying an after-dinner cognac. Both Charles and David were dressed formally in dark suits and tie. Matt, living up to his collegial dress, wore a navy blue blazer, no tie, and jeans.

David stood and said, "Welcome to my humble abode."

Charles stood and offered Matt a Comandon XO Cognac. "Thanks, I'd love one," Matt said and took a seat beside David on the sofa facing the fireplace. Matt sipped his drink, gazing at the logs burning brightly, trying to focus on anything other than his shaking hands.

"Charles and I felt a need to open up to the press and allow a peek into our private lives. We wanted to share a few stories and episodes in our personal and financial journey. We want to demystify all the swirling rumors associated with us." David paused and added, "And we thought of you."

"Why me? I thought our last meeting at the Pink Lady went rather badly. And you have abundant access to the *Chicago Tribune* and the *Los Angeles Times*, newspapers much more sympathetic to your cause." Matt took another slow sip of cognac.

"We need press coverage from an organization not

associated with us. We want a candid look at our rise to power," Charles said.

"I'm … shocked and honored," Matt said. The cognac was beginning to take effect. He felt relaxed for the first time in days.

"We want to invite you on an adventure," David said. "In one week, Charles and I are going to raft the Missouri River." David stood, approached the bar, retrieved the bottle of Comandon XO Cognac, and refreshed his drink. He then poured another drink for his brother and Matt.

"We are going to make a trip down memory lane," Charles said. "Our story begins on the Missouri River. As teenagers, we rafted the river and found intrigue and mystery at every turn. We want to retrace our steps, relive those early years of innocents. We thought you'd bring a fresh and thought-provoking voice to our quest."

"You want me to go along for the ride?" Matt's instincts took over. There was certainly a story here.

"Are you in?" David asked.

"I'm in." Matt wasn't sure of what just went down.

That night at the Holiday Inn, he relived the evening's conversation for the tenth time. It made little sense. At the back of his mind came the same lingering, unanswered questions. *Are they on to me? Did they know about the break-in? Am I being set up?*

Chapter Forty-Six

David and Charles met Matt Tyson in Sioux City, Iowa, where they were chauffeured by limo to the Missouri River fifty miles south of Lewis and Clark Lake. Here they met Jim Connolly, who transported the trio to an encampment along the west side of the lake. David said, "Wow," when he spotted the raft tethered to a dilapidated dock. The dock had long ago been abandoned, but it was secure enough for their needs. The raft was a sophisticated version of the bamboo raft that David and Charles lashed together as kids. The updated version didn't use discarded cordage found behind a local hardware store near the Berrigan brothers' boyhood farm. The twenty-first-century raft was a twelve-foot by ten-foot bamboo craft with wooden bench seats, enough storage space for supplies, and equipment for their journey. There were bottles of cognac, a cooler stocked with beer, beef jerky, dehydrated soup, baked beans, and Dorito chips. It wasn't fine cuisine and spirits, but the Berrigan brothers wanted to turn back the clock and rough it.

"Beer by day," said David, "and cognac by night will keep our spirits bright."

"And the Doritos, beans, soup, and jerky will keep our bellies from growling," chimed in Charles.

Matt had been appointed cameraman. He would interview and video their rafting party. The Berrigan brothers had the stage and would tell the tale of their rise to power, from adolescent dreamers to Wall Street tycoons. Matt Tyson was in charge of creating a documentary about two boys destined for greatness. That's how the brothers billed the adventure. But Matt was haunted by the thought that the rafting trip was a ploy, a sinister act of deception, one designed to put an uppity reporter in his place. Did the brothers really want a candid telling of their rise to financial power or was this just one more subversive act? But Matt, forever the optimist, was game. He was a sucker for a good story.

David and Charles had changed clothes at the temporary encampment, trading in their travel clothes for coonskin caps, jeans, work shirts, knee-high fishing boots, and a large bandana loosely tied around their necks. Charles chose a navy blue bandana; David opted for red. Matt decided on a more contemporary look. He felt more comfortable wearing lightweight safari clothing, hiking boots, and a New York Yankees baseball cap. The safari attire dried out quickly and was comfortable.

Matt had a Cannon .35 MM SLR Camera and a pocket Cannon Power Shot as a backup. He threw himself into the role of official documentarian. This could be a perfect lead into his pirated data clandestinely obtained from the Montana compound. Every time Matt flashed on the Shangri-La raid, paranoia set in. The Berrigan brothers were no hay seeds. They were sophisticated "Robber Barons," ruthless men capable of murder. He had evidence downloaded on his laptop that linked them to the murders of Senator Elizabeth Huntington and Supreme Court Justice Helena Bartoletti. His death would be just another colorful feather in their cap.

As a backup and safety net, Matt had alerted Max Milner of his adventure. Unknown to the Berrigan brothers, the ex-Navy Seal had rented a power boat and would shadow the trio's journey.

With bamboo poles, Charles and David pushed the raft from the dilapidated dock. Matt waved goodbye to Jim Connolly, who snapped pictures as the trio set off. As they entered the current, the raft picked up momentum. It didn't take long for David to pop open the first beer. Within fifteen minutes, the trio had downed their first Miller Lite. It was early afternoon, the sun was fighting through drifting clouds, and the twins were giddy with excitement. Matt still wasn't sure whether he was a reporter or a sacrificial lamb.

"It all started here on the Missouri River," David said as he popped open his second Miller Lite. "In the fall, we'd become sophomores in high school. But as young teenagers, the fall was months away and was of little concern. It was a magical time, the first day of summer."

"It was that first rafting trip that we stumbled upon the cave. If we're lucky, we'll come across it before dark," Charles said as he opened a beer and passed it to Matt.

After several hours of smooth waters, they entered a stretch of water dotted by sandbars, driftwood, and several abandoned docks. As the sky darkened with gathering rainclouds, David pointed to a grouping of boulders and a sandbar stretching several hundred yards adjacent to the shore. "Over there," he said. "We're close to the cave."

David and Charles dug in with their poles, directing the pitching raft starboard. After several tense moments of fighting the swirling water and swift current, they beached the lumbering raft. David jumped out, splashing water about, and secured the front of the raft to a large piece of driftwood. He looked about and exclaimed, "This is it! We're not far from the cave's entrance."

David splashed through some shallow water and began climbing over a series of boulders. Charles and Matt lost sight of David for several minutes before he stood up on a ledge overlooking the sandbar and yelled, "It's here. Bring supplies. Don't forget the beer."

Within twenty minutes, the trio had everything in place. With a bit of sweat and some juicy epithets, they had in place the cooler full of beer, Doritos, beef jerky, and cognac for the party. Blue skies gave way to heavy, dark clouds and the distant sound of thunder. Before they finished their beer, the clouds unloaded their fury. After five minutes of pounding rain, thunder, and lightning, Charles gathered the wood he had piled next to the entrance when they first arrived. It wasn't long before the unlikely trio huddled around the fire, switched from beer to cognac, and began their bull session.

Charles bellowed, "Guns don't kill people, people do." He motioned to the rear of the cave where the pro-gun graffiti was illuminated by the flickering firelight.

"Remember our blood oath?" David said. "We shared blood right there at the entrance to the cave."

"I do indeed. Do you remember what we said?" Charles asked.

David replied, "Simper fi."

"And with that, we exchanged blood," Charles said proudly.

"In body and soul, we are still of one mind," David said.

"Right on," Charles echoed.

Matt had been busy recording the twins. The sincere exchange of fidelity would make great documentary footage.

Suddenly, two bright lights illuminated the cave. Matt squinted and shielded his eyes. David yelled, "Who goes there?"

A coarse, deep-throated voice answered, "We have orders for the arrest of Matt Tyson and David and Charles Berrigan."

"Says who?" yelled David.

"So says the FBI."

Two men stepped through the mouth of the cave. They were wearing tan pants and blue windbreakers embossed with FBI. The taller of the two men showed his credentials. David and Charles looked them over and said in unison, "Arrested for what?"

"We have a search warrant for your compound in Montana. We have a court order to detain the three of you."

Another man entered the cave dressed in jeans and a blue FBI windbreaker and quickly cuffed the three rafters. Their mission had been aborted. David and Charles were hustled up the embankment and down a muddy road to a waiting van. Matt was hustled off to a second van. The vans were unmarked.

Matt was alone and bewildered. Had the twins pulled a fast one? Something wasn't right. Thunder struck, soon followed by lightning. Rain pelted the windshield of the van, making for poor visibility. Matt sat in the backseat, cuffed, wet from the rain, and numbed from what just went down. The driver and the FBI agent riding shotgun were quiet.

The last thing he remembered was drinking some coffee offered to him by the FBI agents.

Chapter Forty-Seven

Max Milner had struggled to focus his high-powered binoculars as Matt and the Berrigan brothers had entered the cave. The motorboat had bobbed like a cork while raindrops splattered the binoculars, making visibility a challenge. After an hour wait in the heavy rain, he had seen headlights above the cave. Ten minutes later, the GPS tracking device he had made Matt wear signaled that Matt's location had changed. Max synched up his hooded rain jacket and pulled hard on the throttle. The driving rain pelted his face for nearly an hour before Max found the dock. He jumped into his rented Jeep and took off. Matt was receding from Max's location by the minute.

Eleven hours later, he was back in Bozeman, Montana. His GPS indicated Matt was headed toward Montana's Bitterroot Mountains. It was a no-brainer; Matt was on his way to the Berrigan brothers' Montana compound. Max alerted the FBI. He was put through to Director Tom Parker, who immediately contacted Agent Alex Martini. Within an hour, FBI SWAT team members were assembled and put on high alert. Agent Martini agreed to meet with Max Milner at his Bozeman office at three in the afternoon.

At 3:00 sharp, Agent Alex Martini was in Max's inner office, bent over his laptop. In less than a half hour, he was convinced that Matt Tyson was in serious danger, so he alerted the assembled SWAT team at the FBI Bozeman Field Office. "The mission is on. We launch operation Bitterroot immediately," Agent Martini barked into his cell phone.

Agent Martini and Max Milner followed the FBI convoy by helicopter. The retired Navy Seal was pumped. Within two hours, the SWAT team surrounded the Montana compound. An FBI chopper hovered overhead as Agent Martini used the loud speaker to announce their presence. "Come out with your hands raised. This is FBI Agent Alex Martini. The compound is surrounded."

Matt's GPS tracking device had him squarely in the middle of the main lodge. Agent Martini instructed the helicopter pilot to make several passes over the compound, swooping close to the US, Montana, and NRA flags flapping in the light evening breeze. The sun had dropped behind the Bitterroot Mountain Range, casting shadows across the grounds. Since Agent Martini got no response from the loud speaker warning, he gave the go-ahead for Operation Bitterroot.

Within five minutes, fifteen FBI agents surrounded the compound with weapons drawn. Two federal agents in tactical gear, olive-green uniforms, matching green helmets, goggles, and bulletproof vests fired several rounds into the front door lock. Both men hit the door with lowered shoulders, dislodged the lock, and broke open the door. The first federal agent stood aside while the second agent peeked in. The go-ahead was signaled by the first agent to enter the compound.

The first two agents were followed by three more SWAT team members. They stealthily swept the ground floor with M4 carbines at the ready. After securing the bottom floor, two SWAT team members climbed the stairs to the second level and entered the spacious family room. Across the room were double doors leading to the outside deck. There they discovered Matt, unconscious, stretched out on a brown leather couch.

A medic was immediately alerted. Within five minutes, Matt Tyson was awakened. He was initially dazed and confused, but elation set in when he discovered that this time he was in the hands of real FBI agents. Matt was alone; whoever had abducted him had fled the scene. Within an hour, Matt had regained his senses. The attending FBI medic cleared Matt to drink coffee and stand and slowly walk about. After a welcomed handshake with Agent Martini, Matt led him to the War Room. The SWAT team used electronic equipment to bypass the locked door. Agent Martini got his first look at the nerve center of the Berrigan brothers. Matt Tyson, still sluggish from the knock-out drug, watched with sober fascination as two members of the SWAT unit activated the computers, monitors, and surveillance system. The room sprang to life.

A treasure trove of incriminating evidence was at their disposal. So they thought. After long hours of investigation, nothing incriminating was found. The computers had been wiped clean. Only official business records from Berrigan Industries were found.

*   *   *

Within forty-eight hours of the raid, Agent Alex Martini had arranged for a meeting with the Berrigan brothers at David's 740 Park Avenue residence. It was ten in the morning on Friday when Agent Martini sat down in the study with the brothers. Both Charles and David were wearing dark gray business suits, red and navy blue striped ties, and highly polished black leather, Italian designer, dress shoes.

"Agent Martini, my brother David and I are dismayed at the raid on our Montana retreat. It's a beloved retreat," Charles said as he sat next to his brother on the sofa.

Agent Martini settled in across from the twins in a wingback chair. He retrieved some notes and said, "I've a lot of questions. First, who were the men who abducted you and Matt Tyson?"

"We have no idea. We were evidently drugged. We awoke beside the Interstate in a van. The FBI agents were gone. After coming to, I used my cell phone to call for help. Iowa Highway Patrol picked us up, interviewed us at an Iowa Sheriff's substation, took down our story, and released us. We arranged for transportation back to New York City." David cleared his voice and then added, "We are at a total loss about events of that evening."

Agent Martini asked, "How do you explain why Matt Tyson was drugged and found at your Montana retreat?"

"We're completely confounded by all that went down. We feel like we're the victims of a sinister plot to blacken our good name. We have been victimized," Charles said. His face turned red, and his hands trembled slightly.

"Well, maybe with the help of Matt Tyson, we can clear all this up," Agent Martini said.

"How's that?" David asked.

"He has some material he'd like to share with you." Agent Martini paused and then added, "He's right outside. He accompanied me this morning. But I wanted to get the okay from the two of you."

"We didn't give our permission for this," Charles said.

"I thought you'd be excited to see your friend," Agent Martini said.

"Well, if he's here, show him in," David said, his tone cold.

Agent Martini excused himself and talked briefly with the butler. A few seconds later, Matt entered the room carrying his laptop. "Gentlemen, I'm happy to see you're both okay," he said, smiling. "I've got some material I'd like to share with you."

The twins sat silently as Matt opened up the laptop and began reading portions of the files linking Charles and David to the deaths of Senator Elizabeth Huntington and Supreme Court Justice Helena Bartoletti.

Both twins stood, and David said, "This meeting is over. This is a grotesque charade and a travesty of justice. We'll say nothing before we consult our lawyers." David paused and then said, "Now, gentlemen, please leave."

Agent Martini cleared his voice and said, "You'll have plenty of time to consult your lawyers. But now we have legal cause to arrest you. You are apprised of your Miranda rights. You have the right to remain silent, anything you say may be used against you in a court of law, and you have the right to retain a lawyer."

At that moment, three FBI agents enter the study, cuffed the stunned twins, and curtly escorted them from the room. Matt Tyson and Agent Alex Martini smiled broadly.

After the Berrigan brothers left the study, Agent Martini said, "It's a good day."

"It's a hell of a good day," Matt Tyson said. "We've both seen a lot."

Chapter Forty-Eight

Two phone calls by the Berrigan brothers set their legal team in overdrive. Within twenty-four hours, the Berrigan brothers' attorneys had challenged the confiscation of computers from their Montana retreat. It was stolen property, illegally obtained evidence, material acquired in direct contradiction to the United States Constitution. Besides, nothing incriminating was discovered.

The law firm of Bernard, Olson, and Flanagan, argued that the Fourth Amendment of US Constitution had been shredded. The Berrigan brothers' attorneys argued that the Fourth Amendment had been drafted by our founding fathers to create a constitutional buffer between US citizens and the intimidating power of government and law enforcement. The rationale of the Fourth Amendment rested on three important ideas. First, it made clear that US citizens have privacy interests; citizens ought to be "secure in their persons, houses, papers, and effects." Second, the citizens' privacy interests prohibit unreasonable intrusions that are not authorized by a proper warrant based upon probable cause. Third, the Fourth Amendment stated that no warrant may be issued to a law enforcement officer unless that warrant describes specifically the place to be searched and the persons or things to be seized.

Within forty-eight hours, the Berrigan brothers were released. The confiscated material was judged to be obtained without a proper warrant. The probable cause and objects seized by the FBI were in violation of the US Constitution. The Berrigan brothers were free, but Matt Tyson had not played his last card.

* * *

Agent Martini was mystified. Alexis Williams had been a big part of his life for the last half year, sending him around North America, from Washington D.C., to California, Puerto Vallarta, and Mexico City. He sensed she was troubled, but the depth of her troubles eluded him. Now the chase was on once again. She had escaped the Twin Towers in downtown Los Angeles and had hooked up with her old boyfriend, Allen Carter. They had been on the lam for a week. The FBI discovered the ZR1 Corvette in a Los Angeles used car lot. The dealer had been contacted by phone. The manager said that a man sold the car to him for five thousand dollars under wholesale. Paperwork showed that the man desperately in need of cash was Allen Carter.

Agent Martini's investigation of the Berrigan brothers had cooled because lawyers had now taken over the investigation. The Berrigan brothers and the US Justice Department were engaged in a legal war. He was enjoying his second day off, the first weekend off in six months, when his cell phoned chirped. He checked caller ID. It was his boss.

"Good morning," Alex said.

"It may good for you, but we've a slight problem," FBI Director Thomas Parker said.

"What's new," Agent Martini said wryly.

"I want you on that West Coast disaster. Alexis Williams and Allen Carter. You're close to the case. The US Justice Department is tackling the Berrigan brothers. Chop, chop! Get your ass out west. I want those two lunatics in custody."

* * *

While Allen was checking into the hotel, Alexis gazed at the tropical fish lazily gliding about the saltwater tank behind the front desk. She had read that the indoor coral reef was home to nearly 450 fish from eighty-five different species. When Allen suggested they launch their road trip in Las Vegas, she insisted they stay at the Mirage Hotel on the strip.

The graceful movements of the fish transported her back to another time and place. She flashed on her therapy sessions with Dr. Hollingsworth, the hypnotic sessions, and her revelations about the clown in the black box. The flashback sent chills through her body. Her inner voice once again returned, whispering warnings.

"I've got our room. Let's go up, freshen up, and hit the casino." Allen grabbed the luggage and said, "Come on, times a wasting."

Alexis blinked several times and gazed over her shoulder at the tropical fish. Allen's excitement and sudden burst of energy brought Alexis back to the moment.

Within an hour, the giddy couple was hopping from

one black jack table to another, cleaning up. Allen won five hundred dollars at the twenty-five-dollar table; Alexis played more conservatively but won three hundred. The couple had radically changed their appearance. Allen had slicked back his thick, dark hair and hadn't shaved in a week. Alexis had dyed her hair black, wore little makeup, and dressed in jeans and a Hello Kitty blouse. Allen couldn't help notice the male attention Alexis got as they moved about the bustling casino. Leaning in close to her at one of the blackjack tables as the dealer shuffled the cards, he whispered, "You're the sexiest woman in the casino. And that's not all. You look younger than ever."

Alexis smiled and said, "You are indeed a sweet talker. But I do feel good. Why don't we call it a night? I can think of a better game."

"You're on!" Allen collected his chips, and they headed for the cashier to cash them in.

Up in their suite, they put play on hold and did a bit of homework. On Allen's laptop, they had been following the latest on the Berrigan brothers. Their Internet searches had paid off. A recent article in the *Chicago Tribune*, now owned by David and Charles Berrigan, had railed against the US government's violation of the billionaire's constitutional rights. The article, sympathetic to the Berrigan brothers' cause, ended with David Berrigan saying, "My brother and I are doing well, and we've retreated to our summer house for some much needed R and R." Allen now had a specific target. He also had a plan.

Allen looked at Alexis as she combed her dark hair. He once again felt close to her. They were bonding, not so much out of love, but out of necessity.

"Come here, baby." Allen flashed Alexis a warm smile.

Alexis moved seductively toward Allen, who was stretched out on the bed wearing only Jockey briefs. "What do you have in mind?" Alexis purred.

"I love your Hello Kitty blouse. But I lust for what's underneath the cute little kitty." Allen smiled and added, "How about you show me what you've got."

Alexis was nearly in the bag, having consumed three margaritas and a joint in less than two hours. "How much have you got, big boy?"

"All you can handle."

The hotel room rocked for nearly thirty minutes with sexual abandon. Alexis and Allen were made for each other, desperate souls that substituted unbridled passion for love and compassion. They only knew and appreciated the raw edges of primitive desire.

Alexis's brain injury was a thing of the past, Gotham City was alive and well, and the former lovers were once again of one mind and purpose. They had a score to settle. The NRA and the Berrigan brothers were in their crosshairs. The crazed couple was sinking into a mad world, a world where comic book characters and sensibilities ruled. Allen had a plan; Alexis had a new object of hate. Allen had convinced her that the Berrigan brothers were the root of all their problems. Her inner voice now chanted, "Death to the evil twins."

Motley Wag ruled once again. Their shared anger and delusion fused into a formidable will. They were ready for a fight. Moody Muse and Motley Wag had a date with the Bitterroot Mountains and the evil Berrigan brothers.

Chapter Forty-Nine

FBI Agent Alex Martini entered the sales office of Coliseum Motors on Figueroa Street in Los Angeles and asked for Robert Morales. The secretary summoned the manager to the front desk. Agent Martini scanned the cars on the front lot. Most of them were beaters, cars that commuters used to get to work on the mean streets of L.A. They were practical cars, battered from rough use, good for getting from point A to point B.

A middle-aged man with a large, dark moustache approached Agent Martini and asked, "How can I help you?"

"I'm Senior Special Agent Alex Martini. We spoke on the phone the other day. I've a few follow up questions."

Robert Morales looked over Alex's FBI credential and said, "Yes, I recall our phone conversation. Listen, I run a clean ship. We play by the books."

"I hope so, but I'm not here about you. Do you know this man?" Agent Martini showed Manager Morales a photo of Allen Carter.

"Yes, sir. As I said on the phone, I bought his 2012

Chevrolet Corvette ZR-1 from him and sold him a Honda Accord."

"May I see the paperwork?" Agent Martini followed Robert Morales to his office. Within ten minutes, he had in his possession important numbers: engine number and license number.

Agent Martini contacted Director Thomas Parker with the news. An all-points bulletin was immediately released with updated information on Allen and Alexis. They were in a 2012 white Honda Accord with California plates.

*   *   *

Before leaving Las Vegas, Allen traded in his clean 2012 Honda Accord for a 2012 black Lincoln Town Car. He preferred the comfort and luxury of the Lincoln. They had some hard driving to do, and he didn't want to leave a trail. Surely the feds were hot on their tail.

Allen did his homework and found a two-year-old Internet article about David and Charles Berrigan, featuring their Montana summer house. He did some further digging and discovered the deed and property tax records on the Montana compound. They headed for the Bitterroot Valley where they rented a cabin for the night.

"Tomorrow we'll talk to locals about fishing and hunting. But we won't let on to what we're really hunting and fishing for," Allen said.

Alexis pumped her arm with gusto. The excitement was building. The big day was close at hand. "Justice will be done," she said.

Before Allen and Alexis went out for dinner, they

visited a local hardware store. Within a half hour, they walked out with two Winchester Super X Magnum 12 gauge shotguns and several boxes of ammo. They also picked up a rod and reel. If everything unfolded as planned, they might do a little fishing on the Bitterroot River.

* * *

David and Charles Berrigan switched from beer to cognac. They sat out on the rear deck and enjoyed the close of day. The sun had just dipped behind the mountains. A red-tailed hawk made a steep nose dive and caught a small rabbit near the pond tucked amid the pines. The dying sunlight illuminated the rabbit's futile struggle.

"The little guy didn't have a chance," remarked David.

"The little guy rarely does," quipped Charles. They both laughed, and then Charles added, "And the feds better lay off of us. We ain't the little guys."

"We've got another pressing score to settle," David said.

"Are you thinking of Matt Tyson?" Charles grinned.

"Bingo." David sipped his cognac, enjoying the dying of the light. As the last hint of sunlight faded, the Bitterroot Mountains receded into the darkness of night.

"Do we pull the plug on the man or his reputation?" Charles asked.

"How about we orchestrate a slow death, one that we can savor?" David finished his cognac and poured another.

"Have you got the details?" Charles asked.

"I'm working on it. Any suggestions?"

"Let me sleep on it. I'm sure I'll come up with something

suitable for Mr. Big Mouth." Charles laughed and added, "We'll show him who rules."

*   *   *

Allen Carter studied the Google Map of the Bitterroot Mountains, narrowing his focus on the Berrigan brothers' compound, and then he and Alexis visited a sporting goods store in the Bitterroot Valley and picked up supplies. They found the essentials: fifty feet of climbing rope, two six-inch hunting knives, hacksaw, file, halogen flashlights, two flairs, light leather gloves, and a map of popular fishing spots. "Any suggestions for good trout fishing?" Allen asked the owner.

"Hand me your map," the owner said. He unfolded the map and with a red marker circled his favorite spots. "I've fared well at these fishing holes."

"Thanks for the tip." Allen smiled and gathered up his gear.

"Good luck. There's mighty tasty fish in them there streams." The owner turned to attend to his sidekick, a Malamute with pale blue eyes. The dog, a gentle giant, rubbed up against his master, his tail wagging playfully.

Motley Wag and Moody Muse were fired up. By the time they reached the Berrigan brothers' compound, the sun had set. Allen located the dirt road running along the high log and wood fence and parked the Lincoln amid thick pines. Alexis pulled out a backpack and removed her Moody Muse outfit. Allen opened the trunk and removed the Motley Wag attire from a black bag. Within twenty minutes, the crazed duo had transformed themselves.

Alexis was simply stunning; her voluptuous figure had

319

never looked better. She was adept with her make-up. The black mask, white painted face, and full red lips mirrored her costume. The skin tight red and black costume showed off her toned body, high lighting to perfection her bubble butt and full breasts. Alexis was the court jester turned vamp. She was electric.

Allen did his best with the make-up; after all he had plenty of practice. After ten minutes of applying the essentials, and with a little assistance from Alexis, the transformation was complete. He gazed into the rear view mirror of the Lincoln. Staring back was Motley Wag, the wide mouth, painted red, distorted by scars into a permanent smile. It wasn't his best make-up job. But it was effective.

Empowered by their favorite comic book heroes, the determined couple moved confidently through the shadows and found a place along the wall where a log post extended a foot above the fence top. Allen fashioned a loop and on the third try lassoed the stubby post. The two ascended to the top and rappelled over the other side, struggling a bit, carefully balancing the sawed-off shotguns slung around their shoulder. Allen had spent over an hour the night before using a hacksaw to cut the barrel and stock of the newly purchased firearms. He knew the smaller size had its advantages, especially when conducting a night raid of a walled compound.

In less than two minutes, they had cleared the wall and were headed for the huge log structure. The full moon was bright enough to light their way. They agreed to not use the flashlights unless absolutely necessary. After stealthily circling the rear of the compound they targeted the garage, spotted a side door, and were instantly relieved that it was unlocked. Inside, the masquerading marauders moved about a bright yellow Hummer, a black Jeep, and three dirt bikes.

Motley Wag put his ear to the inner door. The duo waited a few moments and then slowly opened the door and entered a mudroom off the kitchen. The small room had a row of hooks where jackets and rain gear hung. On the floor were several pairs of boots.

Motley Wag and Moody Muse moved silently through the ground floor before arriving at the stairs to the second level.

"I can make out three distinctive voices," Motley Wag said.

"We better be sure. Let's take a look." Her court jester hat bobbed as Moody Muse tilted her head.

At the top of the stairs, they leaned against the wall. Motley Muse peeked in. There he immediately recognized the trio. David and Charles Berrigan sat facing the fireplace. William St. George sat across from them, a half-empty glass of wine on the coffee table in front of him and a lit cigar in his right hand.

"Let's wait until they're drunk." Motley Wag smiled.

Moody Muse nodded. Out in the hall, the flickering firelight coming from the living room accentuated Motley Wag's diabolical appearance. The eerie look made Moody Muse shudder. It unnerved Alexis. She could hear a faint voice whispering, "You two are fucking evil. You're made for each other."

Chapter Fifty

Agent Martini got a hot tip. FBI agents had swarmed the Pacific Northwest, and one unit talked to the owner of a sporting goods store in the Bitterroot Valley. A bearded, white-haired owner by the name of Charley Whitehorse sold climbing rope, hunting knives, and a hacksaw to a couple of city slickers. The couple said they were going camping, hoping to do some hunting and a little fishing. Charley said they were likable enough. But they didn't look like hunters and fisherman. "No, sir," he had said. "But the woman, she was a looker."

When Agent Martini found out they were now driving a black Lincoln and were headed north to the Bitterroot Mountains, he flew into action. He phoned his boss and got him on the first ring. The call was short and effective. "There's only one point of interest in the Bitterroot Mountains for Allen Carter and Alexis Williams. They're making a beeline for the Berrigan brothers' place," he said. He got the immediate okay from Director Parker to assemble an FBI SWAT team.

"Better be right this time. Chop, chop, and get the bad

guys." Director Parker signed off without a good-bye. He was under mounting pressure from the US Justice Department.

* * *

The Berrigan brothers and William St. George hit the bar for fresh drinks, cognac for the twins and Cabernet for the NRA's front man. Before leaving the bar, David asked, "Do you know why a handgun is better than a woman?"

"No, why?" Charles picked up his drink and headed for the deck.

"Because you can buy a silencer for a handgun," David answered. They all howled, and the party moved through the double doors to the outside deck.

Motley Wag and Moody Muse waited in the shadows of the hallway before silently slipping through the living room. Staying close to the wall and bar, they crept slowly toward the double doors leading to the deck. Peering through the partly opened doors they caught a glimpse of William St. George. The ambient light from the full moon accentuated the pasty hue of his well-known face. His skin looked unnatural. St. George's gaunt look together with the Berrigan brothers' political tirades and sophomoric humor ticked off Motley Wag. *Let's just see who has the last laugh*, he thought.

"It's time," Motley Wag whispered to Moody Muse.

Motley Wag barged through the double doors, raised the sawed-off shotgun, and yelled, "Surprise! It's time for a little fun."

The Berrigan brothers dropped their drinks. William St. George nearly fainted. He was white as a sheet.

"What the fuck is this!" David yelled.

When Charles Berrigan tried to stand, Motley Wag barked, "Sit the fuck down! Nobody moves unless I say so."

"Who are you? How'd you get in?" David blurted. He gripped the sides of the deck chair, face reddening. "Why the charade?"

"I heard on the street that the only way to stop a bad guy with a gun is a good guy with a gun. Now *here's* the million-dollar question: who's the good guy? Why of course, it's the one that's got the gun." Motley Wag waved the shotgun in a slow circle, flashed the horrified trio a wicked grin, followed by the smacking of lips. "Hell, I kind of like my chances here."

"This is outrageous. Put the damn weapon away!" Charles screamed.

"You call this a weapon? Please, this is a *sporting gun*, great for pheasant and duck hunting. Some like to take a crack at clay pigeons. Jeez, I think this is *my* lucky night. Three clay pigeons all lined up for a good guy to hone his firearm skills," Motley Wag said.

"You're a crazy-ass lunatic," cried William St. George.

"Well, Mr. St. George, you should have called for better background checks. The NRA forgot about Motley Wag. The NRA has assured me of my rights. Even Motley Wag has a Second Amendment right." Motley Wag stepped around the back of William St. George and aimed his shotgun at the Berrigan brothers. "Moody, please stand back a bit. I don't want to splatter your attire with their vile blood." His orders were slow and deliberate, eerily embellished by lip smacking and his rolling eyes.

"Stop! Time out! We can talk this out," David howled. His hands trembled as he squirmed in his chair.

"Talk? It's time for action. You've had your say. The Berrigan brothers own the press. Everyone knows the *Tribune* is in your back pocket. Besides, you call the shots in congress and at the NRA. Hell, in California, NRA stands for 'Nuts, Racists, and Assholes.' Why talk when this can be settled with a pull of the trigger?"

Suddenly, the sounds of approaching helicopters hovering above caught their attention. The intruding sound of chopper blades was deafening. A searchlight crisscrossed the rear grounds as the FBI helicopter's loud speaker boomed. "This is the FBI. Don't move. Put your hands up. I repeat: This is FBI Agent Alex Martini. Don't move."

Motley Wag sprang to the double doors, grabbed Moody Muse, and ducked inside. The twins and St. George were motionless, caught between the crossfire of the feds and two fictional comic book characters.

"It's time!" Motley Wag took aim and fired. He hit William St. George in the chest. His eyes instantly glazed over, and blood spurted from his heart, nearly hitting Motley Wag in the face.

Moody Muse fired, knocking Charles Berrigan out of his deck chair. Motley Wag didn't hesitate and fired his second volley, removing half of David Berrigan's face. A fountain of blood shot out onto the deck.

Motley Wag and Moody Muse each emptied six shells from their sawed-off Remingtons, flooding the deck with more NRA blood. They reloaded, hustled downstairs, and ran back into the garage.

"Let's fire up the Hummer," Motley Wag yelled. He opened the driver's door, but no keys were in the ignition.

"What about the dirt bikes?" Moody Muse yelled.

"You ride?" Motley Wag looked surprised.

"You bet!"

They were in luck. The keys were in the ignition. Motley Wag fired up both bikes, hit the door opener, and within seconds, the crazed comic book characters screamed out of the garage and headed for the front gate. A second helicopter approached the compound flashing its searchlights. Shangri-La had turned into a laser show. But Motley Wag and Moody Muse slipped into the night undetected. The chopper's searchlights flooded the compound, missing the escape by mere seconds.

"It's the Keystone Cops!" Motley Wag laughed manically.

With the headlights of the dirt bikes off, they raced along the perimeter wall and found a gate undergoing repair. Workmen had been replacing a large log gate with an iron gate. The chain securing the gate had a lock, but it was unfastened.

"Moody, follow me." Motley Wag jumped from his bike, removed the chain, remounted, and rode through the gap. Moody quickly followed.

Within five minutes, they found the Lincoln, ditched the bikes, threw the shotguns in the backseat, and drove off. With headlights off, Allen could barely see, barreling ahead blindly, slamming through brush, trees, and ruts on the uneven road. Half the time they were spinning through loose dirt, fallen logs, and heavy brush and trees, only occasionally veering back on to the bumpy dirt road. They navigated purely by the light of the full moon.

They hit the main highway and continued their escape with the headlights off. A half mile back, they could see the

FBI laser show. Two choppers were still hovering over the compound.

"I think we dodged a bullet." Motley Wag laughed. "The road trip lives on."

"Won't they run us down with the choppers?" Moody's hands were shaking. Her eyes were wide open with excitement.

"They think we're still inside the compound. We'll pull off the road at the first house we see." Motley Wag put the pedal to the metal, following the white stripe down the middle of the road.

Within five minutes, they spotted lights of a house about a quarter mile off the highway. They made a hard right, the Lincoln throwing rocks into the air as they sped down the gravel driveway. Motley Wag, with headlights still off, slowed and pulled the black Lincoln alongside a small barn next to the log cabin. Motley Wag peeked in the barn and saw an old by-plane used for crop dusting.

"Hey, Moody, see what I see?" Motley Wag grinned; his makeup had shifted a bit, distorting his mouth even more.

"Are you serious?" Moody shook her head. "You haven't flown in months."

"Hey, you're looking at the Red Baron." Motley Wag motioned toward the log cabin. "Let's see what we've got."

Motley Wag and Moody Muse crept slowly through the darkness, around to the rear of the modest cabin, and peered in the back window. At the kitchen sink was an elderly man with full, gray beard and long hair pulled back into a ponytail. He was the spitting image of Willie Nelson.

"Let's go say hello to old Willie," Motley Wag said. "He appears to be home alone. I think he's lonely." Motley Wag laughed, pulled Moody close, and whispered, "Let's have a party."

Motley Wag tried the front door. It was unlocked. He slowly opened the door, and the two fugitives, with shotguns at their side, moved silently past an old Franklin fireplace. At the entrance of the kitchen, Motley Wag knocked on the wall. "Hey, anybody home?"

The old man spun around, dropped a dish he was washing, and blurted, "Who and what the hell are you?"

"We were just in the neighborhood and thought we'd drop by." Motley Wag laughed and introduced himself. "I'm Motley Wag, and this here is my sidekick, Moody Muse."

"Is this a fucking joke?" The old man's mouth gaped open.

"We like a good joke, but this is no joking matter." Motley Wag motioned to the living room with his shotgun. "Let's go in by the fire and visit a bit."

"I don't know you." The old man shook his head in disbelief. "Is this a robbery?"

"No, sir, but I do have business proposition for you. Come on, let's get comfortable." Motley Wag stepped aside and let the old man pass by. The old man ambled to a rocking chair across from the Franklin stove and sank down.

Moody Muse paced about the living room, stopping occasionally to warm her hands near the Franklin stove. Her shotgun was now slung around her shoulder.

Motley Wag kept his shotgun leveled at the old man and asked, "Does the by-plane work?"

"I flew it last month." The old man frowned. "Why?"

"I'd like to rent it for a day or so. I've got cash." Motley Wag waved the shotgun in a slow, circular motion. He smacked his lips and rolled his eyes.

"It's not for rent!" The old man was emphatic.

"Say, may I call you Willie?" Motley Wag slowly licked his lips.

"My name *is* Willie," the old man said.

"Excellent. You remind me of Willie Nelson. He's my kind of guy—likes pot and makes good music."

"Get to the point," Moody snapped. "The feds are on our tail." She hadn't stopped her pacing, moving back and forth in front of the old Franklin. Her jester hat bobbed as she moved.

"Moody's right, so here's my proposition. I've five hundred in cash for a twenty-four-hour rental of your plane."

"No way!" The old man sneered.

"Well, either that or I'll use this. We can handle this as two gentlemen or resort to this," Motley Wag laughed, pointed the shotgun at his head, and wagged it about. "Come on, times a wasting." He rolled his eyes slowly and then puckered his lips.

Willie got up, ambled slowly to a small desk in the corner of the living room, and retrieved some keys from the top drawer. He turned and tossed them toward Motley Wag, who snatched them and said, "Good move. Let's check out the plane."

The next ten minutes were a blur of activity, fueling the plane, going through the preflight checklist, and firing up the engine. Motley Wag jumped in the two-seater and taxied toward the runway. They bumped along to the end, turned, and revved the engine.

The old man hobbled after them in an uneven gait. "You're on a suicide mission," Willie yelled. "It's dark, you've no lights, and there are trees, power lines, and other looming obstacles. You're crazy ass lunatics."

"To each his own," yelled Motley Wag.

Within five minutes, the crop duster had warmed up. The vintage plane revved its engine, lurched forward, and barreled into the blackness. The old man shook his head in disbelief.

Chapter Fifty-One

When the Berrigan brothers' property was secured, Agent Martini climbed the stairs to the second floor to check out the death scene. Out on the deck, the full moon cast an eerie light on the horror caused by Motley Wag and Moody Muse. He stared in numbness at the carnage. Blood was everywhere, on the deck, table, chairs, and log walls. He shook his head and thought, *Perhaps the American people have been spared an embarrassing and expensive trial. The men slaughtered here were cold-blooded killers. They knew no bounds.*

The SWAT team canvassed the enormous structure and sprawling grounds, skipping nothing. Closets, storage areas, basement, and the War Room were inspected. Agent Martini ordered the choppers to do a thorough search of the vicinity. He also received a few startled looks when he did an impromptu imitation of Tommy Lee Jones. "What I want out of each and every one of you is a hard target search of every gas station, residence, warehouse, farmhouse, henhouse, outhouse, and dog house in that area." *The Fugitive* was one of Alex's favorite movie thrillers.

* * *

Motley Wag laughed with glee as the crop duster headed for the light show. The Berrigan brothers' compound was on the horizon. Flying blind was difficult, but the feds made a hot target. Two choppers were hovering over the compound, spotlights playing hide and seek, focusing light on every inch of Shangri-La. The pinpointed beams of light bounced around like ping pong balls in a lottery drawing machine.

Moody Muse yelled into the intercom, "Where in the fuck are you going?"

"It's show time." Motley Wag howled.

"You're going to get us killed!" Moody Muse shrieked. "The feds will slaughter us."

"I'm not going out with a whimper." Motley Wag banked the crop duster and headed directly for the center of the compound. When they were within two hundred yards of the entrance, Motley Wag let go of his pay load. Pesticides dropped from the tank, spraying the driveway, entrance, heliport, NRA banner, and log home. He climbed a hundred feet, motor sputtering, banked hard, and made a second pass of the compound. An FBI chopper approached, loud speaker shouting something indistinguishable.

Motley Wag dropped his second load, spraying two agents on the ground running for cover. Allen Carter was living his dream. He laughed hysterically while Alexis screamed bloody murder. She was losing control, hurling toward the unknown, scared and alone. Allen had deserted her once again.

An FBI chopper suddenly veered directly in front of the vintage crop duster. Shots rang out, hitting the crop duster's vertical stabilizer. Motley Wag fired back, hitting the tail of the chopper. It was a dog fight, a crop duster from back in the day versus a Bell 412 tactical helicopter. Motley Wag was outnumbered and had less fire power and maneuverability, but he was fearless. *If I had Napalm, I'd use it,* he thought.

Motley Wag fought the controls of the crop duster as it veered out of control, desperately trying to evade the FBI chopper. He banked once again, this time dropping fifty feet and plummeting toward the front entrance of the compound. Old Willie's by-plane lurched up, barely missing the roof, and suddenly pitched upward toward the full moon. The crop duster went belly up, banked hard right, and headed directly for a pursuing chopper. In an instant, the crop duster and chopper collided, exploding into a ball of fire.

Both aircrafts feebly tumbled from the sky, lighting up the night with burning bodies and fuel. The second chopper made an emergency landing while SWAT team members rushed to the crash scene. Shangri-La had become a killing field. Burned bodies lay lifeless amid the twisted and mangled metal parts from the incinerated aircraft. The night air reeked with the pungent aroma of burned flesh and industrial pesticide. For the next hour, FBI personnel scrambled to rescue any survivors. There were none. Five SWAT team members perished from the explosive crash. Motley Wag and Moody Muse were found sprawled across the ground under the flag pole. Ironically, the only flag flying over the tragic death scene was the NRA banner. This was not lost on Agent Martini. He looked at a fellow FBI agent and said, "The NRA always has the last word." The agent looked up at the banner and shook his head in disbelief.

Agent Martini bent over and examined Motley Wag's face. His makeup had smudged, but the look on his face revealed his feelings before death. The eyes were wide and glazed over; his mouth was twisted in a sinister sneer. The charred but still vivid colors of his costume, the purple blazer, green vest, blue collared shirt, funky orange tie, and gray and purple striped slacks gave the scene a comical look. But there was nothing humorous about tonight. He next checked out Moody Muse. Her partially burned attire, the black and red jump suit, fluffy collar, eye mask, gloves, wrist ruffles and red and black jester hat, provided vivid illustration of the couple's madness.

Agent Martini sadness deepened when he checked on the fallen SWAT team members. He had lost some brothers tonight. Evil had been played out by demented souls who had extinguished the lives of hard working men dedicated to their profession. He felt angry, but powerless to change what had happened.

*　*　*

Matt Tyson folded up the *Washington Post* and dropped it on the table. He was at Starbucks, down the block from his Washington D.C. condo, getting his early-morning jolt of java. Two columns in this morning's opinion section addressed the pure madness of the Montana massacre.

One writer compared the recent mass murders to the Saint Valentine Day Massacre. The 1929 prohibition era conflict came to a head when the South Side Italian gang led by Al Capone squared off with the North Side Irish gang led by Bugs Moran. Seven mob associates were gunned down execution style.

The editorials are provocative, Matt thought, *but they only skim the surface of what really went down. There's much more at stake than two gangs in a fight over territory.* Matt had not fully digested what had happened. The air disaster and assassinations at Shangri-La seemed surreal. It wasn't about people he had read about or briefly met. He knew these people. These were lost souls who had befriended evil.

Matt had waited long enough to tell his story. He had documents in his hands, downloaded material taken from computers at Shangri-La. The documents might not be admissible in court, but they had the Berrigan brothers' fingerprints all over them. The public had not yet heard of the inner circle and Fire Power. They didn't know that one of Alexis Williams's victims worked for William St. George. He had enough hard facts to bring the Berrigan Industries to its knees.

Matt flashed on the late-night bull sessions with his roommates in college. He recalled his love affair with Buddhism, his first go around with the idea of karma, the idea of cause and effect and personal responsibility. To this day, he believed that you get what you give. There was no day of judgment meted out by a cosmic judge.

Matt Tyson shook his head. He had a story to write.

Today he would pen an obituary in *The Socratic Rag*. He would write about the Berrigan brothers, William St.

George, Moody Muse, and Motley Wag. He would entitle the piece, "Shangri-La," but he knew, in some twisted way, they had the last laugh. The NRA was alive and well. The joke was on us.

Matt was about to leave Starbucks when his cell phone buzzed. It was Agent Alex Martini. "Good morning, Alex," he answered. "I was just thinking about you."

"I hope they were good thoughts. Say, I just wanted to touch base with you. I was wondering what you thought about the disaster at the Berrigan brothers' compound."

"I'm at Starbucks revving up my engine. I've decided to write an obituary." Matt looked about Starbucks. The place was packed, bustling with early-morning energy.

"An obituary?"

"It's time. It's time to reveal to the public what I discovered in Shangri-La. It's time I drop my literary bomb." Matt took his last sip of coffee. A young woman in a dark business suit asked if she could borrow his newspaper. He nodded yes.

"You're going to stir up a hornet's nest," Alex said. "Say, I've got a question."

"Shoot." Matt smiled at the young woman who borrowed his paper. She reminded him of his high school sweetheart.

"What do you know about Allen Carter's circle of friends, the group he partied with, the partygoers that dressed up as comic book heroes?"

"Nothing. I met them at the costume party, the affair where I dressed as Hypnos."

"Well, if something comes back to you, let me know," Agent Martini said. "One more question: do you think Allen Carter was insane?"

"I'm not a doctor," Matt said. "Insane? No, I think crazy fits better."

"What about Alexis Williams?"

"Perhaps insanity fits here. But I'd opt for evil." Matt got up and gestured that the young woman could keep the newspaper.

"I'm looking forward to reading your next piece in *The Socratic Rag*. It should raise some eyebrows."

"I was hoping to land a few white-collar types in prison," Matt quipped.

"Good luck with *that* one. Keep in touch. I'm heading out to California. I'm going to look up some masquerading comic book heroes."

"Good luck with *that* one." Matt signed off. He had a story to write.

His phone immediately buzzed again. It was an unknown number. "Matt Tyson, how may I help you?"

His phone erupted with laughter. It was a crazed laugh—a sinister, mocking laugh. "I hope I didn't disappoint you." The laugh became louder and then trailed off. "How'd you like my last act?" A second round of laughter exploded in his ears and then died off, followed by the eerie sounds of lips smacking. The message ended and restarted. It was a recording.

It was Motley Wag. *I guess he got the last laugh*, Matt thought. *But I'll have the last word.*